The Psycho

John Hagen

Dedication

To Ileana, the love of my life.

Acknowledgment

After almost 40 years as a practicing general surgeon, I've learned that even with a flawless operation, the recovery process can still bring unexpected complications and anxieties for the patient. Reviewing the videos when complications occur often cannot reveal the specific technical issues causing surgical problems. The complication, stemming from patient factors, still often leads to surgeons blaming themselves. When the patient's family blames the surgeon, their accusations add to his already considerable angst and guilt, a heavy weight of responsibility pressing down on him. The sleepless nights, filled with regret and self-recrimination, can leave the surgeon feeling drained for days. But an angry family member can haunt the surgeon for years.

This novel explores those avenues with depth and insight, revealing hidden connections and unforeseen consequences. This novel is a work of fiction, and any resemblance to actual events or persons is entirely coincidental. I would like to express my sincere gratitude to my colleagues at the hospital, where I dedicated 37 years of my life, for their unwavering support while managing the complications I faced following a surgery I performed. The kindness and concern they showed eased my burden considerably.

I would also thank Janet Gyenes, my editor, for her frank comments and help with the manuscript. Any mistakes in the text are mine.

About The Author

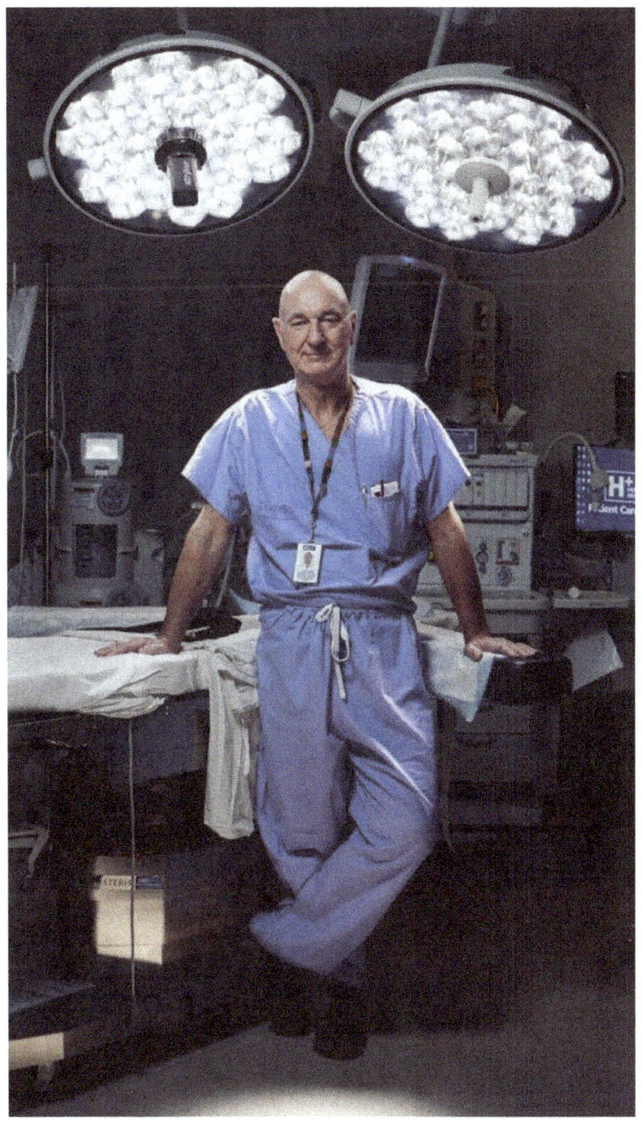

Dr. John Hagen completed his doctor of medicine (honours) degree from the University Of Alberta in 1979, later attaining specialty training in areas such as endoscopy. He's spent much of his practice in Toronto-area hospitals in roles such as attending surgeon, division head of general surgery, surgical director of bariatrics, and chief of surgery, chief of staff, among others. Now retired from practice, Hagen has taken on several instructor responsibilities such as reviewing videos of trainees operating and offering them advice. Since 2005, Hagen has lectured widely and delivered myriad courses and live demonstrations, particularly in laparoscopic and bariatric surgery, in Canada, the US, UK, Europe, Mexico, Nepal, Colombia and China.

The Psycho is Hagen's ninth novel, following eight other medical thrillers, *The Junkie (*2025), *The Downfall,* (2025), *The Heir*, (2024), *The Clinic*, (2024), *The Embryo* (2023), *The Mission* (2024), *The Complication* (2024) and *The Sailor* (2023). Along with being a dedicated lecturer and volunteer at medical missions with his wife, Ileana, the couple are avid travelers and sailors. They live in King City, Ontario, and spend time taking excursions on their 51-foot sailboat, *Ileana,* having sailed to the Caribbean and the Bahamas for the winter months. Read about his sailing adventures on www.dreamingofileana.com

Contents

Chapter 1

Larry Klapman had completed the surgery, a complicated colon resection in a 22-year-old university student. As he scanned the waiting room, his eyes fell upon her father. Larry made his way towards the older man, observing him spring to his feet in surprise.

"Jacob, I finished the surgery," Larry said, "and Melodie is in the recovery room."

Standing at six and a half feet, Jacob looked down at Larry with an unreadable expression on his face, his imposing height making the surgeon seem smaller by comparison. Appearing to be in his mid-fifties, he sported a salt-and-pepper stubble beard that mirrored the colour of his full head of hair, which was neatly gathered in a ponytail at the back of his head. The darkness and intensity in Jacob's eyes revealed his distrust of the surgeon and seemed to pierce deeply into Larry's very being.

A shudder ran through Larry's body as the thought of Jacob's creepy nature washed over him, leaving him feeling unsettled and disturbed. The handshake revealed a powerful grip that hurt Larry's hand. The sheer size of his biceps, straining against the fabric of his Harley Davidson T-shirt, showcased his heavily muscled form. In a deep voice, tinged with the subtle lilt of Eastern Europe, Jacob inquired, "So, tell me, how did everything go?"

"Why don't we sit down for a moment?" Larry politely suggested.

Still in his early thirties, Larry was only in the first year of establishing his surgery practice. Because he had been diligently training for a 70.3, a race also known as a half-Ironman, he, too, was in excellent physical condition. His short, cropped hairstyle served to effectively diminish the visual impact of his premature balding, making it less obvious to observers. His consistently pleasant demeanour, combined with a deep compassion for his patients' suffering, earned him the utmost respect from his surgical colleagues and the nurses with whom he worked. Throughout his training and short career, Larry had found that speaking to families in an intimate and less intimidating manner after surgery was always a more effective and comforting approach. If he said something that alarmed them, sitting face to face could often lessen the impact. Larry pointed to the cushioned chairs in the corner.

"I prefer to stand," boomed Jacob. "Now tell me, how did the surgery go?"

Larry looked up into Jacob's eyes and sighed. "By resecting 18 inches of the intestine, we successfully removed the cyst from the right side of her colon. We started laparoscopically, but it was stuck to the retroperitoneum, the space behind the colon. We needed to make a large incision. It was the only safe way to remove the cyst.

I asked another surgeon, Dr. John Hegland, to come to the operating room, and he agreed this method was the sole solution. We took a video of the laparoscopic part, and I am happy to show you and Melodie the surgery if you like."

Jacob listened intently, remaining completely silent and not uttering a single word throughout the conversation after learning about the surgery. He shook his head from side to side subtly, as if his brain were actively working to process and understand the recently received information. Larry felt increasingly uneasy under the intense, unwavering gaze of his eyes. He waited expectantly for Jacob to speak, but when Jacob remained without words or even a grunt, Larry broke the silence.

"The cyst itself, which is what we term a duplication cyst, is a developmental abnormality that is not frequently seen. The condition was causing her significant pain in her abdomen and episodes of bowels obstruction. I believe that now that we have removed the source of her discomfort, she will feel significantly better."

Again, Jacob's eyes met Larry's, a stony silence hanging heavy in the air between them, thick with tension. Larry shifted uncomfortably as the dark eyes continued to bore into him, their intensity making his skin crawl. He looked away, a slight flush on his cheeks, and mumbled, "Do you have any questions?"

After a moment, Jacob replied, "You said you would do the surgery with small incisions. Now you are telling me you made a large incision. How large?"

Larry held up his hand and spread his fingers to show about six inches. "The anesthesiologist put in an epidural to help with the postoperative pain. We'll remove it in a few days after she feels a little better. In the meantime, we'll try to get her up to walk to reduce the chance of a blood clot developing in her legs. The Foley catheter in her bladder will get removed at the same time as when we remove the epidural."

Jacob's face went red, and his voice became loud. "You didn't tell us this would happen—a tube in the bladder, a needle in the back, postoperative pain, possible blood clots. What else didn't you tell us?"

Jacob's breaths were shallow and ragged, each one a painful struggle as his distress mounted. Larry backed away as the unsettling agitation continued, his heart pounding in his chest and a cold sweat breaking out on his brow.

With a sudden movement, Jacob's hand clamped down on the V-neck of Larry's scrub suit, the unexpected contact sending a jolt through him. With a smooth, effortless motion, the larger man lifted Larry off the ground, the surgeon's feet dangling loosely. Larry gasped, his larynx constricting, each breath a desperate struggle. Jacob slammed him against the wall, the rough brick scraping against his back, and roared, "If anything happens to her, I swear I'll kill you."

He dropped Larry. With a soft thud, he crumpled onto the cold linoleum floor as Jacob stormed out of the waiting room, slamming the door behind him.

"Code white, code white, code white!" screamed the intercom. "Surgical waiting room."

A sharp pain shot through Larry's neck as he touched it. He could feel a burning welt forming where the rough, starched cloth of the scrubs had chafed his skin. He sat up, his heart pounding in his chest, still disoriented from the events that had just transpired. Looking around the sterile, brightly lit waiting room, a few startled families stared at him, their faces imprinted with concern.

"Dr. Klapman, are you alright?" asked Ben. The young floor cleaner's brow furrowed with worry as he looked at the doctor's pale face. "I saw everything. That psycho attacked you. I think you should go to the emergency room."

Larry shook his head. "No, I'm alright," he croaked. "Thanks, Ben."

The team from security rushed into the waiting room. Larry watched as they surveyed the people sitting in chairs and then approached Larry. "What happened?" asked the security guard closest to him.

"I'm OK," said Larry again, still a little shaken up.

The security guard said, "We need to make a report. Can you tell us what happened?"

Larry sat in a soft fabric chair in the sterile waiting room, the low hum of fluorescent lights filling the air. One security guard, his face grim, escorted the others who had witnessed the attack into the adjacent room to take their statements. The air hung heavy with dread. Alone with the security guard, Larry felt the tightness in his chest, a lingering physiological effect of the events' tension. The security guard held his pen poised above the clipboard.

"I told the father of my patient, Melodie, about the surgery," said Larry. "With a sudden, violent movement, Jacob Ashinoff picked me up and hurled me against the wall, the impact jarring my whole body. His eyes seemed to burn with rage—and he made a threat that he would kill me if anything happened to her."

"The usual procedure now is to file a police report," said the security guard. "We can't have him coming back into the hospital."

Larry thought about that for a moment. "Let's just forget about it. Something I said upset him. I don't want to be a bother."

The security guard wasn't having it. "We need to file a police report and get a restraining order. He might do a lot more damage next time. It is hospital policy to do so. We'll do it with or without your help. Maybe it will be a nurse that gets hurt, or one of your colleagues."

"OK, OK," said Larry, resigning to the wishes of the security guard. "I get it. I'll agree with whatever is necessary. Let me know what to do."

"We'll call you when the police officer arrives," he said. "And Dr. Klapman, thank you for doing this."

Exiting the hushed waiting room, Larry walked down the hall to the recovery room, the sounds of medical equipment faintly audible. The manager, Leslie, immediately met him at the door, her expression serious.

"Are you OK?" she asked, leaning closer to get a better look at his face and neck. "I heard that Melodie's father assaulted you! That it was a terrible, violent scene. I'm so sorry. Melodie's recovering nicely and is feeling up to talking."

Larry sauntered into her room and made his way to the bed. The rhythmic beeping of Melodie's heart monitor was a steady pulse in the otherwise quiet space where the nurses attended to her. Her worried eyes, wide with apprehension, looked up at him. Larry reached out, his fingers brushing lightly against her hand before giving a gentle squeeze.

"You are going to be fine," he said, his voice a warm,

calming presence beside her. "We resected 18 inches of your intestine. It was likely a duplication cyst that was kinking your bowel and causing an obstruction. I think you'll feel better now."

"Thanks, doctor," she said, smiling. "There's no cancer?"

Larry gave her a look of surprise and said, "Definitely no cancer. But we had to make a large incision to perform the surgery safely, so you'll have more pain than usual for a while. Our anesthetist inserted an epidural catheter to help with the pain, so we placed a catheter in your bladder. We will remove both in two days. You can get up and walk around in a few hours. I would want you to eat a normal diet when you get to the surgical floor."

A tear, glistening like a pearl in the fluorescent light, rolled down her cheek. Larry gently passed her a soft tissue, and with a trembling hand, she wiped it away as it traced a path down her cheek.

After Melodie had settled somewhat, he said, "Ahhh, you were so worried about the result. You are going to be fine now."

With a long, slow sigh that released the tension in her shoulders, she regained her composure. "That's not why I'm crying," she said, her voice choked with unshed tears after a moment. "The nurses told me that my father had injured you."

"I'm OK." said Larry. "Don't you worry about that. I'm fine.

He was just worried about you. All you need to concentrate on is getting better. I am going to take excellent care of you."

Melodie sighed. "My dad is a little crazy. He doesn't trust anyone. I am happy you are looking after me."

"I will do the best I can for you," replied Larry. "See you tomorrow."

Melodie smiled as Larry walked away. He felt better after seeing Melodie and ensuring that she was doing well. His cell phone chirped. It was a text from an unknown number:

REMEMBER WHAT I TOLD.

Chapter 2

"The cyst is right there," Larry said, pointing to it on the computer screen with the mouse icon. The four surgery residents and a medical student sat in the small conference room with doctors Larry Klapman and John Hegland, the air thick with the smell of old coffee and anticipation. They watched the 60-inch screen on the wall, mesmerized by the vibrant colours and sharp details. Here, surrounded by the quiet concentration of their colleagues, they reviewed their laparoscopic cases, each image on the screen a potential lesson in how to perfect their approach.

"It looks like it is stuck to the retroperitoneum," said John, pointing to it with the mouse. As the current chief of surgery at the hospital, he held laparoscopic surgery video sessions at least once per week as he began his day. The purpose was to improve the quality of surgery by reviewing the cases with the benefit of hindsight. Although in his late thirties, his youthful appearance and short brown hair, with its hint of auburn in the sunlight, made him look a decade younger. But his expertise commanded respect from his colleagues.

"The problem I faced was I couldn't identify the correct line of dissection," said Larry. "I was concerned about damaging the ureter, or the iliac vessels. Look what happened when we injected the ICG intravenously and then through the ureteric catheters."

The vibrant green glow of the ICG dye Larry mentioned illuminated the iliac arteries. A few seconds later, the ureters, their bright green outlines stark against the surrounding tissue, lit up.

"Those deep structures, nestled within the dense retroperitoneal fat, risked damage had we continued the laparoscopic approach," he said. "With the benefit of hindsight, the conversion to a laparotomy was clearly the best course of action, preventing further harm."

Jake, a final-year surgery resident, put his hand up to speak and said, "Dr. Klapman, did you consider mobilizing the hepatic flexure of the colon and entering the retroperitoneum that way? It appears less inflamed up there."

"Look here, Jake," replied Larry as he advanced the video image. "We identified the ileocolic vessel pedicle, the blood supply to the right colon where the cyst was located, but look how thick the retroperitoneum is here? Had we persisted, we could have injured the duodenum. Mobilizing the hepatic flexure would have landed us in the same thick tissue around the duodenum. We might have injured it had we tried what you suggested. I could not find a safe place to enter the retroperitoneum to mobilize the cyst to facilitate the resection."

"I agree it was the best decision," said John thoughtfully. "Larry asked me for my opinion during the case, and I too felt a laparotomy was the safest approach. This case highlights several important teaching points for the residents. In the high-pressure environment of the operating room, encountering the unexpected is commonplace. When this happens, don't hesitate to ask for advice from a trusted colleague. The urgency of the situation demands clear communication and collaboration among the medical team. Although we often pride ourselves on performing complex laparoscopic dissections, the patient's safety must remain our top priority. If that means converting to a laparotomy, even in a 22-year-old, that's the correct surgical decision, prioritizing patient safety above all else. Finally, I would encourage all of you when you are in practice to videotape your cases so you can review the surgery to see if you could have done anything differently."

The residents and medical student nodded in agreement. Larry could feel the relief of tension in the room as the trainees sensed there was no shame in asking for help when a difficult intraoperative situation arose. Larry had trained under John's guidance and had benefitted from his wisdom. Jake was presenting the next video case, a difficult gallbladder operation, when the overhead paging screamed, "Code blue, room 1723; code blue, room 1723."

Larry immediately jumped up from his chair when he realized the significance of the medical emergency call. "Shit!" he cried. "That's Melodie's room!"

The Psycho

The team of surgeons and trainees, their faces grim with urgency, raced from the conference room to the elevators. Larry punched the code blue button; a high-pitched ring filled the air as the elevator arrived within 10 seconds, taking them to the 17th floor. When the doors opened, a wave of noise and excitement pushed them toward room 1723. Melodie lay in bed, her skin as white as the sheets, her breathing shallow.

As they entered, a frantic student nurse glanced at them, her white coat stained, her breath catching in her throat. "I helped her up to go to the bathroom, but the effort was too much; she collapsed, her body hitting the floor with a soft impact." Her finger jabbed towards the damp, dirty bathroom floor. A dark, viscous pool of blood coated the tiles, the coppery tang of blood mixing with the sickeningly sweet smell of decaying stool and sulfurous gases.

Larry walked over to Melodie. With a gentle touch, he calmly took her hand. Her wide eyes, dilated with fear, stared up at him, blinking incomprehensibly. Eyes darting, they scurried about the room, her breath held, as if searching for danger. Larry stared intently at the vital signs displayed on the wall-mounted monitor, the rhythmic beeping a steady pulse in the silent room. A flashing 140 on the monitor indicated tachycardia, likely caused by blood loss. The monitor recorded the blood pressure at 70/30. The thermometer read 36.9°C. At 95 per cent, the oxygen saturation was within the normal range.

Larry's gaze darted over Melodie in a quick examination, his hands hovering near her. A noticeable distension of her abdomen was present, yet palpation revealed minimal tenderness. He reassured himself about the epidural catheter in place to manage pain, understanding that assessing tenderness might not signal any issues with the surgery.

"I suspect you're bleeding from the site of the anastomosis we created at the time of surgery," Larry explained, his brow furrowed in concern as he gently touched his patient's abdomen. "That's where we attached the small intestine to the colon using staples. Occasionally, a minuscule blood vessel will rupture, resulting in a subtle, scarcely noticeable trickle of blood. Usually, the bleeding stops by itself, the wound slowly clotting and the flow of blood ceasing. If the problem persists, we can intervene, but this would mean another surgical operation. Right now, we're going to administer intravenous saline—that's a clear, sterile solution—and draw some blood to check your hemoglobin, a measure of your red blood cells. In the event of critically low hemoglobin levels, we will administer a blood transfusion to restore your blood to healthy levels."

After a brief nod, Melodie gave Larry's hand a squeeze. "Dr. Klapman," she whispered, her voice trembling, "I'm scared." Tears formed in her chestnut-coloured eyes and slowly spilled down her cheeks.

"I'm going to take care of you," said Larry. "The blood team is here to take your blood. I'll be back to see you shortly." He gave her a reassuring squeeze of her hand and walked out to speak with Jake, the senior resident who was looking after her.

"What do you think is going on with her?" asked Larry.

"I agree with you," Jake replied, having overheard the conversation Larry had had with Melodie. He nodded his head in affirmation. "It is likely that the cause of her condition was a bleeding vessel resulting from the anastomosis. I hope it will stop on its own. Given her life-threatening blood loss, I'm requesting an emergency blood transfusion from the blood bank; time is of the essence."

"Sounds good," said Larry. "Let's discuss her again in half an hour. If you think we need to take her back to the OR sooner than that, call me."

With a sigh, Larry headed to the shared surgical office, the quiet hum of the hospital a constant backdrop to his day, punctuated by the occasional unexpected surgical complication like Melodie's. The silence of the empty office pressed in on him as he sat, considering his next steps. When an unexpected complication occurred, his practice was to phone the family, sharing the details in a clear, concise manner to ease their concerns. He knew he couldn't reach out to her father after the earlier assault. Except for the name

Jacob Ashinoff, the next of kin section was blank, an emptiness on the official form. His responsibility was to care for Melodie, ensuring her safety and well-being.

Larry finished the dictations that had been overdue from the medical records department and then glanced at his watch. It had been half an hour since he had last assessed Melodie, so he took the elevator to her room on the 17th floor. Jake was standing by the bed, squeezing blood into the intravenous line by hand. He stopped temporarily as Larry walked in. Melodie was lying quietly on the bed and smiled weakly when she saw Larry.

"Could I have a word with you outside?" asked Jake. Larry nodded.

When they were far enough away from Melodie that she couldn't hear them, Jake said, "She's not settling," his voice slow and urgent. "I am struggling to raise the systolic blood pressure above 80. After receiving four units of packed cells, she had two more bloody bowel movements. Given the amount of bleeding, I think we need to return her to the operating room immediately."

Larry sighed. "I think you're right. What would be your plan?"

Jake frowned as he thought, and then replied, "I would open up the old incision and have a look at the anastomosis. If there are no other obvious areas, I would resect it and make a new one."

"I agree with you," said Larry. "How could we be certain the anastomosis is the source of the bleeding and there is no other explanation, such as a bleeding duodenal ulcer?"

"It will be tough, because the anastomosis will look deceptively normal, even under magnification. If a bleeding duodenal ulcer were present, blood would fill the small intestine—a condition that resection of the anastomosis wouldn't fix. In case of any uncertainties, we have the option of performing an intraoperative gastroscopy. Taking the liberty of calling the operating room, I informed them we were bringing her down for a laparotomy. The urgency of Melodie's condition necessitated bumping Dr. Gould's room. He was not happy. I suspect you will get a call from him in a few minutes complaining about the inconvenience. I made a request to have the endoscopy cart, with all the necessary equipment, on standby."

A slow smile warmed Larry's face, softening his features. With his surgical training nearly complete, Jake's competence was evident in his precise movements and confident demeanour. Larry trusted his judgment, a calm confidence settling over him as he made his choice. "I'll go talk with her while you head down to the OR, prepping the room, and getting the surgical team ready."

Jake headed over to the elevators when Larry called out to him. "One more thing, Jake." Larry walked over just as the elevator door opened. Jake put his foot in the door to stop it from closing.

"The father, Jacob Ashinoff, assaulted me after I spoke with him following the first operation. He threatened me if anything happened to her, well..." Larry paused before he continued. "Please make sure no one from the surgical team has any contact with him. I don't want to put anyone else in his sights. I've already talked to the police. They have prohibited him from entering the hospital, but I doubt that will stop him."

Jake nodded and the elevator doors closed, taking him down to the OR.

With a deep breath, Larry walked back to the quiet solitude of room 1723 to talk to Melodie and explain the upcoming plans for another operation. When he entered the room, the hushed atmosphere was heavy with worry. Jacob was standing vigil by Melodie's bed. His eyes, burning with an inferno of rage, fixated intensely on Larry.

Chapter 3

"You need to take these passengers," barked Gustav Schroder, captain of the St. Louis, his words sharp against the cries of gulls overhead and the lapping of waves against the hull. "Their Cuban visas guarantee them entry; they've all got them." At the far end of Havana Harbour, the 174.90-metre passenger ship settled into the water, its anchor chain clanking against the hull as it found purchase on the seabed. The 937 passengers awaited disembarkation, their faces revealing a mixture of exhaustion and excitement, their conversations a low drone.

A weary sigh escaped from the harbour master as he shook his head. "With a stroke of his pen two weeks prior, President Federico Laredo Bru silenced the world by cancelling all visas, leaving many asylum seekers stranded and heartbroken. We are strictly limiting access to individuals possessing valid American citizenship documentation. The escalating tensions and promise of war in Europe have forced us to close our doors to any more refugees seeking shelter."

"But the German government stripped all these people of their citizenship," said Gustav. "They have nowhere to go. If I take them back to Germany, the secret service police will kill them."

The harbour master took Gustav aside, getting them away

from the prying eyes of the passengers, who strained to hear the conversation. "Look, they are Jews. Nobody wants them. Why do you even care? You are a German captain of a big ship. You have your whole life in front of you. My advice is to take them back to where they came from."

Gustav shook his head. "I cannot do that. They are all decent people. Many were prominent doctors, bankers and lawyers. Unlike the others in my country, they guided their lives by a distinct and fervent religious practice and a commitment to help those less fortunate. Take the time to speak with several of them. Their stories might surprise you. They strive to uplift the less fortunate. Their actions are driven by empathy and a desire for a more equitable world. Imagine that! They desperately want to help others, but the inability to secure even a place to live is a cruel irony, a heartbreaking roadblock to their compassion. My loyalty to them is unwavering; I'll stand by them through thick and thin."

"There's nothing I can do," the harbour master sighed, the creak of the dock a mournful accompaniment to his words.

"Yes, there is," Gustav said, his voice low and steady. "Among them, 22 individuals hold American visas, while four are Spanish citizens, and two are Cuban citizens. At a minimum, you must permit their entry into the nation."

The harbour master stared at Gustav and said, "OK. Bring me their paperwork and I'll see what I can do."

The Psycho

Gustav went to the enormous deck of the ship, where all the passengers waited expectantly with their luggage. He turned on the microphone so all 937 passengers could hear him. His voice was clear and strong. "The authorities cancelled all the visas two weeks ago, without our knowledge. They will not allow refugees into the county. That is the county's firm decision. Despite the restrictions, they will allow entry for those with Spanish and Cuban passports, as well as the 22 of you possessing US visas."

The crowd erupted in a loud murmur, a sea of voices rising and falling like the tide. Sobbing, the sounds of their muffled cries and ragged breaths filling the air as they sought solace in one another's arms. Others, although silent, their eyes spoke volumes: full of fear, widening and reflecting the horrifying events.

Gustav continued, his voice firm, "I am not abandoning you. In just 90 miles, I will take you to the sunny shores of Florida, a land settled by immigrants, just like you. At that point, I will formally petition the US authorities for permission to enter, hoping to present a compelling case. My resolve is firm; I will not cease in my efforts until you are safe. The weight of my concern for you lies heavily on my shoulders. I give you my solemn promise."

***

Ebenezer Klapman and his wife Gloria hugged their four-year-old son, Abraham, tightly, whispering words of love into his soft hair. They had a plan in place, a contingency for this exact scenario, if they would not let them enter Cuba and the authorities stood firm in their refusal. Gloria sobbed uncontrollably on Ebenezer's shoulder, hot tears streaming down her face.

"Honey," he said, his voice thick with emotion, "you know it is the only way. Our top priority, above all else, is ensuring Abraham's safety. If we can make even a small, positive impact on the world, we should seize this opportunity. You know Sybil will care for him as tenderly as a mother would, ensuring he's well-fed and comfortable."

"I am going to miss him... so... much..." Gloria blubbered, tears streaming down her face. "The thought that he might believe we abandoned him because he wasn't loved enough cuts me to the core." Her sobs escalated, shaking her whole body.

"You know that will not happen," consoled Ebenezer. "We will make it our life's mission to find him when we are in a position to do this. For now, this is his best option."

Ebenezer carried Abraham through the hallway and into the Sybil's cabin. The worn wooden floorboards creaked under his weight as he approached Gloria's cousin. Her American visa, a golden ticket to Cuba's rich culture and history, set her apart from many.

The dark confines of Sybil's luggage were familiar to

Abraham. The young boy had practised hiding in among Sybil's clothes in the wooden chest as a game during the long passage from Hamburg. Now, he remained motionless, listening intently to every creak and bump of the chest as if counting down the seconds until his freedom. With serious faces, Ebenezer and Gloria stressed the life-or-death importance of obeying Sybil, their words an inaudible murmur of reassurance about their eventual return. Ebenezer shut the lid of the wooden chest, with his son hiding among the clothing at the bottom. Tears filled his eyes as he wondered if he would ever see his boy again.

Gloria and Ebenezer watched, their eyes brimming with tears, as a powerfully built Cuban, his face scrunched with exertion, wrestled the heavy, iron-bound chest from the ship and onto the rain-slicked docks. The sound of wood scraping on wood was audible even over their sobs. As the Cuban walked past the customs official, a sudden flurry of activity erupted—whispers, shouts, and the clatter of dropped luggage. Ebenezer and Gloria couldn't make out the words. The officer's frantic hand gestures, however, spoke volumes, leaving them breathless while they watched from above on the ship's deck. The man was eager to see what treasures or secrets the old, ornate chest held, and prepared to inspect its contents.

Gloria and Ebenezer watched in horror as Sybil desperately tried to prevent the officer from opening the trunk. He shoved her aside as he brutally forced the locks open. The sounds of metal groaning echoed in the tense silence. Observing his unsettling smile, they saw him nonchalantly grab a pair of Sybil's underwear, sniff them, and slyly conceal them in his jacket. The lid of the heavy chest slammed shut with a resounding thud, rattling the old wooden frame. With a grunt, the Cuban hoisted it onto his shoulders and set off, following Sybil.

Ebenezer and Gloria let out an enormous sigh as the tension finally left their bodies. Abraham was safe. The feeling of knowing his son was finally out of danger of the world's madness washed over him.

***

For Larry, the story of Abraham's survival never got old. Abraham's gravelly voice, vibrating with age, had repeated the tragic events to Larry, his grandson, countless times as he grew up. Following the US and Canada's refusal of entry for his great-grandparents, Ebenezer and Gloria, the two eventually had returned to Europe, where they became refugees in Holland, facing uncertainty and hardship. The Nazis swiftly rounded up the Jews, herding them along with others. They and six million other Jews tragically lost their lives at the hands of the Nazis.

The irony of Abraham's success always brought a smile to Larry's face. His grandfather had started in such humble beginnings, eventually making his way to Canada to become a leading medical scientist. At the time, a high-ranking minister and architect of the cruel Canadian policy that turned away the Jewish refugees seeking asylum, callously declared, "Allowing none was too many." His words dripped with the indifference to human suffering. The statement, sharp and cruel, revealed the depth of antisemitism in Canada.

As Larry watched the raw hatred burning in Melodie's father's eyes, a calm, familiar presence settled over him like a gentle hand. His dedication to helping others, a cornerstone of his Jewish heritage, was a part of him that even the most hateful couldn't erase; it was woven into the fabric of his being, a strength born of his faith.

"I'm taking Melodie to the operating room now," was all he said.

Chapter 4

With a hopeful expression, Melodie looked up at Larry, her eyes searching his for reassurance as he spoke. "Everything will be alright," he said. "Picture in your mind a really wonderful and special place you would love to visit and be present right at this very moment. Allow yourself to imagine it clearly. As the anesthesiologist administers the propofol injection, you can anticipate experiencing incredibly pleasant and vivid dreams. I will see you in the recovery room for a conversation about an hour from now."

A smile touched Melodie's lips as her eyes rolled upward, then gently closed, a look of serene contentment settling upon her features.

Larry and Jake made their way over to the scrub sinks to thoroughly wash their hands while the anesthesiologist was intubating Melodie and attaching her to the equipment necessary for anaesthesia. Entering the operating room following the completion of his surgical scrub, Larry observed the circulating nurse preparing the patient's abdomen with chlorhexidine, meticulously draping the operative field to prepare for the procedure. With practised movements, Larry and Jake carefully put on their gowns and gloves.

"Let's do the time-out, to ensure we have the correct patient and the correct procedure," announced Larry, his voice confident and in control. "The patient is Melodie Ashinoff and the hospital ID is 000489667. She has signed consent for a laparotomy and possible resection of a bleeding anastomosis."

Larry turned to the anesthesiologist. "Could you give her two grams of the antibiotic, Ancef, but hold giving her heparin, the anticoagulant? Does anyone have anything to add?"

The anesthesiologist said, "I've got four more units of packed cells in the fridge, but her last hemoglobin was 84, so I'll hold off giving her anymore blood for now. She is hemodynamically stable. I suggest you get started."

Larry intended to be Jake's surgical assistant. He would defer major intraoperative decisions to him unless a critical situation arose. Jake's five years of surgical training, filled with long hours and intense procedures, finished in a few short months. Larry found him to be a competent and careful surgeon, whose steady hands and precise, skilful movements inspired confidence. Each movement was deliberate and thoughtful.

Jake removed the first set of surgical clips. Larry, observing from the other side of the operating table, noted the slight scent of antiseptic and the faint whisper of movement in the room. He felt at home in these serene surroundings, where the rest of the world seemed to fade away as they focused on the surgery. Gaping open, the wound revealed the deeper, gleaming blue sutures that held the fascia together. Jake cut the suture, which came free with a gentle tug, and he handed the severed length to the scrub nurse. Only the soft clinking of instruments broke the quiet of the operating room. Opening the abdominal wall exposed the intestinal contents. With a gentle touch, he carefully extracted the intestine with the anastomosis from the abdomen.

"As expected," Jake confirmed, gently probing the area with his gloved fingers, "the anastomosis looks perfectly fine—strong, stable, and with no leakage. The small intestine is notably free of blood, in contrast to the colon, which contains a considerable amount of blood. That significantly reduces the probability of a bleeding duodenal ulcer. I think we should proceed with a gastroscopy. It's the only way to be absolutely certain about the diagnosis."

Larry simply nodded in agreement.

The rhythmic beeping of heart monitors filled the operating room as Jake moved toward the patient's head, where the circulating nurse had the gastroscope prepared. He removed his blood-soaked gloves and the stiff fabric gown and tossed them into the overflowing wastebin. Then he put on a fresh set of gloves and skillfully inserted the gastroscope into the mouth, guiding it down the esophagus. The image, sharp and clear, blazed across the four monitors, each one reflecting the pink mucosa of the esophagus. With a steady hand, Jake manoeuvred the gastroscope through the pylorus and into the duodenum, systematically inspecting each quadrant for any abnormalities. With a sigh of relief, he carefully repositioned the gastroscope into the stomach. Jake inspected the stomach lining and found no ulcer. He thoroughly checked every area for other abnormalities. The esophagus, too, appeared healthy and normal upon examination. He finally removed the gastroscope.

After going through the same scrubbing and gown donning process as the first time, Jake returned to his side of the operating table. "Although the original surgery looks perfect, I think we should resect the anastomosis and create another one," he said. "I'm sure a small open blood vessel is leaking into the anastomosis."

Again, Larry nodded in agreement.

The rhythmic hum of the ultrasonic scalpel was a steady counterpoint to the quiet tension in the operating room as Jake meticulously divided the blood vessels around the anastomosis. With precision, he used two stapling cartridges to divide the bowel before passing the specimen to the scrub nurse. The final anastomosis required the use of two more sets of stapler cartridges. With a final suture, Jake finished the surgery in under thirty minutes. Once again, the rhythmic beeping of the heart monitor filled the room.

"Don't put the specimen in formalin," instructed Larry to the scrub nurse. "I want to take it to the pathologist. Hopefully, he can pinpoint the source of the bleeding under a microscope."

Leaving the sterile environment of the operating room, Larry carried the specimen, wrapped in surgical towels. Having witnessed Jake's exceptional surgical competence firsthand, he felt comfortable leaving him to close the abdominal incision, confident in his steady hands and precise technique.

"Could you look at this specimen?" asked Larry. With a sigh, Dr. Guido Consoni gazed up from his microscope, his horn-rimmed glasses perched precariously on his forehead. He was a small man, his grey goatee soft to the touch, framing a face worn with the passage of time, each line a testament to a life lived. Larry knew, with absolute certainty, that his skills surpassed all other pathologists at the hospital. His diagnoses were always precise and thorough.

Guido didn't speak. He simply pushed back from his cluttered desk, the chair legs scraping against the floorboards scratched up over time, and walked with Larry to the specimen room, its door slightly ajar. He carefully opened the anastomosis with a pair of sharp, gleaming scissors, the metallic scent of blood filling the air. With a rush of cold water from a nearby tap, they rinsed the old blood and stool from the surgical site, leaving behind a clean surface as they both leaned in to look at the specimen.

"Look here," said Guido. "There is a tiny ulcer right in the staple line. You can see the end of a small open vessel. I suspect that was the source of your bleeding."

"Wow," Larry murmured, his head shaking from side to side, a low whistle escaping his lips. "Such a small, insignificant vessel could cause such devastating grief? That's incredibly unlucky. It's like a series of unfortunate events."

Larry walked back to the brightly lit operating room and updated the team about the pathology findings. "I suspect she'll be fine now," Larry said, a hint of relief in his voice. "The chances of experiencing significant bleeding from an anastomosis are minimal, at less than 1 per cent. She was one of the unlucky ones, I guess."

With Melodie on a stretcher, Larry left the operating room, the hushed tones of the medical staff following him as they moved toward recovery. Carefully, he dictated the operative note, ensuring he meticulously recorded every detail from the incision to the closure. He could still feel the weight of the father's anger, the trouble brewing like a storm. Yet the second encounter with Jacob, in Melodie's room before the surgery, felt like a stroke of luck. The arrival of the OR transport team, he was certain, had prevented another assault. Jacob had stormed out of the room, his anger a palpable thing in the air, leaving Larry to watch as they wheeled

Melodie away on the gurney. Although he felt a surge of gratitude, he knew this was not the last he would see her father.

Melodie was awake, her eyes bright, when Larry arrived in the recovery room, the beeping of machines filling the quiet space. He held her hand, his touch gentle as he spoke to her. "The surgery went very well," he said, a relieved smile on his face. "We found a tiny ulcer in the anastomosis, with a visible vessel at the end, which appeared to be where the bleeding originated. I think you're going to be OK now; the worst is over. I looked at the specimen with the pathologist."

Melodie managed a weak smile. "Thank you, Dr. Klapman," she whispered. "I'll try not to bleed any more..."

This last comment made Larry smile. "I am sure you'll do your best!" he laughed. Larry stood up from the edge of the bed where he was sitting and headed for the door to leave. When he heard Melodie speak, Larry turned around.

"Dr. Klapman," she said, her voice thick with sorrow, "I'm so sorry about my father. I told him not to come back to the hospital. He's not the type of man anyone can tell what to do. I don't want him to hurt you, and I told him so. You are very kind to me."

Larry walked out of the recovery room, blinking in the bright hallway light, and almost ran into the distraught father. Jacob reached up, his fingers gripping the rough fabric of Larry's his scrub suit collar, and hoisted him effortlessly towards the ceiling. His voice was a low growl, thick with menace, as he spat out, "If you touch her again, I swear I'll kill you."

With a sickening thud, Larry hit the floor, the sound amplified by the emptiness of the hallway. He landed with a heavy finality. Larry watched as Jacob walked away, not even turning around.

Chapter 5

"Look," Larry said sharply, his eyes darting around the room to Sergeant Mendez, the police officer tasked with obtaining his statement, "his daughter's illness has left him distraught and upset." Muffled sounds of the anesthetic monitors from the surgery taking place in the operating room came through the walls of the small, cramped office. With a blue ballpoint pen, Sergeant Mendez diligently recorded Larry's statement in a black notebook. "That's the extent of it," Larry said firmly. "Filing charges is not something I intend to do. I will simply steer clear of him. I don't want any trouble."

"This is the second time he has attacked you," Mendez stated, his eyes hard and filled with seriousness. "There's no way we can effectively prevent him from entering the hospital. He's determined and could easily slip past security. It is a public building with multiple points of entry. He could come back and try to hurt you—again."

"We will probably discharge Melodie within a few days, and I will have no more dealings with him thereafter," Larry stated, his words carrying a sense of relief. "I don't want to push him any further, to risk inciting his already simmering anger. I suspect he has a multitude of his own difficulties that he's currently handling."

With a barely perceptible sigh, Mendez shook his head, his eyes betraying a hint of weariness. "Just so you know, I'm going to have a very unpleasant conversation with him. It won't be pretty. He needs to know we are watching him. I will warn him that if he comes near you again, we'll take him into custody."

"OK, then. We're finished?" asked Larry.

Mendez stood, shook Larry's hand, and then exited the stuffy office. Larry exhaled slowly, letting out a long sigh, then reclined in his chair, fingers laced behind his head, staring up at the pale ceiling. The memory of another time, when angry men had surrounded him, flooded his thoughts. He recalled the heavy smell of sweat and fear imprinted on his brain as if it were yesterday, and how his calm demeanour had defused their aggression 10 years earlier.

***

Larry had proudly displayed his University of Toronto computer science degree to the medical school interview committee. It was the culmination of four years of late-night coding sessions and challenging exams. He'd achieved a solid 4.0 GPA, reflecting his hard work and academic excellence. His MCAT scores, which are used for entering American medical schools, were in the top 95th percentile, a testament to his rigorous studying and preparation. When he applied to medical school at the University of Toronto, the admissions committee lauded his exceptional grades, but expressed concern about his lack of real-world experiences that would shape him into a compassionate and well-rounded physician. With his grandfather Abraham's enthusiastic support, Larry joined the Israeli army's boot camp.

Having flown on El Al to Tel Aviv, Larry felt the dry desert air as he immediately boarded a bus with fellow recruits. The journey to basic training was a blur of activity and anticipation. The first part of the exercise, medical and psychological testing, began with a battery of physical and cognitive assessments. This ensured the army's needs aligned perfectly with each soldier's skills and aspirations. All recruits had to endure the gruelling four-month Rifleman 02 basic training program, filled with early mornings and rigorous physical challenges. The plan was to match recruits to their best-suited roles, weighing the results of their medical, cognitive, and psychological evaluations, ensuring optimal placement.

Bright fluorescent lights buzzing overhead woke Larry on the first day of training camp. He glanced at his watch, its face a blur in the reflecting light. At 4 a.m., the world outside the window was still and quiet. But inside was different.

His drill sergeant, Yuri, yelled, "Everyone up!" his voice booming across the barracks, making the bunks rattle. Larry, now awake, watched as Yuri glanced around the barracks, noting the rough-hewn bunks and the sounds of snoring soldiers. With a sigh that Larry could hear, Yuri took in the 40 new recruits, their nervous energy palpable in the air. Larry and the recruits scrambled out of bed, the rough fabric of his crisp new army fatigues scratching his skin as he pulled them on, the rigid leather of his brand-new boots pinching his feet. Dressed in their uniforms, they stood at attention, their bodies stiff, while Yuri meticulously inspected them.

Six inches separated Yuri and Larry in height. Yuri's head barely reached Larry's shoulder. His face was smooth, freshly shaven, with his short hair neatly cropped close to his scalp. Larry thought Yuri was a few years younger, in his late teens. With his arms held stiffly behind his back, the drill sergeant moved with the quiet assurance of someone in command. The air crackled with unspoken power. As he walked down the line of recruits, inspecting each one with a curt nod, he paused abruptly when he reached Larry. The silence hung heavily in the air as Larry braced himself.

Yuri glanced down at Larry's new boots, as if noticing an imperfection. He roared, "Klapman!" the sound sharp and urgent. "I see a scratch on your left boot, a nasty gouge that looks freshly made. Your duty is to have them polished and ready for my morning inspection—I expect perfection. Now hit the deck and knock out 20 pushups."

Yuri's face was within two inches of Larry's neck. Larry could feel the hot, wet spittle of Yuri's saliva and the rasping breaths on his neck as he yelled. The sharp, barked command startled Larry. He froze for a moment before continuing to look straight ahead, pointedly avoiding the drill sergeant's eyes.

"Klapman!" he roared, his voice reverberating through the cavernous space. "Are you having trouble hearing me? Hit the deck and do 20 pushups—now!"

With a thud, Larry hit the floor, and though he powered through the exercises, his muscles screamed in protest as he fought for the last two. Arms burning with a fiery ache, he attempted to stand as he finished, but the unmistakable pressure of Yuri's boot on his back prevented him. He could feel the sharp edge of the sole digging into his flesh.

"That was not fast enough," Yuri cried, the frustration evident in his voice. "I need you to complete another 20."

Larry felt a jolt of anxiety, like a fist clenching in his chest. His mind raced, a whirlwind of thoughts, as he felt his pulse quicken, a frantic drum against his ribs. He doubted he could handle another 20 repetitions. Already his muscles screamed in protest. Overwhelmed, he knew arguing was futile. With a surge of determination, he forced himself past the burning pain, completing the 20 pushups. This time, when Larry got up, Yuri did not stop him. He simply resumed his careful examination of the other recruits, his eyes sharp, his expression unreadable.

The first day of training, Larry remembered, hadn't been the worst—yet the sounds of shouting instructors and heavy breathing were still fresh in his mind. Every day for the next four months, the familiar sting of Yuri's criticism would fill Larry's ears, leading to another punishment, a heavy weight on his spirit.

Near the completion of his boot camp training, exhausted after 15 miles of a 20-mile hike with a 50-pound pack, he set his rifle down on a smooth, grey rock to ease the straps that had dug into his shoulders.

Yuri's sharp eyes, like a hawk's, instantly spotted the mistake. "Never let go of your rifle!" he yelled, his voice echoing through the canyon. "You are going to run the last five gruelling miles to the base. Now get going. We haven't got all day! I will know if you stop for any reason, and in that case, you'll need to start over."

Ignoring the weary sighs of his fellow recruits, Larry started trotting off, carrying his heavy pack on his back and the rifle in his arms. The dust rose in little puffs around his boots. He smiled, a smug, knowing smile, as he left. This wouldn't be a problem for him. Not at all. Four months of Yuri's brutal punishments had sculpted him into a muscled machine, a body honed to perform any physical task. The methodical pounding of his feet could outrun the relentless criticisms of the sadistic drill sergeant, who verbally attacked him daily. In his mind, each word was a searing brand imprinting on him. While Yuri had pushed him to the limits of his physical endurance, his ragged breathing was a testament to the exertion. He felt resilient, a powerful surge of energy coursing through him, ready for any challenge. With renewed determination, Larry picked up his pace, his steps quicker and more powerful.

The wisdom gained during the relentless training proved to be Larry's most treasured and impactful life lessons. When encountering angry men who felt they were in a position of power, Larry would typically adopt a calm, nonconfrontational demeanour, defusing the situation with measured responses. He possessed the remarkable ability to transmute his anger, using it as a catalyst for becoming a better and stronger individual. Larry had witnessed others from which bitterness and unhappiness radiated, those who couldn't channel negative energy constructively. Their discomfort and grief were palpable, a heavy weight in the air.

Later, after boot camp was over, Yuri confided in Larry, sharing that the psychological testing had revealed he was blessed with a specific trait. Following the psychologist's interpretation of the results, Yuri received the austere instruction from his superiors to relentlessly push Larry to his breaking point. This would transform him into a stronger and better person. It would also make him a better soldier.

Chapter 6

Larry came by on rounds to find Melodie's bed unoccupied. A half-finished crossword puzzle lay on the nightstand, and the room was unusually quiet. Since her last operation, she'd been progressing nicely, the previously troubling bleeding having ceased completely. Two days prior, with her pain managed, the Foley and epidural catheters were removed, leaving her feeling more mobile, allowing her to walk around in the hallway. Yesterday, though, Larry had noticed a disturbing redness around the wound, along with a slight warmth to the touch, increasing his concern for infection. He recalled their conversation from the day before about the possibility of having a wound infection, the weight of her words still heavy in his mind.

"You don't use antibiotics?" Melodie had asked. Melodie gazed at him.

"So, I'm going to wait another day," Larry had said, sighing, "to see if the wound settles on its own." Inspecting the incision, he carefully felt the edges, his fingers searching for the telltale softness, suggesting a pocket of pus forming under the skin.

The question about antibiotics hung heavy in the air, thick with unspoken worry. She had just finished a breakfast of warm blueberry pancakes. The sweetness lingered in her breath. A warm smile spread across Larry's face as he looked at Melodie, noticing her improved condition and her eagerness to learn more about her treatment. He outlined everything in fine detail.

"We administered antibiotics before the surgery started to help prevent postoperative wound infections. At the time-out, a moment of quiet pause before the procedure, the anesthesiologist administered the antibiotic, a necessary precaution against any oversight. Despite antibiotic treatment, some wounds become infected, marked by redness, swelling, and throbbing pain. To treat the infection, we must open the wound to release the pus, which often has a foul odour," he said, noticing her grimace. He smiled gently. "A nurse will pack the wound with sterile gauze to promote healing, and it could take up to four weeks for complete closure. Administering antibiotics after a wound infection has already taken hold not only fails to aid healing but may also negatively affect the recovery process."

Today Larry was keen to inspect Melodie's wound to determine if he needed to drain any infection. When he saw she was not in her room, he went looking for her. Larry found Melodie chatting with a kind-faced elderly woman in the softly lit patient's lounge, the smell of antiseptic and chamomile tea mingling together. A peal of laughter erupted between them as Larry approached.

"Hi, Melodie," said Larry, a warm smile gracing his lips as

he greeted her. "I was looking forward to taking another peek at your incision. Should you prefer, I could come back this afternoon — say, around four o'clock, when things are a bit quieter."

"No, no. Let's go back to my room." She smiled at Larry and then at the elderly woman. "I hope you don't mind," she said. The elderly woman shook her head.

"You seem so much better," said Larry as they walked to Melodie's room. She lay on the bed and covered herself with the white sheet. Larry donned a pair of gloves and removed the dressing. The wound was now angry looking with red on the edges. It was swollen, and the softness indicated an infection.

"Melodie," said Larry softly, "I'm going to remove the surgical clips and then gently open the wound. As I discussed yesterday, the treatment is to let the pus out. Is that OK with you?"

"Yes," Melodie replied, her voice barely a whisper. "I had a feeling that was the case. You explained it to me yesterday, and I am prepared, so go ahead. Do what you need to do."

"I'm going to get the dressing and stapler remover. Returning shortly."

Within the next two minutes, Larry returned. With gloved hands, he placed the cool, blue absorbent pads around her incision, a naked contrast to her warm skin. Then, after re-gloving, he removed the 13 clips, feeling the slight give of the skin as each one came free. Using his index finger, he gently probed the wound, releasing a thick, yellow pus that ran down to the blue pads; the smell was acrid and sickening. He packed the wound with saline soaked gauze and put a thick dressing over the top, taping it in place.

"I think you will feel better now," he said.

"Do you think I'll be able to go home tomorrow still?"

"If you think you're up to it, I don't see why not," he replied, a slow, thoughtful smile playing on his lips while he removed the soiled dressings and his gloves. "I will take care of the paperwork so that a nurse can be scheduled to change the dressing at your home on a daily basis. I can see you in my office next week to check on your healing progress, and we can discuss any concerns you may have."

Melody nodded, smiling weakly. "See you tomorrow then."

***

The following morning, Larry made his rounds, greeting the residents in the small office on the ward with a smile and a cheerful "Good morning."

"Melodie's hemoglobin level is at 100," Jake informed the team. "The white blood count came back as normal at 9.6, and her electrolyte levels and the rest of the blood chemistry also show no abnormalities. There are no issues with her bowel movements, and there is no sign of blood. Her temperature is 36.9°C, and she does not have a fever."

"Do you think it is safe to send her home?" asked Larry.

With a scratch of his coarse beard, Jake muttered, "Well, we are not doing anything for her here except for the dressing changes. Home care nurses can provide this service directly, offering personalized attention in familiar surroundings. Besides, she had all her belongings packed and was excited to head home. You could practically feel her anticipation."

"OK," said Larry. "I'll just say goodbye to her. You can carry on with your rounds on the rest of the patients."

Larry sauntered into Melodie's room, his footsteps barely audible on the thick linoleum. Sitting on the edge of the bed, she was dressed in blue jeans, paired with a white cotton blouse. Her fashionable short boots, with their intricate stitching and subtle sheen, were a perfect complement to her outfit. She had zipped her wheeled hand luggage and pulled up the handle, ready for departure. The faint scent of lavender hinted at a sachet inside.

"I guess you are ready to go," laughed Larry.

Melodie grinned, nodding.

With a reassuring smile, he gave her his business card and

said, "Here's my cell phone number. Call anytime, day or night, if you have any worries at all. If you need anything or have questions, please don't hesitate to call. My cell phone is always within reach. I carry it everywhere. I'll look forward to seeing you in the office next week. Please call the office number to set up an appointment."

Larry turned to leave. "And Dr. Klapman," Melodie said, her voice a little shaky, "my father is picking me up. He's waiting for me in the front of the hospital. I deeply regret the disrespect he showed you. His behaviour was unacceptable." A single tear traced a path down her right cheek before she dabbed at it with a tissue.

Larry looked at her and said, "Melodie, this journey is all about you. Don't you worry about me. Just make sure you get better and that is all that I need from you."

Larry offered a warm smile, a flash of white teeth, before quietly leaving her room. He made his way to his busy office, the sounds of phones ringing and people chattering already filling the air. The list showed there would be 50 patients to see today.

Larry sighed, a long, weary sound escaping his lips. The hum of the computer and the rhythmic tap-tap-tap of his keyboard were the soundtrack to his long day. He knew he wouldn't be leaving his office until after 7 p.m. Settling into his large leather chair before the aged oak desk, he reflected on the satisfying feeling of successfully navigating Melodie's intricate surgery, especially the tricky bleeding anastomosis. Sometimes, when unforeseen complications arise, the consequences can be far more catastrophic, leaving a trail of wreckage in their wake. He felt a surge of relief this time, as she left the hospital with just a minor wound infection—a small bandage on her incision, a testament to a near miss—that would clear up in a few weeks. Knowing she had her entire future ahead, full of untold adventures and experiences, filled Larry with satisfaction. The waiting room buzzed with nervous energy as he began seeing patients, the ticking of the clock a counterpoint to the hushed anxieties.

A call arrived at 11 a.m., interrupting the quiet hum of the office. He glanced at his cell phone. The caller ID flashed Jake's number, a familiar string of digits. Larry answered, and Jake immediately started speaking.

"Melodie just arrived in the emergency room with absent vital signs." Jake paused. "We did everything we could to resuscitate her. I'm sorry, Dr. Klapman... She just died."

Chapter 7

Ethan Dreyfuss, the training camp commander, had dark, penetrating eyes that seemed to bore into Larry's soul, reading his every thought. His short, salt-and-pepper hair, sharp nose, and jaw, etched with the deep lines of years in the military, commanded instant respect. The very air around him felt charged with authority. Larry sat in the unforgiving wooden chair, the rough grain digging into his thighs, opposite his cold metal desk. He'd finished four gruelling weeks of basic training, but the meeting with his supervisor to discuss the next eight months loomed. For a new recruit, a meeting with the base commander—a man whose booming voice now filled the bare, white office—was highly unusual.

"Your cognitive and psychological tests suggest Unit 8200 might be what you are best suited in the Israel Defense Forces," said Ethan Dreyfuss. "Do you know what that is?"

Larry nodded slowly, a thoughtful expression on his face. He gave a quick, respectful, "Yes, sir."

Unit 8200, a clandestine IDF cybersecurity branch, had highly skilled personnel. It was the largest unit in the force, with thousands of recruits. This placement was exactly what Larry had been hoping for. A feeling of overwhelming relief washed over him. Typically, the unit attracts 18- to 21-year-olds with quick learning skills and proficiency in computer programming, a demographic known for their adaptability and innovative thinking. Many in the unit, sworn to secrecy under threat of imprisonment, monitor internet traffic worldwide, often late into the night. The thrill of gathering intelligence, the risk and the secrecy, was what attracted Larry to this type of work.

Dreyfuss continued, a glint in his eye, "We believe your expertise would be invaluable in our fast-paced cybersecurity developmental unit. It's a challenging but rewarding environment. We need your help in creating a worm that can interfere with the centrifuges used in nuclear weapons production in Iran and other hostile regions posing a threat to Israel. Do you have any questions?"

"No sir," replied Larry, his heart pounding and voice trembling slightly with barely suppressed excitement. This surpassed even his wildest expectations.

"You can go now," Dreyfuss said, the words sharp and clipped, leaving no room for argument. He glanced down at the scattered papers on his desk, the rustling sound a clear sign for Larry to exit.

***

The next morning, a dusty army jeep, its engine rumbling, arrived to collect Larry and two others. They drove across the sun-baked expanse of the Negev desert, finally reaching Beersheba, where rows of identical military barracks housed the new recruits. They ushered Larry into a cramped, stuffy office, redolent with the smell of old paper and stale coffee. There he met his next in command.

"Hi," said the man, his smile warm, inviting, and youthful, barely a day over 20. "I'm Benjamin. It's customary to call each other by our first names in this place, making interactions feel more personal and relaxed." His curly black hair sprang up from his head, and his long, curved nose gave his face a striking profile. His warm smile and kind eyes hinted at a sharp, intelligent mind.

"Larry," he said, extending his harm for a firm handshake.

"Let's get right down to it, then," said Benjamin. "Our mission is top secret, which means we cannot discuss with anyone except the 10 of us on the team. Iran has always been a nuclear threat, but we are close to stopping that. We need your help to finish the programming."

For the next eight months, Larry burned the midnight oil, the glow of his computer screen illuminating his face as he coded late into the night. The plan was to unleash a 500-kilobyte computer worm, designed to silently infect every Windows operating systems globally, spreading like wildfire through networks. Next, it searches for the Siemens S7 system—a Windows-based program used to control industrial equipment like centrifuges—its interface a familiar blend of clicks and beeps. With a sickening shudder, the worm causes the centrifuge's high-speed rotation to become unstable, ripping it violently apart. The worm's widespread internet presence, and subsequent transfer to USB drives for offline propagation, are key to its effectiveness. Unseen by the operator, the worm duplicates itself relentlessly, a silent digital plague seeking its target. The false certificate from a well-known company easily bypasses standard virus protection, giving the software an air of legitimacy.

The worm then scans for Siemens-made industrial control systems, verifying if the machine is a target. Nuclear fuel-enrichment systems, like the ones in Iran, rely on high-speed centrifuges for the process. The worm remains dormant, silent, and inactive unless the system is recognized as the target. If the system is a target, a newer version downloads, aiming for the system's logic controller. The process is silent and swift. By subtly observing the system, the worm gains knowledge of the centrifuge's inner workings, leading to its malfunction. It feeds the outside world false data, masking the true state of affairs until it's too late for intervention.

Larry's smile widened as he relished the depth of his access into the cyber-minds of those seeking to harm Israel. His pivotal contribution was essential to the project's success. Larry programmed the worm's download function, allowing it to fetch the latest version from the internet, a crucial part of its operation. The project was ongoing, a continuous cycle of revisions and refinements. The public revelation of their actions triggered a rapid response from cybercriminal gangs, who attempted to reverse-engineer their worm, adapting the malicious code for their own nefarious purposes. Containing the escalating security breach required more painstakingly written lines of complex, error-free code to prevent this from happening.

***

Laughter and cheers filled Dalet, a bustling campus bar, as the 10 teammates celebrated their win with drinks. Although none of the Unit 8200 army recruits could discuss the project among themselves, many others from different units eagerly joined in.

"I'm not sure what all the excitement is about," said Jasmine, a recruit working on monitoring the internet traffic for intelligence. Standing near a bar stool next to Larry, she was halfway through her second beer, the condensation clinging to the glass. With a flick of her wrist, she brushed her long, inky curls away from her face, revealing eyes the colour of moss, alight with playful mischief. Her head only reached to his shoulder, a distinct difference in height. He bent low, the raucous laughter and clatter of glasses a deafening roar around him, as she whispered into his ear. When she spoke, the delicious smell of lilac, heavy and intoxicating, filled his nostrils. Larry had noticed her before, the scent of her perfume a faint, sweet note carried on a gentle breeze. In the darkness of the bar, the shadows in her dark hair and eyes hinted at secrets buried deep within her, a mystery as compelling as a hidden treasure.

"We are saving the world from the shadowy, evil forces that threaten to consume us all," Larry declared, his voice ringing with righteous conviction. A warm smile spread across his face as he basked in the glow of Jasmine's attention. Amid the throng of young, fit soldiers in the bar, she had chosen him to talk to.

Jasmine subtly scanned the bar, her eyes darting around, gently pulling him toward her amid the boisterous chatter and clinking glasses. "Your name," Jasmine said, lowering her voice, her face grave, "came up on the dark web." The words hanging heavy in the air.

Larry stopped lifting his glass as he was about to take a drink. "What does that mean?" he asked. "You're the expert."

A deep, weary sigh escaped Jasmine's lips, carrying the weight of unspoken words. "I'm not sure. Sometimes, it's just a meaningless whisper in the wind, leaving no trace. Or it may mean something more serious, such as a significant security breach, perhaps even a data leak. I have to report this to my superior. It's my duty. I felt it was important for you to be aware."

Larry paused, a thoughtful expression on his face, the possibilities of the significance pressing down on him. "Two weeks from now, I'll be jetting back to Toronto. My acceptance letter to medical school arrived, confirming my admission—it's my dream realized. The next two weeks I'm spending at my distant cousin's kibbutz in the south, near Gaza." He looked around the bar and then back at Jasmine. "I don't want to be targeted. Once information is on the internet, it's there forever, a permanent digital footprint in the vast expanse of the web. My involvement in this cyber-project could have lasting consequences if the internet identifies me as one of the masterminds; my career and personal life could be severely affected."

"I understand," said Jasmine.

"I guess you'll let them know if you uncover any further details?"

"So far, there is nothing," she said. "But I'll keep looking."

The Israeli army poured significant resources into bolstering its cybersecurity capabilities and developing sophisticated internet intelligence gathering techniques. Employing computer models and algorithms, they could differentiate between genuine threats and those posing minimal risk, utilizing the most advanced methods available. The army kept secret the names and details of everyone involved in the operation, working diligently to maintain anonymity.

Breaches could come in many forms, ranging from data leaks to physical intrusions, each with its own unique set of vulnerabilities. Larry filled his emails to his family with stories of basic training—the intense physical challenges, the camaraderie among his fellow recruits, and the ever-present tension of the daily routines. The army meticulously scanned all emails for security breaches, but anyone with access to the University of Toronto's records—a trove of sensitive data—would undoubtedly know about his computer science degree. It was a small, almost insignificant step for someone to assume his involvement with the Unit 8200. He was a soldier in a modern war with the computer surveillance and internet as his weapon. Larry always knew that he might become the next target.

Jasmine and Larry clinked glasses with a satisfying ting, and swiftly drained their ice-cold beers, the foamy residue clinging to their lips. The next day, Larry found himself in the sun-drenched south of Israel, experiencing the communal living of a kibbutz, the sounds of Hebrew conversations and laughter mingling with the bleating of sheep.

Chapter 8

In Finnigan's bar, a few blocks from the hospital, the clatter of glasses and indistinct murmur of conversation faded as Abraham and Larry focused intently on the flickering images of the newsreel. Larry made it a point to see his grandfather at least bi-weekly, typically after a grueling day in the operating room, the quiet moments of their visits a welcome respite from the sterile atmosphere of the hospital. Larry, his voice hoarse from explaining, finally finished detailing his troubles with Jacob Ashinoff to Abraham.

"Don't be so quick to judge him," said Abraham. "The man sounds like he has a lot going on in his life. Dismissing him as merely a psycho ignores the complex, possibly traumatic experiences that shaped his life. One can't judge without knowing the full story..."

Larry interrupted the conversation. "Look at that." He pointed to the television screen.

Both Larry and Abraham focused their gaze on the screen. The newly elected prime minister of Canada sat next to the President of the United States in the oval office of the White House.

"This is a monumental chance to join the US, becoming its 51st state, a momentous occasion brimming with potential," beamed the president. "You'll pay significantly lower taxes, leaving more money in your pocket, and enjoy access to world-class healthcare. Unlike the rest of the world, you won't face any tariffs."

"Some things are not for sale," responded the prime minister. He swept his arm around the room. "This house, for example, will never be for sale. The Canadians have spoken in no uncertain terms by electing me. We will remain a sovereign nation."

"Well, the tariffs will remain intact until you change your mind. We don't need Canada, anyway." The president shook his head, disappointed.

"Respectfully, Mr. President, Canada is your largest trading partner. Severing trade ties with Canada would cause your country significant economic hardship. US income taxes, with their complex brackets and deductions, often exceed their Canadian counterparts, leading to a greater tax burden for many Americans. While your healthcare is excellent, the price tag is twice as high as in Canada. You'll pay a significant premium for this quality. Canadians benefit from a publicly funded healthcare system, eliminating the need for personal payments at the point of service. In line with other developed countries, the government provides funding for health care."

"We'll see how you feel about this after the bite of tariffs takes hold. You will know what to do..." The president stopped talking and looked around the room as if confused. "I... I don't know..."

The cameras stopped and flipped back to the CNN studio. "Incredible," said the host, "The president seemed to have lost his flow of thoughts in the middle of a conversation with the prime minister."

Larry and Abraham stared at each other and tuned out from the CNN news report.

"I'm 81 years old," replied Abraham. "I can relate to that. It happens to me too. Sometimes, my mind goes blank, the train of thought derailed by a sudden, inexplicable distraction. I might head to the kitchen to get something, only to stand there amidst the familiar clutter, a vague sense of purpose dissolving into the quiet hum of the refrigerator, trying to remember what it was I came for."

"It happens to everyone. You are not running the country with rules you have made up as you go," laughed Larry.

The sounds of the room faded as Abraham went quiet, his face falling into an expression of deep thought. "It is not so funny what is going on right now. Your Canadian life has been one of quiet comfort and gentle winters, far removed from harsher realities. The weight of a tyrant's rule, the stifling silence, the pervasive sense of dread—none of this is familiar to you. It all begins like this. With the suspension of Habeas Corpus, a blatant violation of the

Constitution, the tyrant delivered executive orders designed to harm his critics; rampant corruption flourished openly. The list seems never-ending. Each event is more egregious than the last, a crescendo of horrifying actions. Each event, with its attendant chaos and fear, further cements his iron grip on authoritarianism. This feeling is hauntingly familiar; I've navigated these treacherous waters in the past, and I know what it takes to overcome it."

"Surely it is different now. He supports Israel. He is not antisemitic. As a Jew, we are safe."

"His anti-Palestine stance is solely driven by his vindictiveness to retaliate against Harvard. They refused him entry over 50 years ago, their words sharp and dismissive, because he was not smart enough. He will switch his pro-Israel stance when it suits him, or when a Jew criticizes something he says."

"What do you think will happen?"

Abraham ran his hand through his hair before he replied, a move he does after a great deal thought has gone into his answer. "He declared his ambition to make Canada the 51st state, voicing his unwavering determination to achieve this goal. It's a battle for dominance, a struggle for control over resources and influence. For him, there's no moral compass, only the fleeting whim of the moment, speaking impulsively without consideration of the consequences."

"My psychiatric colleagues at the hospital, after observing his cognitive decline and memory lapses, have diagnosed him with early-onset dementia. Because of his narcissistic personality disorder, he's incapable of recognizing or accepting his flaws. Is there no one in a powerful US position who can prevent his dangerous actions?"

"Edmund Burke's prescient quote highlights the cyclical nature of political decay, a phenomenon currently visible in the United States. 'The only thing necessary for the triumph of evil is for good men to do nothing'. Never has this statement held more weight than it does today, as we witness the unfolding events and their significant impact on us."

Chapter 9

With a grim expression, the coroner inquired, "Explain to me precisely what occurred in that operating room."

Larry sat next to Dr. Alton in a small, sterile office next to the chaotic emergency room, reviewing Melodie's medical records as the fluorescent lights hummed overhead. A local family doctor, Alton, moonlighted as the coroner, his familiar face a comforting presence despite the grim circumstances. He adjusted his black-rimmed glasses, which had slid down his nose, to read the small font on the computer screen. He had a substantial potbelly, making it difficult for him to lean close enough to the computer screen to see it properly. Glancing up at Larry, who sat quietly, he brushed his long blond hair back behind his ears; the strands catching the light.

"The operative reports contain all the details," said Larry. "Jake, my chief resident, and I each dictated our separate operative reports, which convey the same message. Our general surgery division reviewed the video of the first operation. We observed the sterile environment and the meticulous techniques. No significant points or ideas emerged during the discussion. It was rather uneventful. You can get a copy of the video through the medical records department."

With a creased brow and a hushed tone, Dr. Alton said, "The

autopsy uncovered an unexpected anomaly. It revealed an ulcer in the transverse colon, far from the surgery site. The pathologist notes a large, distended arterial blood vessel at the ulcer's base. Its compromised integrity suggests a massive hemorrhage caused the death, a conclusion supported by the enormous quantities of blood in the colon. Thirty minutes—the journey to the emergency room—was all the time she had left. She bled out, her body's vital fluids escaping in a tragic, silent rush. Is it possible that the bleeding following the first operation stemmed from this issue?"

Larry ran a hand over his grizzled beard, the act a familiar comfort as he pondered the problem. "I think it's highly improbable that the ulcer you found during the autopsy caused the first postoperative hemorrhage. The anastomosis bleed, which we treated by resection, was slow, a mere trickle of blood. A gradual internal bleed developed over 24 hours, ultimately less significant than the massive hemorrhage causing her death. At the time of surgery, I personally took the specimen to the pathologist, and we looked at it together. During our examination, we identified a small, open arterial vessel in the staple line. Both of us deemed this vessel to be the likely cause of the observed blood loss. Throughout the entirety of her hospital stay, there was no recurrence of bleeding whatsoever. The bleeding stopped immediately, providing further evidence that we removed the correct portion of the colon that caused the bleeding."

"Why didn't you do a colonoscopy to confirm no other sources were present?" asked Dr. Alton.

"The risk is considerable," Larry stated in response, "when we perform a colonoscopy on someone with a recent anastomosis. Distension of the colon from pumping in air could blow the anastomosis apart. The other concern was the colon had filled with blood, and it would be unlikely we could see anything."

"Huh," said Dr. Alton. "I see." The computer monitor displayed a long list of medical records, and the coroner methodically scrolled through them, pausing occasionally to examine specific entries.

"Upon discharge, all aspects of the patient's records and care appear to be complete and accurate, showing that everything is in order," Dr. Alton continued. "All her blood tests came back normal, and likewise, all her vital signs were within the normal range. The surgical team meticulously explained and provided her with the typical postoperative care instructions, covering everything from wound care and pain management to activity limitations and follow-up appointments. A review of the medical records revealed no indication whatsoever that the patient was imminently close to death just hours after her discharge from the hospital."

"Is there a problem?" asked Larry.

"Well, the cause of death is obvious: massive hemorrhage

from an ulcer in the colon," said Dr. Alton after a thoughtful pause. "Given the absence of any information in her hospital records that would suggest a predictable death, I do not feel an inquest is required. The root of the issue, the source of the difficulty, lies with Jacob Ashinoff, the father. He has reached the conclusion, and fully convinced himself, that you are the individual responsible for causing her untimely demise. I plan to inform him that a thorough review of both the records and your management practices reveals no evidence that could have reasonably predicted this outcome. In such circumstances, we typically advise the complainant to speak with the College of Physicians and Surgeons if they are not happy with what we have told them. If he goes this route, you can expect a complaint investigation, which is never a pleasant experience."

"Thanks for the warning," said Larry. "He told me if anything happens to her, he'll kill me."

Dr. Alton's eyes widened in astonishment as he looked at Larry, his features betraying his surprise.

Larry continued. "Although the police strongly encouraged me to file charges against him, I decided against it to avoid further provoking him and escalating the situation. Rather than resorting to violence, I'm hoping he will pursue a legal course of action, a far safer and more constructive approach to resolving this conflict."

"Considering that someone threatened your life, it's

remarkable how calm you are."

"In life, you often must manage with the cards dealt to you. Despite my efforts to provide Melodie with the best possible care, the outcome was unfortunately the worst imaginable. That describes the existence of a surgeon—a relentless cycle of high-pressure situations, intricate procedures, and unwavering commitment to patient care. Even when the operation is successful, a possibility of unforeseen and negative outcomes always exists. Despite the profound sadness and self-recrimination we experience in the aftermath of a preventable death, we must persevere and continue providing care for our patients. Even months later, it's not unusual to experience the sudden, involuntary recurrence of memories and feelings related to a past traumatic event, what we call flashbacks. Makes me wonder, though, why we do this kind of work." There was a sense of melancholy, as Larry shook his head sadly.

They exchanged goodbyes, leaving Larry alone with his swirling thoughts. Melodie's father, Jacob Ashinoff, filled his mind. Afraid of his vengeance, Larry desperately searched for more information to plan a defence. With a sigh, he opened his laptop and googled. The familiar logo greeted him on the screen.

Having defected from Russia years earlier to escape persecution, Jacob presented himself in Canada as a scientist, a new identity carefully constructed. With only a few scattered details online, many questions remain unanswered. The tribunal had denied his refugee status because of insufficient evidence supporting his claim of being a scientist. The process was rigorous, demanding substantial proof of his professional background. Without the proper paperwork, they deported Jacob back to Russia. He had one child, Melodie, who was born in Montreal, after his deportation, while his wife remained in Montreal where Melodie lived with her mother. Melodie was eight when her mother passed away. They sent her back to Russia to live with Jacob, the father. Over the next five years in Russia, she experienced the biting winters and the fleeting beauty of the brief summers. Jacob's defection from Russia to Canada was a clandestine operation. He brought Melodie with him, their escape shrouded in secrecy. The internet search yielded only that much information, a meagre and unsatisfying amount that left Larry wanting more.

Melodie had never discussed details of her father's story with Larry. And his sole responsibility as her surgeon was to meticulously oversee her care in the days leading up to and following her operation, ensuring her comfort and a successful recovery. Larry had feared a heated debate about her father's aggression would create a deep chasm between them, a situation he wanted to prevent. A sense of foreboding washed over him as he realized the scarcity of information he had on Jacob, making him feel unprepared for the challenge ahead.

With a sigh, Larry stood, the weight of the day settling on his shoulders as he prepared to leave. Streetlights flickered to life, casting long shadows as it grew past 7 p.m. The unexpected death of Melodie had left him in a state of emotional turmoil. The day had been long and arduous. A familiar ache of "what ifs" throbbed in his chest as he reviewed the events, a pointless exercise he knew, yet the sounds of his own self-recrimination were a mournful symphony of his grief. He walked towards his Tesla in the parking lot. The car gleamed under the last low rays of sunlight, its battery fully charged and ready to go. Before he got in the car, a high-pitched chirp from his phone announced the arrival of a text message, its vibrations a gentle buzz against his thigh.

My promise to you is forever in my memory; I haven't forgotten. Your death will be slow and agonizing, each moment a torment. I see you in your sleek, black Tesla, the engine humming quietly as you prepare to leave. I will be a shadow in the night, and you will not see me coming.

Larry's hand trembled as he slipped behind the wheel, quickly pulled out of the parking lot, and drove his Tesla to the nearest precinct to file a complaint about Jacob Ashinoff.

Chapter 10

"And this is the first time you are telling me this? A maniac threatened to kill you?"

Chantelle, Larry's wife, was livid, her voice rising in a furious crescendo. Her Latin Italian heritage was evident in the flash of anger that sparked in her almond-shaped eyes, their dark depths filled with fiery emotion. Her thick, curly black hair rested in perfect ringlets on her bare shoulders, smelling faintly of peach and apple shampoo. Larry's steady presence was a calming influence amid her emotional turmoil. He remained a rock of stability as she raged. It was the intoxicating mix of her fiery spirit and emotional turbulence that drew him in from the start.

After spending a year with the army, Larry had two weeks of spare time before leaving Israel. His grandfather, Abraham, had encouraged him to visit a kibbutz to get more in touch with his Israeli origins.

"They live in harmony with nature, their lives dictated by the rhythms of the land, unlike our structured society," Abraham had explained thoughtfully. "The community acts as an extended family, nurturing the children while their parents work, creating a supportive environment for everyone. Originally, they shared everything—fields, houses, and tools—but now, individuals own everything. Many still work the land, their hands rough from years of tilling soil and harvesting crops," he said, pride showing in his voice. "Max, a distant cousin I haven't seen in years, still works in the orchard. The scent of ripe fruit is always heavy in the air. Did you know that certain desert oases support orange trees? Their vibrant fruit is a testament to resourceful cultivation techniques. A kibbutz offers a transformative experience. You need to immerse yourself in its communal lifestyle, from the shared labour to the evening gatherings. Once you have completed your year in the Israeli Army, remember to schedule some time with Max before heading back to Canada."

Though doubts, like shadows, clouded his mind about visiting Max, Larry couldn't bear the thought of his grandfather's crestfallen face if he declined. He walked into the kibbutz, past the sounds of children playing and the scent of orange blossoms, to Max's small house and knocked on the door. The air grew cooler as Max opened the door, the last rays of sun casting long shadows across the ground. Larry surmised, from Max's obvious aches in his bones and the wrinkles across his face, that he must be in his eighties. As he embraced him, his small, furry white head barely reached Larry's chest.

"Abraham has told me so much about you," Max said, a smile playing on his lips as he recalled their conversations. "Welcome to paradise!"

Larry looked around the room at the sparsely furnished space with the empty chairs and tables against the walls. A wave of regret washed over him for his impulsive decision. The adrenaline rush of the past eight months of the successful cyberattack had left him jittery. He worried the following two weeks of inactivity would be unbearable. The old wooden chair creaked softly as he sat, facing the scarred wooden table, its surface a tapestry of scratches etched by countless hands and meals. Max retrieved a cold bottle of water, still beaded with condensation, from the refrigerator. He twisted off the top and plunked it down in front of Larry.

"Drink," Max urged, his brow a landscape of worry lines, the words barely a whisper. "You don't want to get dehydrated. The desert sun is relentless."

Larry downed the entire bottle of water in four quick gulps, the cool liquid soothing his parched throat. Just as he was about to express his gratitude to Max, a sudden chaotic noise erupted outside, making him jump. A woman chattered animatedly, her loud words tumbling out in rapid-fire Italian, while a man shrieked, his high-pitched voice piercing the silence. The door creaked open, and a woman with a warm smile entered the room. With a burst of energy, she raced over to Max, planting a quick kiss on each cheek before embracing him in a warm hug.

"Hi, Max," she said, the forced cheerfulness in her voice a

strained contrast to the angry words she'd just spat at someone outside. "Sorry about the outburst. That crazy guy from the market tried to pinch my butt again, but I kicked him in the balls. Italian women learn from a young age to defend themselves. I'm sure he won't bother me again."

Her olive complexion shone with tiny beads of sweat catching the light on her forehead. A short tan skirt revealed her long, shapely legs, which ended in stylish cloth sandals. The crisp white cotton of her T-shirt clung to her perfectly sculpted body, accentuating every curve. Long black hair rested on her shoulders in soft curls. Her smile was radiant, her perfect white teeth reflecting the light.

Larry watched in awe at the beautiful woman who had focused her attention on Max. She appeared passionate and animated. Never before had he witnessed such breathtaking beauty contained within such a vibrant, energetic personality. Her eyes sparkled, and a smile played on her lips. Her movements were fluid and captivating.

Max reached out to Larry and grabbed his hand. "I want you to meet Chantelle. She's visiting us from Italy."

Larry was speechless. His mind was racing, and no words could escape his lips. Chantelle's beauty and grace mesmerized him. Her smile was captivating, and her body moved with smoothness and elegance. In that fleeting moment, a warmth spread through him. He knew she was the one. Her face broke into a curious smile, eyes twinkling with amusement, as though she possessed the power to peer into his very thoughts.

That first stolen kiss under the moonlight later that evening marked the beginning of their passionate love affair. They spent the first night together in Chantelle's room, but Larry snuck back into his own room before it got light. At dawn, Max awoke them and fed them a breakfast of fresh fruits, yoghurt, and toasted bagels.

"You two look like you didn't get any sleep," winked Max. "You do not have to sneak around in my house. If you want to sleep in the same room, go ahead. My house is your house."

A shared smile bloomed on their faces as Larry and Chantelle glanced at each other, their eyes sparkling. Though they had tried to stifle their moans, Larry was certain the sheer intensity of their passion had boomed through the thin walls of the house.

"Get your sunhats, sunscreen, and long-sleeved shirts," said Max. "We're going to the orchard today."

They walked towards the neatly spaced rows of orange trees heavy with fruit, evidence of Max's 20 years of tending. That the succulent, sun-ripened citrus could grow in the harsh, dry desert was a testament to modern agricultural technology's advancements.

"The world, with its dismissive whispers and scoffs, declared it impossible," explained Max, a glint of defiance in his eye. "And yet, here we stand, amidst the sweet scent of orange blossoms, a top global orange producer, ranking 16th in worldwide orange supply. Imagine that! A tiny, sun-baked parcel of desert yielded surprisingly bountiful crops."

Larry looked at the rows and rows of orange trees, their leaves a vibrant green, the fruit glowing like tiny suns. "Your job today is to prune the lower branches," said Max, gesturing to the overgrown shrubs with their green shoots. "Chantelle, you prune row 19. Larry, you prune row 20. Let's schedule to meet for lunch in three hours from now." Max winked at Larry as he walked away.

The following two weeks were a blur of shared experiences for Chantelle and Larry, filled with laughter, sun-kissed skin, and lasting memories. With the orchard baking under the summer sun every afternoon, it was too hot to work, so they escaped to the local coffee shop or to the relaxed atmosphere of Max's living room, enjoying their time together. They would spend countless hours at night experimenting with different methods to satisfy their desires.

The day before Larry was to leave, they sat in the shade of Max's front porch. The clinking of ice in his glass mixed with the sound of Chantelle and Max's hushed laughter as they enjoyed the iced tea away from the heat of the sun. Max had been recounting tales of his and Chantelle's grandfather's wartime experiences. His voice was low and filled with a sense of awe and respect. The afternoon air hushed as he spoke of the grandfather's bravery. The buzzing of his cellphone diverted Larry's concentration. Not wanting to change the flow of the conversation, he quietly removed the phone from his pocket and glanced at it.

The caller ID showed a number he recognized, his friend Jasmine, from Unit 8200. "I better take this call," he said, as Chantelle and Max glanced up at Larry with concern.

"You need to get out of there!" Jasmine shouted into the phone. "We have been monitoring internet traffic, and your name keeps coming up. Hezbollah has targeted all 10 of you involved in the last project. We have contacted most of the others. There will be an attack on the kibbutz tonight. They have mobilized the Israeli army to protect everyone and get them to go to the bomb shelters."

Larry told Max and Chantelle about the phone call. They decided the best decision was for Larry to leave as soon as possible.

"I'll post my departure on Facebook and Instagram to deflect some of the immediate outrage," he said, hoping to lessen the intensity of the backlash. "I'll say I'm going to Jerusalem to throw them off, but my true destination is Ben Gurion Airport in Tel Aviv. Jasmine has booked me on a flight to London tonight."

Chantelle and Larry embraced passionately, tears streaming

down their faces as they said their last goodbyes. They exchanged promises to see each other again within a few months, the unexpected intensity of their sobs reflecting the sadness of their parting. Chantelle was a computer science student at the University of Milan, and although she had two years left of her studies, she promised to make time to visit. The army jeep picked up Larry a few minutes later. Max and Chantelle headed off to the bomb shelter.

At the airport, Larry called Chantelle. "My flight leaves in 10 minutes. I wanted to make sure you're alright."

"Yes, Max and I are perfectly fine," Chantelle replied, her voice calm and reassuring. "A few hours ago, the earsplitting wail of air raid sirens shattered the stillness, followed by the distant rumble of a few bombs—a weak attack, we're told. I think your diversion worked."

"Look," said Larry. "I have to go. They are calling my flight. I love you. I miss you."

Heartbreaking, ragged sobs shattered the silence on the other end of the phone. Chantelle finally whispered, "I love you, too," her voice barely audible above the cacophony of the airport departure lounge.

Two years of long-distance calls and emotionally intense visits finally ended when Larry convinced Chantelle to move to Toronto. They got married after he started his gruelling general surgery residency, a time filled with long hours and intense pressure. Their two children, four-year-old Abe and six-year-old Sheldon, were a handful—a whirlwind of boisterous energy and adventurous spirit, constantly on the go. Chantelle dutifully drove their kids to school and appointments. The rhythmic thump of the tires on the road constantly accompanied her as she temporarily shelved her career aspirations.

Today, the news of Jacob's threat against Larry's life ignited Chantelle's fiery temper. Her voice rose sharply. Larry, always calm, rationalized, "He seemed over protective about his daughter. When a loved one suffers a catastrophic event causing death, anger is frequently the response. His harsh words, a result of his grief, may not carry the weight of genuine threats."

"The thought of that maniac coming after our kids for revenge sends a shiver down my spine," Chantelle yelled, a thin, reedy sound choked with terror. "It's like the saying goes, 'an eye for an eye,'" she muttered, her voice tinged with bitterness. "Italian culture, unlike yours, instilled values where taking a life for retaliation is considered honourable."

"I've reported it to the police," said Larry, the weight of the situation heavy in his tone. "A warrant's out for his arrest because of the threats he made—a serious charge, in their view. I have a peace bond."

"Huh," Chantelle laughed, a throaty chuckle that shook her shoulders. "They'll never find him," she whispered, the words catching in her throat. "I've met men like that before; arrogant and full of themselves. They play by different rules than us."

Larry nodded, then replied, "We'll keep the doors locked and remain vigilant."

With a weary sigh and a shake of her head, Chantelle completed the task of making the kids' lunches, the sounds of cartoon characters blaring from the TV in the background.

Larry had taken the morning off to prepare for their upcoming adventure, the aroma of freshly brewed coffee and the quiet hum of his packing efforts filling his home. An exciting trip loomed for them. He checked his list of items to pick up before their Saturday departure: groceries, a new spinnaker halyard, and a first-aid kit were at the top.

John Hegland, the chief of surgery, had invited Chantelle and him on a sailing trip in the British Virgin Islands, promising turquoise waters and gentle breezes. Moored securely in Nanny Cay, Roadtown, Tortola, John's dad's vessel, a 51-foot sailboat, was available for the week. John had intimate knowledge of the British Virgin Islands' capricious winds and sun-drenched beaches. Having visited the Caribbean islands countless times, he volunteered to be their captain. For the first time in six years, Chantelle and Larry were looking forward to a child-free vacation, a much-needed break.

Larry checked his phone when it chirped. A Facebook message notification popped up on his screen. He would normally ignore it, but the bold, almost aggressive capitalization of his name made him pause. His eyes quickly scanned over the words:

Dr. Larry Klapman is a butcher. He killed my daughter and now he must face the consequences.

Chapter 11

The sails billowed as the wind propelled the sailboat effortlessly across the brilliant blue waters. The rhythmic creak of the mast was a steady beat against the sounds of the sea. A gentle warmth spread through the cockpit as the early morning sun illuminated the space, casting long shadows across the wood panels. The sun beat down on Chantelle's face as she sat at the helm, her wide sunglasses and sunhat doing little to hide her deep smile at Larry. A carefree expression made her pretty face even more stunning. She looked every bit a movie star. The bright yellow shorts and halter top were a vibrant contrast to the rich, dark gleam of the teak floor under her bare feet. Eyes wide, Larry gazed at her, mesmerized by her beauty.

Ten years into their relationship, the sight of her hair whipping in the wind still gave him a jolt of excitement and arousal, his pulse quickening as if it were the first time. She flashed a playful wink. A silent spark of flirtatious energy shot through him like electricity, though she seemed utterly unaware of her effect on him. Feeling faint, Larry sat down heavily, his vision swimming as he continued to stare at her.

As they approached Deadman's Bay, the gentle rocking of the boat and the salty tang of the sea air filled Larry's senses as he gazed at the rich green of Peter's Island, anticipating their mooring for the night. The champagne-coloured sand stretched out before them, deserted except for a few scattered seashells and the gentle lapping of waves. Protected from the wind and waves, the tranquil bay offered a mirror-like surface, its stillness urging him to dive in. They had scuba gear, complete with tanks and regulators, and snorkelling equipment, including masks and fins. Their plan was to take the small dinghy to the Indians, a cluster of small islands a short distance away, where they would explore vibrant coral reefs teeming with colourful fish after securing their boat to the mooring ball.

They had discussed cancelling their trip after the last threatening Facebook post, but Meta had taken it down, and the police were actively looking for Jacob Ashinoff. Larry had convinced himself it was just a grief process that Melodie's father was going through and would likely pass with time. Larry's parents had agreed to take care of Abe and Sheldon and actively encouraged them not to cancel the trip. Besides, John Hegland was depending on them to help transport the boat to the Dominican Republic. After spending three or four nights cruising in the British Virgin Islands, they would journey to Samana, a two-day sail across the Caribbean Sea. It was too late for John to organize someone else to help, so they both felt obligated to venture into this tropical paradise.

"I'll grab the mooring ball with the boathook," said John calmly, the boat rocking as they slowly approached the ball.

With the jib furled and the mainsail dropped moments before, the quiet hum of the engine was the sole sound as Chantelle steered the boat towards the ball. They were the only sailboat in the quiet mooring field, the winds barely ruffling the water. Chantelle selected the mooring closest to the beach. Larry's job was to grab the thick wet rope attached to the mooring ball once John had hooked it. With practiced ease, he threaded their mooring lines through the eye of the rope, feeling the familiar rough texture of the lines, and secured them to the cleat with a decisive tug. Chantelle brought the boat to a gentle stop, expertly positioning it for a flawless exercise, and turned the engine off before the boat settled into the calm water.

In seconds, Chantelle had slipped into her bright pink bikini, sunning herself for a few minutes, face turned up to the sky, before she jumped into the clear water from the stern of the boat. The salty air filled their lungs as John and Larry, now dressed in their swimming shorts, leaped in, too. Larry floated on his back, the sun warming him, the azure Caribbean water enveloping his body. Any residual worries seemed to melt away as he gazed up at the fluffy white clouds, their shapes shifting in the blue sky.

Giggling, Chantelle swam up to him. After a playful splash, she ducked his head under the water. With a swift turn, Larry wrapped himself around her in a warm bear hug, his lips meeting hers in a tender embrace. The water churned around their legs as they used a scissor kick to maintain their position. Chantelle's kiss was passionate as she explored his mouth with her tongue before moving her hand to his crotch and giving it a firm squeeze. He became instantly hard. She giggled again and swam back to the boat. John, already in the cockpit, was meticulously coiling the ropes, the musical thud of his actions a counterpoint to Chantelle's small grunts as she hauled herself up onto the swim platform. Glancing back at Larry, she smiled playfully and flipped her hair, her eyes revealing a teasing, sensuous glint.

After a quick dry-off from their swim, they climbed into their small dinghy and motored toward the dive site with their dive gear, the sun warm on their skin. Scuba diving in the Indians, a group of spectacular rocks, was alive with coral reefs and colourful fish. Turtles floated by, their smooth shells gleaming in the sunlight. A group of sergeant fish, flashing black and yellow stripes, darted in and out of the coral, protecting their territory as Larry's hand approached, a ripple disturbing their careful dance. Sleek moray eels, strangely shaped puffer fish, and large schools of groupers created a mesmerizing underwater ballet. With a slow, graceful dance, the large underwater fans waved in the gentle currents, their surfaces shimmering with the play of light and shadow.

As the pressure gauges neared 500 psi, indicating near-empty scuba tanks, they began their ascent, surfacing with a gentle *whoosh*. Waves rocked the dinghy, making it a challenge to climb back in, but the inflated buoyancy compensator, secured to a rung, provided a makeshift step. Once on board, they motored the short distance to the sailboat.

The underwater scenery left Chantelle sighing. "That was the most breathtaking dive ever." As the sun dipped below the horizon, painting the sky in fiery hues of orange and red, they sat in the cockpit, sipping their red wine and enjoying the view. The sky blazed with a kaleidoscope of reds and oranges, the fluffy clouds catching fire in the reflected light, creating a spectacle. John had set up the barbeque. The aroma of freshly grilled steaks filled the cockpit as they ate their dinner of striploins with Bearnaise sauce, mashed potatoes, and green beans, clinking their wine glasses in celebration when the sun made its final disappearance.

"The perfect meal to end the perfect day," said Larry. As evening settled, a hush fell over the mooring field. The only sounds were the faint creak of rigging and the distant cry of a gull. They had Deadman's Bay entirely to themselves. No other boats had settled for the night in. With the salty air still clinging to their skin, they made their way to their cabins. They fell asleep early, dreaming of the next day's journey.

***

Larry woke with a start, his heart pounding as he heard John at his bedside whisper, "There's someone on the boat," his voice barely audible above the gentle lapping of the waves. He'd had slept soundly beside Chantelle in the cramped, dimly lit forward cabin, now completely awake, his heart pounding. Larry glanced at his watch: 2

a.m. Chantelle was awake now, too.

"Wait here, Chantelle," Larry instructed, his voice barely above a whisper.

He and John quietly crept into the main salon. To stay cool during the night, they'd kept the companionway door open, letting in the refreshing night air and the sounds of the waves. From above, on the deck, came the soft, almost imperceptible squeak of rubber soles. John slipped into the aft cabin as Larry stared through the open companionway to the cockpit. Against the moonlit sky, he could see two shadows that had entered the cockpit and were approaching the entrance to the main salon. He gulped, his heartbeat in overdrive. Larry slowly pulled opened the utensil drawer and grabbed a sharp knife.

With the blade glinting in the dim light of the cockpit, Larry yelled, his voice resounding in the confined space, "Get the fuck off the boat!"

The squeak of the rubber soles against the wooden deck ceased, leaving an unnerving silence. A rustle came from the aft cockpit as John searched for something in its cabin. Then he heard a faint, unsettling whisper, punctuated by the creak of the boat and the slap of waves against the hull. The silence, heavy and suffocating, swallowed Larry's sharp command. "Who the hell is up there?"

No answer. Larry remained motionless, his heart pounding in his chest, unsure of his next move. The cockpit was silent and utterly devoid of movement. Then Larry saw it. His breath caught in his throat. A slow motion of a hand rising. A cold, steel barrel, glinting faintly in the dim light, pointed directly at him from the shadows.

"He's got a gun!" shouted Larry as he leapt to the floor to get out of the line of fire.

The sharp crack of a gunshot echoed through the night. Within seconds, a searing pain shot up Larry's right leg from his calf, the intense heat making him gasp. He let out an involuntary scream, a raw, primal sound that ripped through the silence and startled even himself. A jolt of agony shot through his calf as he attempted to stand. He doubled over, unable to support his weight.

A bloodcurdling wail sliced through the cockpit, followed by a sickening thud as something heavy like a body hit the floor. A hollow sound reverberated, someone running to the stern of the boat. Feet thudded on the polished teak. The sputtering start of the dinghy engine, followed by a rising whine as it pulled away. The salon lights flickered on, illuminating John bending over Larry, the sudden brightness making both of them squint.

"Are you OK?" John asked, his voice full of concern.

"I think someone shot my right calf," replied Larry. "It hurts like hell."

John looked at Larry's bare limb. Thick dark blood oozed from a ragged hole in the back of his leg. Larry sat up, groaning slightly, and watched John's stunned reaction. He recovered quickly, getting into doctor mode. John lifted the leg, his fingers searching for the popliteal pulse behind the knee, then tracing the leg down to find the fainter beat of the anterior tibial pulse.

"Your pulses are strong and steady. I see an entrance and exit wound on the calf's leg. I suspect it is just a soft-tissue injury."

John's gaze lingered on Larry for a moment before he rose and walked to the medicine cabinet, the wood creaking slightly beneath his weight. He picked up the small dressing tray and filled the basin to the brim with the pink Chlorhexidine. John carefully flushed the wound with the cool antiseptic solution, then gently wrapped it with sterile gauze and a layer of cling dressing.

"I think I got one of them with the speargun," said John. "I pointed it through the aft cabin window and pulled the trigger. I'm going up to check. Will you be OK?"

"Yes, I'm fine," said Larry, still stunned at the dramatic turn of events.

John cautiously approached the companionway entrance and peered into the cockpit. "Shit!" he shouted.

With a shaky breath, Larry pushed himself up on his good leg, his heart hammering a wild rhythm against his chest. He hauled himself partway up the narrow companionway, the rough wood scraping against his hands, trying to see what had startled John. Ignoring the throbbing pain in his right leg, he pulled himself up the last, creaking step.

John stood over the man, his breath shallow and ragged, unsure if he was still alive. The speargun's shaft had pierced through the crotch and protruded out of the abdomen. A length of twine, taut and black, ran from the spear outside, through the open aft cabin window, to where the gun rested on the cabin floor. The man lay on his back, his body still and silent, as if carved from stone. The darkness of the cockpit was absolute, and Larry could barely make out his own hand in front of his face, let alone see if the man was breathing. He peered closer and saw John's fingers graze the man's neck, his touch light as he sought the telltale beat of a carotid pulse.

John looked up at Larry, his eyes wide with disbelief, and said, "He's still alive."

Grunting with effort, Larry heaved himself along the hard cockpit bench, his knuckles scraping against the fibreglass paint to get a better look. He leaned over and his heart skipped a beat.

Jacob Ashinoff lay sprawled on the cold cockpit floor.

Chapter 12

"It seems a little unlikely," the police officer said, his voice rising in incredulity, "that an unconscious man, with the jagged spear of a speargun protruding from his abdomen, would somehow regain consciousness, yank out the weapon, and then leap from the side of your boat—all the while bleeding profusely, then disappear without a trace."

Larry looked at the beach about 100 feet away, the sun sparkling on the wet sand. Chantelle was sitting beside Larry in the cockpit, trembling and pale. She clutched his hand; her knuckles were white. A dozen police officers, their faces grim, meticulously combed the sand and rocks, the sun's rays bouncing off their metal badges as they searched for any trace of blood or clothing. Half a dozen inflatable dinghies, each bearing the word Police in bold black letters, rested at a jaunty angle on the beach.

"Look," said Larry. "John and I both witnessed the spear piercing through his body. When we saw him last, he was alive, though his skin was pale and clammy. We both came back into the cockpit and called the mayday on the VHF radio. When no one answered us, we used our cell phone to call you. While we were on the phone with you, we heard a splash. The gun jammed on the window and the force of gravity must have caused the spear to tear through his body and spring back into the cockpit. We left the gun and spear where you found them."

The police officer again shook his head and made a few more notes on the pad he used. "Did you see the other intruder?" he asked.

John replied, "No, it was too dark. As soon as Jacob got impaled by the spear, the other guy took off."

Larry spoke, an indistinct murmur barely audible above the din. "We heard him run, the pounding of his feet on the wooden planks of the stern, before the 10-horsepower engine roared to life. We heard the engine rev and the powerful sound vibrating through the water as he sped away."

"How do you know it was a 'he' and not a woman?" asked the police officer.

"What?" John asked, his brow furrowed in confusion. His voice was rising in frustration. "You sound like you don't believe us. I stated we hadn't seen the intruder. The 'he' was merely an assumption. Larry clearly identified Jacob as the man who John shot with the speargun."

The police officer said, "Look at it from my angle. I have someone shot in the calf. There is no gun. Maybe it was the speargun that went through your calf?" The officer pointed to Larry. "Perhaps you had a dispute? Perhaps the wife got angry about something? Then you come up with a cockamamie story about a man wanting to kill you because of a surgical misadventure? It sounds too fabricated to be true."

Larry, John, and Chantelle stared at the police officer, their mouths agape in disbelief. A shared look of astonishment passed between them. The officer's dismissal of their account was utterly perplexing. "What about the blood splattered across the cockpit?" John shouted, his voice reverberating across the water. "If you test it, you'll find it does not belong to any of us. On the salon floor, though, you'll discover Larry's blood. That's the dark stain spreading from where the bullet pierced his leg."

"Where's the bullet?" he demanded, his voice tight with suspicion. "The team searched high and low, under furniture, and behind walls. Even so, they couldn't find it."

"This is complete and utter bullshit!" Larry roared, his face reddening with anger, his voice a guttural bellow that rang through the room. "I'm the victim here, and you refuse to listen to our side of the story!" Larry's eyes blazed bright with a furious anger. He was practically spitting fire. Clenching his jaw, he took a deep breath, trying to keep his emotions in check.

Ignoring the shouts and angry words, the police officer continued to write his report. In a low voice barely audible above the crashing waves, he said, "You have 12 hours to leave the British Virgin Islands. You are correct: I find your statement hard to believe. The details don't add up. Our economy is based on tourists visiting us and renting sailboats. If this unbelievable tale ever became public knowledge, it could severely cripple our already fragile economy, sending shockwaves through the tourist markets. I won't allow that outcome. The consequences are too severe. Let me be clear. Another visit here, and you'll face arrest for your malicious mischief. I will ensure you get prosecuted."

He stood up and walked to the stern of the boat. Stepping into the dinghy, he started the engine and sped off. When he got close to the beach, the boat slowed down. Larry saw him talking into the radio. Within the next two minutes, the rest of the police dinghies left the beach and headed back across Sir Francis Drake Channel to Roadtown, the principal town in Tortola, where the precinct was located.

Larry watched the police, the sound of their motors fading as the flotilla of inflatable boats disappeared over the horizon. "Don't you find it strange," he hissed, "that he showed so little concern for my bleeding wound? No offer to take me to the hospital; no questions about how I felt; and no concern about whether the leg gets infected from the bullet. The thought of the public backlash and the long-term damage to his reputation was what would keep him up at night. That was his biggest concern."

"It could be worse," John stated, a grim set to his jaw

betraying his true feelings. "He might have charged us with mischief, throwing us into a cold, damp jail cell for who knows how long."

"What now?" asked Chantelle.

Larry gazed across the stunning bay, its turquoise waters undisturbed and silent except for the occasional cry of a seagull. The sound of the waves and the feel of a 12-knot breeze on their skin beckoned him to the open ocean. Golden sunlight streamed into the cockpit, warming his face as he sat. The paradisaical waters and beaches of the British Virgin Islands, which had filled him with such wonder and beauty upon arrival, were now tainted by the recent events. The scent of salt air and blooming hibiscus lining the edge of the beach couldn't quite mask the underlying tension.

Larry knew the usual departure process meant a trip to the somewhat distant customs and immigration office, a likely frustrating wait, and the feeling of impending scrutiny. Departure papers were required when they reached the next port. The police officer's threat of arrest made the usual departure process untenable. They would have to forgo the visit to the British Virgin Islands customs and immigration office and take their chances of entering the next port without the papers.

With a decisive nod, Larry barked, "Let's release the mooring ball and get out of here!" The sound of the waves lapping against the hull underscored his command. "We have enough food to last us a week. We have plenty of canned goods, dried fruits, and bottled water. With a few taps and clicks, I can disable the automatic identification system, the Garmin InReach, and the Starlink satellite connection, plunging us into a digital silence. We'll vanish without a trace, leaving no clues to our whereabouts or destination. We will be digitally invisible, untraceable in the vast expanse of the internet."

In less than an hour, with the salty spray on their faces and the wind whipping through their hair, they had the sails set and were heading to the Spanish Virgin Islands, just to the east of Puerto Rico. John gripped the wheel, the worn leather cool beneath his hands, as Larry approached, his right leg dragging slightly across the cockpit floor, each step clearly a painful, audible scrape.

"I cannot believe Jacob could survive an injury like that," said John. "The most likely scenario is that when he launched himself overboard, he drowned."

"The spear would have gone through major blood vessels, intestines, and possibly the bladder," Larry replied, his voice grim as he pictured the gruesome injury. "Even if he made it to a hospital, and even if he underwent emergency surgery, his chances of survival were slim. We have witnessed injuries despite being less severe, still led to fatalities, haven't we? He might have survived if he hadn't pulled out the spear, which would have caused further bleeding and injury."

"Maybe we will eventually come to realize that this might be the best thing that has happened to us," said John. "With Jacob gone, you can resume your normal life, and get back to your surgical practice without a cloud hanging over you."

"It is devastating to lose a daughter and then to lose the distraught father. The grief is almost too much to bear, leaving a life marred by sorrow." Larry sadly shook his head, a sigh escaping his lips as he did so. "Those gruesome wounds are still vivid in my mind. It will haunt my sleep. I'm sure I'll get over it with time. There's something else that happened here for which I am truly grateful."

Larry turned to his friend, a grin spreading across his face, and continued. "You saved my life!" he exclaimed, his voice thick with emotion and gratitude. "He was hellbent on killing me. I could see the dark barrel of the gun with me in its sights. I think it was his partner that had the gun. He almost missed me. Another second, he would have finished me, lying there on the floor in agony, helpless. When you felt the weight of the speargun in your hand, the cold steel against your skin, it must have been incredibly difficult to pull that trigger..."

John said in a low and serious voice, "From my perspective,

the uninvited intruders on the boat should have known they were risking their lives. The weight of the decision about what to do about it rested on my shoulders. I had thought about how to handle intruders if that had happened. It was us or them. No other option existed."

Larry's eyes widened incredulously as he looked at John, a mixture of shock and surprise on his face. As a surgeon, his training instilled in him the unwavering commitment to preserve life above all else. Taking a life was utterly antithetical to his profession. Unlike him, John had no professional military training. Larry recalled the harsh desert sun beating down on him during his Israeli army bootcamp, the memories jarring against the simplistic view he'd once held. In those four months, the relentless drills and brutal exercises had honed him into a killing machine.

"What happened that made your survival instincts kick in?" asked Larry.

"Last fall, I sailed the boat to Antigua with about 100 like-minded sailors on ocean-going sailboats like ours. Throughout our 10-day journey from Hampton, Virginia, to English Harbour in Antigua, the group organizer on shore maintained a watchful digital presence, closely monitoring our progress. Before we left, I had met a couple, Patricia and Robert, who owned a boat, also a Hanse, and we quickly became friends. While sitting at a somewhat disreputable sailor's bar one cold night at the docks in Hampton, we sampled more than our share of the local beer. We told stories of sailing and promised to keep in touch on the journey south."

"Sounds like my kind of sailing friends," quipped Larry.

"Throughout our 10-day trip," John elaborated, "we made it a point to stay connected daily. For several months, I safely secured my boat in its docked position at Jolly Harbour in Antigua while we returned home. They kept a close watch on her, making sure she was safe while I was gone. Returning after Christmas and an overnight sail, we dropped anchor in St. Vincent. When I awoke that morning, the first thing I saw was their boat, *Helium,* bobbing in the calm water near the shoreline. I carefully lowered the dinghy into the water and then nimbly hopped on board to find out what was wrong with *Helium.*

"It shocked me to find Robert had sustained a severe knife wound to his abdomen, resulting in significant injuries. Though he was alive, he was unconscious. A perpetrator had secured Patricia with zip ties, rendering her unable to move. They raped her. Being awake, she was terrified at the thought of them returning. I quickly released her and subsequently transmitted a mayday emergency signal over the VHF radio frequency. In a rush to administer fluids, I raced back to my boat, located the IV bags containing saline solution, and immediately pumped three litres into Robert. Upon the arrival of the police, we immediately transported him to the nearby local hospital for medical attention. I assisted the local surgeon in the repair of a perforation of his small intestine.

"Despite the ferocity of the attack, Robert survived. Thank God. Patricia was emotionally distraught and struggling to cope with the aftermath of that event. They went back to the US, and since that time, despite my attempts to contact them, I have been unsuccessful. I haven't heard from them since."

At this point, Larry's eyes were bulging, seemingly about to pop right out of their sockets. "I'm shocked and surprised that you never shared this story with me before! Who attacked them?"

John glanced across the horizon, checked the instrument panel, and then shook his head. "In the islands, the criminals roam freely. The three who that attacked Robert and Patricia were in jail for murder. They do not lock the jail cells in St. Lucia, and often the criminals will venture out of the compound. They boarded the *Helium*, anchored off the Pitons, and motored all night to St. Vincent. During the trip, they took turns raping Patricia. At one point, Robert freed himself. He used his speargun and killed one criminal. The two others escaped in the dinghy, but not before stabbing Robert, leaving him for dead. Authorities later captured the two remaining escapees and returned them to St. Lucia."

Larry thought about that for a minute and said, "That's

where you got the idea to use the speargun. Are attacks like this common in the Caribbean?"

A high-pitched chirp from Larry's cell phone signalled a new email in his inbox. He swiftly flipped open his phone and accessed his Gmail account. He did not recognize the sender of the message; therefore, he decided against opening it. The email's subject line, despite its brevity, delivered a chilling message:

I am not done with you yet.

With a look of astonishment, Larry glanced up at John and said, "Jacob, despite the terrible injury, somehow lived through it."

Chapter 13

The rough texture of the rock pressed against Jacob's back as he lay on the cliff, gazing down at the beach below. A searing, sharp pain ripped through his abdomen, leaving him gasping for breath. He watched as police officers in crisp blue uniforms meticulously combed the beach, their flashlights cutting through the pre-dawn gloom. They presumably searched for evidence that he'd somehow survived the injury and could corroborate the men's story. He must have passed out near the cliff edge, the wind whipping around him, because he had no memory of the ascent.

Jacob glanced at his ripped clothing, the rough fabric scraping against his skin as he pulled his shirt upward. A ragged hole about the size of a plum gaped open on the right side of his abdomen. A dense, crimson blood clot, still slightly moist and glistening, sealed the opening. The memory flooded back. The jarring wake-up, the cold spray of seawater on his face, and the terrifying sight of the spear point in the dim cockpit light. He shuddered, the weight of the decision pressing down on him like a physical burden, as he recalled the moment he knew what he needed to do.

A sturdy metal flange at spear's tip kept the weapon firmly in place, preventing it from slipping out of its prey. With his fingers, he broke off the metal flange and flipped it into the ocean. When he got to his feet, he reached down between his legs and removed the spear with a sudden motion. He heard a soft *thunk* as the sleek metal, still slick with blood, slid free from his body and landed on the cockpit floor. With a powerful thrust, he launched himself into the inky blackness of the ocean. The water, although warm, shocked his system. He had no memory of reaching the beach, only the feel of the coarse sand between his fingers and the sound of crashing waves.

With the sky ablaze in a fiery orange and soft pink sunrise, the deep rumble of the outboard engines filled the air. Rolling onto his side, he could see the inflatable boats speeding toward Tortola, their motors roaring, leaving the lone sailboat bobbing gently on the waves. In under an hour, he watched as the vessel disconnected itself from the mooring ball and sailed off towards the west. Alone, the only sound he heard was the faint whisper of the wind through the rocky cliff. He closed his eyes, the world fading to a soft, dark nothingness.

Sometime later in the morning, Jacob awoke to a throbbing pain in his abdomen. Though unpleasant, it was tolerable. With a groan, he pushed himself up to his feet. He reached into his pocket and flipped open his phone. Even after his ocean swim, the device continued to work, a testament to its waterproof design and robust construction. Google Maps confirmed his location as Peter's Island, a small dot on the screen surrounded by blue. A quick internet search revealed that the only hotel, the luxurious Peter Island Resort, had opened its doors just two months prior, following seven years of renovations after Hurricane Irma had destroyed it.

"I'd like a room for the next week," he told the receptionist, who answered the call.

"When might we expect you?" she asked.

"I'm on the island now, having left the sailboat. I'm looking down at your resort on the cliffs above Deadman's Bay as we speak."

"Check in time is 3 p.m."

"I need the room now!"

A heavy silence, thick with unspoken words, followed the last statement. The insistent clacking of a keyboard in the background punctuated Jacob's wait. The receptionist, her voice a gentle murmur, said, "We have room 107 available now. When you arrive in the front lobby, I'll be happy to check you in."

The lobby's hushed atmosphere did little to mask the sounds of Jacob's floor-scraping limp as he entered. His makeshift repairs to his torn clothing barely concealed the damage. Aware that his rumpled, blood-stained shirt and pants and messy hair might frighten the receptionist, he looked her directly in the eyes. Hoping to convey calm and confidence, he slapped a credit card down—one with the fake name of Brian Harper. The sharp sound echoed in the quiet lobby. He said, "You have room 107 available for me?"

She swiped the credit card almost defiantly. The machine whirring quietly as it processed the payment. His eyes, like chips of flint, bore into her, searching for any flicker of alarm in her expression. He knew she could feel the silent pressure of his scrutiny.

Relieved to find she remained calm, he said, "I am not to be disturbed for the next week. Skip the cleaning. Just leave the fresh towels on the doorstep. I'll order room service if I need anything."

She simply nodded as he left the front lobby to find his room.

A similar situation had tested Jacob in the past, leaving him with scars both visible and invisible. After his escape from Iran, and safely back on Russian soil, late one night, he walked past a dimly lit alley. Suddenly, someone attacked him. Prepared for a violent payback, a calm settling over him. Using his powerful hands, he snapped the man's neck. He felt the vertebrae give way with a loud crack. He watched the life drain from the man's eyes instantly. It was only when he looked down at the lifeless body lying on the alley's pavement when he realized the man had stabbed him in the abdomen. The knife was up to the hilt in his right lower abdomen. Jacob reached with his left hand and pulled it out. A searing pain ran through his stomach. He fell to the ground until the agony became bearable.

Jacob, his abdomen throbbing with each step, hobbled to his

Moscow apartment, and painfully climbed the stairs to the second floor. He collapsed onto his bed, his body heavy with exhaustion. Two days later, he woke with a start. The sunlight stung his eyes. A severe pain, many times worse than before, ripped through his belly. He could feel the feverish heat radiating from his skin. A powerful thirst consumed him. He chugged a litre of water, the cold liquid burning a path down his throat before he violently vomited it all up. He collapsed on the linoleum kitchen floor, his body hitting the ground with a thud, the last sound he heard.

When he awoke hours later, the abdominal pain had lessened, but a sickly sweet smell of bile filled the air as the green fluid leaked from the stab wound, spreading across the floor. After covering the wound with a kitchen towel, Jacob sat up and winced at the throbbing pain. Although his legs trembled with weakness, he braced himself against the cool metal of the kitchen sink, his head bowed to the chrome faucet. With a desperate eagerness, he gulped down the water, each swallow a minor victory against the burning thirst. This time, the water stayed down.

Using grey duct tape, he hastily attached a ziplock bag to his abdomen to collect the viscous, green fluid leaking from a deep wound. This was something he changed every day without fail. It took a full week, but finally, he was strong enough to venture outdoors. The over fluorescent lights seemed to glare at him as he navigated the aisles of the pharmacy, finally selecting and purchasing his powdered protein supplements. The package, promising a 400-calorie boost, instructed users to mix the powder with 500 ml of water. Jacob bought enough supplies to create 10 packages each day for the next month, a considerable amount of material.

Six weeks later, the incessant bile leakage finally stopped, marked by the absence of its sickly sweet odour. Although he still felt weak, his muscles trembling with the effort, Jacob began a vigorous exercise program at the gym, the sounds of weights and grunts filling the air as he endured his routine. Six weeks later, he had regained 20 of the 50 pounds he'd lost, his body still feeling weak but his appetite returning with a vengeance. Six weeks after that, his usual energy returned, and he felt like himself again.

***

The doorknob felt cold and metallic beneath Jacob's trembling fingers as he opened the door to room 107 of Peter Island Resort. The faint shadow of his previous abdominal trauma experience seemed to fill the silent space. Jacob made his way to the minibar and uncapped a large bottle of water; the sound of the plastic cap twisting off and cracking slightly in the quiet room.

He drank it all, savouring the last drop of the precious fluid. Another bottle of water, its label slightly crumpled, sat on the counter, waiting to be opened. He gulped down the liquid, the refreshing water sliding down his throat. A third bottle, cool and condensation-covered, he placed on the nightstand. He lay on the bed, pulling the rough cotton sheets up against his bare skin, and closed his eyes, wondering if he would wake up this time.

***

Jacob replaced the towel he had tucked between his legs with a clean one. The puncture wound where the spear had entered him in his crotch oozed thick yellow pus. With the draining of the pus, the fever that had burned him for four days finally subsided, its oppressive heat replaced by a lingering chill. Massive volumes of pus soaked the towel, leaving it heavy and dripping within a few hours. Worse, a fetid smell, like rotting meat and stagnant water, filled his nostrils, instantly killing any hunger he might have felt.

However, the situation with the abdominal hole was quite different. The fresh wound was alarmingly close to the old stab wound. Within 24 hours, it too began draining a viscous, green bile, just like before. Despite the sharp, intense abdominal pain, it lacked the familiar, gut-wrenching agony of his previous episode. He could drink litres of water, the cool liquid a welcome relief to his parched throat, without vomiting. For most of the first four days, he slept, his breaths slow and even.

Jacob knew logically that a hospital visit was necessary. He needed antibiotics, a CAT scan to assess the damage, and potential surgery. He carried the weight of his problem—a profound distrust of everyone—like a heavy cloak. The threat was ever-present. People were still out, plotting his demise, their hatred palpable. The sterile environment of a hospital, with its busy corridors and the ever-present sounds of medical equipment, would make it very easy for them to find him if he checked in. Every click, every search, every use of his phone, was a digital breadcrumb, making it simple for the internet to track him. It would be easy for someone to inject a lethal toxin into the IV line, leaving no trace. With steely resolve, he decided his fate rested solely on his own shoulders. To live or die, he would face it alone. Right now, he wasn't certain of the outcome.

Jacob knew too much. The centrifuge disaster from 10 years ago was just the beginning. Now he knew things that could change the world. He had to stop those who planned the destruction before the damage was irreparable. First, though, he had to survive.

Chapter 14

"Jasmine!" shouted Larry into the phone. "I cannot believe it has been 10 years!"

She shouted back, her voice carrying the single name, "Larry! It's great to hear from you! I was just thinking about you the other day. Where are you? Did you finish med school?"

"I am a surgeon in Toronto. Married with two boys. How about you?"

She paused for a moment, as if lost in thought, before erupting into a fit of laughter. "I have to admit, I've had a long-standing, unrequited crush on you, and for years I've held onto the secret hope that you might one day call me. And here you are!"

Larry's face broke into a smile as the sound of her voice filled his ears, a smile that reflected the joy he felt in her words. Jasmine possessed a sharp mind and a personality that was incredibly fun to be around. Plus, she was strikingly attractive. Since his departure from Israel, he had reflected on her countless times, her image frequently appearing in his thoughts. It had been she who delivered the warning that his life was in grave danger, stemming from his involvement in the perilous centrifuge worm project. Jasmine had masterminded his escape from Israel, demonstrating impressive levels of planning and coordination to ensure his successful departure. Larry believed that, had he not encountered Chantelle during his time at the kibbutz, he would have undoubtedly attempted to establish a relationship with Jasmine.

"What's happened with all your internet sleuthing you learned in the army?" he asked.

"Following three years of experience in the army, I established my own cybersecurity company. Many of us from Unit 8200 have done that. Over the past seven years, several companies have merged with ours and we have one of the largest business-based clientele now."

Larry responded with a simple, yet expressive, "Wow! My purpose in calling is to determine whether you can find any information about an individual who is actively attempting to cause me harm." For the next half hour, Larry recounted to Jasmine the complete and detailed narrative encompassing the tale of Jacob Ashinoff, the tragic passing of Melodie, and the harrowing incident involving the violent attack on the sailboat.

"As you were speaking, I was searching the internet for information related to our conversation. Jacob Ashinoff is a Russian nuclear scientist. Ten years ago, he was on loan to Iran when the nuclear centrifuges imploded. Iranian officials held Jacob, the lead scientist, and his team accountable for the failure of the nuclear program, issuing a death sentence for his alleged role in the collapse. He escaped back to Russia, but the nuclear branch of the Soviet government retracted his scientific credentials."

"Wow!" replied Larry. "So he was a scientist, after all."

"There's more," she said. Through the phone, Larry could hear the loud and sharp sound of her banging on the computer keys. "Holy shit! He appears to have issued a contract against you that is dated several weeks ago. This date aligns with the attack that occurred in the British Virgin Islands which you experienced. He claims he will give a sum of $25,000 to any person able to verify the fact of your death. Recent events have brought a renewed focus on the 10 individuals responsible for the destruction of the Iranian nuclear facilities, with increased internet traffic reflecting a significant upswing. The list contains all the nine other people as well."

"That makes no sense," said Larry. "The threats against me started when Melodie had her first operation."

"It's possible that he might have recognized you from a decade prior, don't you think? This wouldn't be the first occasion on which an Israeli operative had been the target of an attack years after a significant event."

"The quiet existence I've cultivated in Canada for all these years makes the shocking reality that my past could somehow catch up. That is something I find incredibly difficult to process and accept. My biggest concern would be for Chantelle, my wife, and my two sons. If you were counselling someone in a similar situation to mine, what protective measures or strategies would you usually suggest?"

"Huh," said Jasmine. "I have been out of the intelligence field for some time now. What I used to suggest was to hire a bodyguard and take extreme precautions to keep hidden. Things have changed so much in the cybersecurity field. There may be a way to target Jacob digitally to give him confusing information that would render him impotent to harm you or your family. Let me check my contacts from Unit 8200 and get back to you."

They both said goodbye and hung up the phone, promising to keep in touch.

Letting out a long, slow breath, Larry felt a wave of relief wash over him. Although he was happy he'd contacted Jasmine, a skepticism lingered within him concerning her capabilities to ensure the safety and protection for himself and his family. Despite an extensive search by the Toronto Police Department, Jacob remained elusive, and they could not find him anywhere. They reported he had just disappeared. During their searches for criminals, they employed the same technology Jasmine used, namely a digital tracking software, thus highlighting a shared investigative approach. Reconnecting with his old friend, Jasmine, however, felt incredibly rewarding, instantly reviving cherished memories of the strong bonds of friendship and shared experiences they had together during their time in the Israeli army.

"So what did Jasmine say?" asked John. They were at anchor

in Bahia Dakiti, Culebra, in the Spanish Virgin Islands near Puerto Rico. Despite the easterly trade winds whipping up waves on the open ocean, the sheltered bay remained calm and peaceful. The warmth of the setting sun felt gentle on their faces as they sat in the cockpit, enjoying a steaming vegetarian chili and rice dish that Chantelle had prepared after anchoring. She was below the deck cleaning up as John and Larry talked.

"Jasmine's diving into the dark web's murky depths to find out more," replied Larry, "but she told me that Jacob put a $25,000 contract out on my life two weeks ago. She thinks it is because he was the Russian nuclear scientist who helped the Iranians set up their nuclear weapons program. When the worm developed by the Israelis irreparably damaged the nuclear centrifuges, the Iranians blamed Jacob and sentenced him to death. He somehow found out I was involved in the Israeli project. I think that's the true reason he wants to kill me."

"Did she have any thoughts on how to protect yourself?"

"She didn't give me specifics, but is looking for a way to attack him digitally, perhaps diverting his attention elsewhere. I am not sure what that means, but things do not look good. I'm thinking of hiring a bodyguard to protect Chantelle and the kids until the threat is over."

John stroked his chin, a thoughtful frown creasing his brow as he mulled over Larry's words. "I suspect we will be safe for a few weeks, though the ominous silence while waiting will make me uneasy.

With such severe injuries, a month is the shortest recovery time Jacob can hope for, if he even recovers at all." With a sharp shake of his head, John dispelled the thought. "I just cannot see how he would survive that kind of injury; the blood loss alone would be enough to kill him."

As Chantelle emerged from the main salon, darkness enveloped the boat. "I couldn't help but overhear your conversation. I concur with John. We have a small window of opportunity to plan a comprehensive strategy. We start our overnight sail to the Dominican Republic tomorrow. Let's put our heads together to devise a detailed survival plan, considering all possibilities. For now, I'm off to bed. We hardly slept last night."

Unable to quiet his racing thoughts, Larry eventually fell into a restless sleep. The companionway door clicked shut, a reassuring sound in the dimly lit passage, and he felt the digital cloak of invisibility settle around them like a warm blanket. Exhausted from the previous night's terrors, his breaths hitched with each shudder before eventually settling into a rhythm with Chantelle's soft and even ones as sleep finally claimed him.

***

Larry awoke to the sun's rays painting the room gold, a gentle warmth on his skin. He softly glanced at Chantelle, peacefully snoring. Quietly slipping out of bed, he padded softly to the galley, where he made a cup of Nespresso. The scent of freshly ground coffee beans filled the air. John was already up and sitting behind the chart plotter in the cockpit, the morning sun reflecting off his aviator glasses. Larry noticed John was studying the route to the Dominican Republic. Vibrant colours filled the map, showing depths and currents.

"When do you want to leave? It's a beautiful day; I don't want to miss it!" said Larry.

"The sooner the better," John replied, a slight impatience colouring his tone. "Chris Perkins, our weather guru, warned of an approaching low-pressure system, a potential harbinger of stormy weather. I calculate, factoring in steady winds and calm seas, we could reach Puerto Bahia Marina in roughly 30 hours of sailing. In about 48 hours, he predicts the storm will hit, bringing with it the squalls with lightning and the thunder. If his estimations are accurate, we should have a comfortable margin of time."

"Let's go," said Larry as he stood up. "I'll raise the anchor as you start the engine."

Five minutes later, they were cutting a path through the waves. The low chug of the engine was a steady contrast to the sharp protests of gulls drifting above as they headed toward Puerto Bahia Marina, 236 nautical miles to the northwest. A steady 15-knot breeze from the east, the familiar trade winds, whispered through the rigging. Once they raised the sails, the yacht sliced through the waves, the wind nudging them along at 8.5 knots on a comfortable reach. John completed his three-hour shift and went to get some sleep while Larry took over.

Thirty-six hours later, just as they entered the Bay of Samana, the turquoise water sparkling under the midday sun, Larry spotted something that took his breath away. A colossal humpback whale, only 100 feet away, suddenly dwarfed the sailboat. Its powerful blowhole sent a 30-foot geyser into the air, a thrilling spectacle accompanied by the whale's soft exhale. The air hung heavy with the thick scent of fish, seaweed, and decaying sea life. Larry could see the dark shadows of the gigantic creatures as they skirted by. They were close to the Dominican Republic. With land in sight, John risked a quick cellphone check, turning it on and off as fast as possible. He glanced at it as it vibrated. A text message appeared on the screen.

I'll be waiting for you. You won't know when or where.

Larry's tired eyes, burning from lack of sleep, stared unfocused at the screen. Forwarding the text message, he sighed deeply, thinking of Jasmine and the distant yet familiar feel of Israel. He'd barely finished sending it to her when his phone vibrated with Jasmine's incoming call.

"Something like a luggage tracker is being used to track you. I can see it on my screen. It appears to be at the boat's bow. Do you have a locker or something like that at the front?"

"We have a sail locker," he replied. "Let me check inside."

With a few steps, Larry reached the front of the boat. Pulling on the creaky latch, he opened the sail locker. He looked around for something out of place. "Damn!" A small, round magnet, about the size of a quarter, clung to the bottom of the door, cool and smooth to the touch. "Jasmine, you are right. A small round object. Should I heave it overboard?"

"No," Jasmine responded. "I've blocked the GPS signal. He cannot follow you now. Stick it onto a different boat when you moor, something like a huge cruise ship, and I'll unblock the signal. That will keep him busy."

"Any thoughts about how I should protect myself when I get to Toronto?"

Jasmine's words trailed off, and a hush settled over the room. "Larry," Jasmine cried, her voice thick with sobs, "I need to tell you something."

It took her a full minute of stunned silence before she spoke again. "Your commanding officer in the Unit 8200... Benjamin... The brains behind the Iranian nuclear project cyberattack... He got kidnapped yesterday morning in Jaffa while walking home after taking his three-year-old son to daycare. They dumped his body in the village square a few hours later. We suspect Jacob Ashinoff's involvement, possibly using money to solicit a Hezbollah operative to execute the plan. Mossad agents apprehended the man who they believe killed him.

They are interrogating him. The sheer volume of internet traffic focusing on Jacob Ashinoff in relation to the latest murder created a digital storm of speculation, with countless articles and social media posts suggesting his guilt. You can expect a call, perhaps a coded message, or even a visit from the Mossad soon. Expect it to be discreet."

Shock washed over Larry, leaving him speechless and unable to form a coherent response. Benjamin, with his infectious grin and unwavering optimism, was the best commanding officer he'd ever known. The weight of realizing Jacob had murdered him for a project orchestrated a decade prior was unbearable. The details replayed relentlessly in his mind. Jacob, if he was still alive, had a reach around the globe. There had to be more to the story than the few cryptic clues he possessed. A deeper mystery lurked beneath the surface.

Chapter 15

"We'll have a car parked in front of your house 24/7," Casper, the stern owner of the security firm, stated. "A loud siren will blare, and flashing lights will illuminate your property if an intruder breaks in, instantly alerting us. We will drive behind the school bus when the kids go to school in the morning and retrieve them with you or your wife in the afternoon. If Chantelle or you decide to go shopping, we'll follow, keeping a safe and unnoticeable distance, naturally. Let us know if there is anything we can do to help you."

Larry guided the two security guards to the backyard, pointing out the intricate details of the house and the meticulously manicured gardens, the scent of roses heavy in the air. The security system, a complex network of sensors and alarms, was supposedly wired directly to the police station. Despite its hefty price tag, the new system did little to inspire confidence in Larry; its clunky operation and frequent glitches only fuelled his skepticism.

Last year while the family was on holidays, the alarm went off. Larry got the alert on his smart phone and immediately called the security firm's emergency number. "It's probably a false alarm," said the man who answered. "I'll send a car around."

"Aren't the police supposed to check it out?" asked Larry.

"Nah, they don't respond to house alarms anymore because 99 per cent are false alarms. We'll call them if we are concerned."

"When will someone check it out?"

"We'll send someone within the hour. Don't worry, we've already turned it off so we don't bother your neighbours."

"Within the hour? Turned it off? What if someone has broken in? They will have run off with all our stuff by the time you get there!"

"As I told you, 99 per cent of the time it is a false alarm."

It turns out it was a false alarm. Or perhaps the sensitive system scared away a potential intruder. The nonchalant attitude of the company they relied upon for safety prompted Larry to get security guards posted until the threat of Jacob went away.

***

A hush fell over Larry's office as he read the email from the College of Physicians and Surgeons, the regulatory body that held his professional life in its hands. "We have received a complaint about a recent patient's death, Melodie Ashinoff, from the father, Jacob Ashinoff. Please send all medical records and an accompanying cover letter explaining your involvement in her care."

The letter was signed, "Jackie Wallace, investigator."

Larry immediately called her and, to his surprise, she answered the phone rather than allowing it to go on to voicemail. Larry told her the story of Melodie's surgery.

"Look," he said, "I have a restraining order against Jacob Ashinoff. He physically picked me up and threw me against the wall when I spoke with him after the surgery. He tracked me down on holidays and shot me. My family has bodyguards around the clock. We fear for our safety. You can't possibly be serious about investigating me and giving his frivolous complaint any credence."

"By law," replied Jackie, "we must take all complaints seriously. Furthermore, we found, upon reviewing the hospital records and discussing the case with your chief of staff, that you released her with an active wound infection. We found no record of antibiotic administration in the patient's file. Maybe if you'd shown more care and concern, things could have turned out better for her. A little more attention to detail might have improved the result."

On the other end of the line, Larry's silence was thick with unspoken words. *Just my luck to have a sanctimonious, ill-informed investigator with little surgical knowledge.*

"It sounds like you have already concluded your investigation before you have heard my side. This conversation is over." With a sharp *click*, Larry hung up the phone, the receiver hitting its cradle hard.

He could feel the heat rising in his cheeks, his body trembling uncontrollably. A complaint, adding to the already overwhelming pile of problems. For years, unfair practices marred the College's history against doctors, cloaked in the rhetoric of public safety, a legacy of misguided actions. Larry felt a chill run down his spine; he knew this was going to end badly. With a deep breath, he contacted the Canadian Medical Protective Association. Their reputation for defending doctors was both a comfort and a source of anxiety.

The next call Larry made was to the chief of staff, David Graham. "I've received a complaint from the father of a patient who died after surgery," he explained. "I spoke to the investigator from the CPSO. The conversation did not go well."

"Maybe we should meet. Can you come to my office?" replied David.

With a determined stride, Larry headed towards the imposing oak door of the chief of staff's office. David, in his expensive charcoal business suit, stood by the window, as if watching the city below. Towering over Larry by six inches, he used his height to intimidate, a tactic Larry expected from their past encounters. Their hands met in a firm, brief handshake. David's grip was a little too strong, Larry noted, a slight wince crossing his face as the larger man squeezed.

"I'm familiar with the case," said David. "I reviewed the medical records. It was me who told Ms. Wallace that I found some deficiencies in the management."

Larry stared at David, a mixture of anger and confusion swirling within him. "What are you talking about? At our last division meeting, we meticulously reviewed the case, each of us adding insights. Following our morbidity and mortality rounds a week ago, we sent the notes to you. We spent time carefully examining the videos of the two operations, analyzing the visual details, and listening to the audio of the procedures. While you may disagree with the video portion, we surgeons find it invaluable for pinpointing areas in our surgical techniques that require refinement."

"I am still investigating the use of videos in the operating room. This stinks. The ethical implications are nauseating and leave a bad taste in my mouth. A patient, desperate and vulnerable, will agree to anything the surgeons ask, so I question whether informed consent is truly being obtained. My recommendations following this review of your mismanagement include a ban on videos in the operating room to minimize distractions and maintain a professional atmosphere. I told Ms. Wallace that as well."

"If you review the video, you will see we went through an extensive time-out procedure where I asked the anesthesiologist to administer heparin and antibiotics. It is right there on the video."

"Well, that is complete bullshit. There is no written documentation that for both operations you gave either. Your videos are worthless."

Larry sat rigid in his chair, every muscle tense. The year of brutal Israeli army training resurfaced, hardening his resolve against his commanding officer's bullying. This was the same frustrating situation. He knew his chief of staff lacked the authority to interfere in using videos in the operating room. As an infectious disease specialist, David lacked the knowledge to dictate OR quality assurance protocols or prevent the surgeon from recording cases.

The medical advisory committee, a group of department heads, possessed that power. Only then, after much deliberation on the legal and ethical ramifications, could they proceed with banning the videos they routinely take in the operating room. He stared at David, his silence heavy with unspoken words, the atmosphere tense.

Larry finally said, "David, I'm on solid ground here. The video in the operating is something you have no authority to control. You and I both know that. I think this conversation is over."

He watched as David's forehead and cheeks flushed crimson, his anger palpable. His face wrinkled, a furious scowl twisting his features as Larry's challenge hung in the air. His voice, tight with barely controlled rage, boomed, "I am going to personally see that you are going down! Your future at this hospital is uncertain, and your time here is limited. Now, get the fuck out of here!"

Seething with anger, Larry stomped away from David's office, the sound reverberating in the empty hallway. Exiting the hospital, he made his way to the parking lot, the smell of exhaust fumes somehow a comforting contrast to the antiseptic hospital.

Larry shook his head as he walked away. He exhaled deeply and unclenched his fists. David's outburst had been pathological; his face was red, veins bulging, and spittle flew from his lips as he screamed. *It's one thing to disagree, but the threat to "take me down"—a venomous whisper laced with barely controlled rage. David is teetering on the edge of a psychotic break.*

Larry had witnessed this similar behaviour. He remembered his Uncle Randy's drunken episodes, the smell of stale beer, and the aggressive shouts. At 15, spending a summer week at his cousins' Muskoka cottage, north of Toronto, promised a welcome escape, the feel of the warm lake water already imagined. Larry looked forward to the carefree days after school was out.

Months at a time, his Uncle Randy was out at sea, the navy's demands keeping him away from home. His life was a rhythm of waves and distant horizons. When he came home on leave, the slam of the door and the clinking of ice in his glass heralded another night of drunken stupor, his words soon thick and slurred.

In the cottage's entrance, an enormous grandfather clock with a mellow, resonant chime would softly announce each passing hour. Its large glass window, framed in gleaming brass, required weekly winding with a long, heavy key. A beautiful reddish-brown mahogany frame, polished to a deep lustre, reflected the light in subtle highlights. More than a century old, the clock's door bore the embossed mark "1923," a testament to its enduring history, the wood worn smooth with age. Uncle Randy would bellow at the clock when it chimed, his voice raging through the room, and threaten to smash it when drunk, his words slurred and menacing. Yet he never stood up and made good on his threat. Perhaps he stayed seated to avoid the risk of falling. Getting up might have resulted in a tumble.

One morning, the remnants of the previous night's alcohol still clung to Uncle Randy like a second skin, even before he started on the Crown Royal. Cornflakes crunched, and the cousins laughed and chatted as Larry and his 17-year-old cousin, Jason, Randy's oldest son, ate in the kitchen. A sudden, sharp crash shattered the peaceful morning. They ran toward the entrance, the cacophony of shouting and crashing growing louder with each step.

Uncle Randy, his eyes filled with madness and hands covered in blood, was fiercely punching the clock, shattering the glass and splintering the wood. The clock's innards, a chaotic mess of gears and springs, spewed across the floor with a clatter. Even after he'd finished pulverizing the clock, Randy's enraged shouts filled the room with senseless cacophony. Hyperventilating, the drunk man glanced at Jason and Larry.

Thinking back on the incident all these years later, the look in his eyes was the same Larry had witnessed when he'd had that disastrous meeting with David. Uncle Randy, though, opened the door to the cottage, hopped into his Ford truck 150, and spun the tires, spewing gravel as he sped out of the cottage driveway.

The memory of his conversation with Jason after the incident chilled Larry to the bone. Every word was sharp and clear, as if spoken just moments before. "The damage my father has caused this family is insurmountable, just like the others in my group," Jason said, his voice coarse with grief. He spoke with maturity, reflecting wisdom beyond his years. "For years, I've attended Al-Anon meetings, the support group for families of alcoholics, sharing stories and finding solace in the company of others dealing with the struggles of alcoholism. They call it 'dry drunk' when, despite sobriety, the unsettling psychotic episodes still occur. Today, my dad displayed it for all to see. The only way for him to change is to confront his mental health condition, commit to long-term therapy, and learn coping mechanisms to avoid relapses. This will take years of dedicated effort. That is something he refuses to do. The support group has us bracing for the inevitable. A feeling of impending doom has settled over us kids like a heavy shroud as we have come to realize this will end badly. The chances are high that he will commit suicide. Survival mode is our family's current state, as we navigate through challenges together. A deep, gnawing anxiety fills me when I think of my younger siblings and the challenges they face. Come September, I'm leaving for college, ready to start a new chapter, and I swear, I'll never come back."

Two years later, Larry learned that Uncle Randy had hung himself in that same cottage. David was exhibiting the same violent behaviour as he had witnessed from Randy. *Was David an alcoholic?* More than a simple personality clash, this exchange felt like a seismic shift, the ground trembling beneath the weight of their animosity. David's threat was a disturbing promise, whispered in a low, gravelly voice. Larry's mind raced, a whirlwind of possible motives, each one more unsettling than the last. *Or is professional jealousy causing these issues? A contest to assert authority and leadership? Anti-Jewish sentiment?* His phone rang.

"Jasmine!"

She skipped all pleasantries. "What the Iranians want," she said, her voice tight with tension, "is any digital information you can provide them about your role in creating the code that crippled their nuclear centrifuges. I have been providing support to the Israel

Defense Forces. I'm still a reservist. This means they can call upon me at any time."

"Huh, I guess once you are in the IDF, you are in for life. What did you find out about me?" asked Larry. "I did that work over 10 years ago. Surely, they could crack that code with reverse engineering?"

"Benjamin had his team inserted several codes to safeguard against that after you left us," said Jasmine. "My online sleuthing has turned up some worrisome information. The internet chatter is difficult to interpret. Some of it has us believing the Iranians, with Russian help, want to do something similar to the American nuclear program."

"How could that possibly affect me? I've got nothing to do with IDF and coding."

"Benjamin was the same as you after he left our unit. But he became a pilot for Cathay Pacific. He had nothing to do with IDF and coding, either. Although we are certain they tortured him into giving information before they killed him. What he told him that could be useful, we do not know. The reason I called was to update you on what I know, which unfortunately is not much, and to tell you to be careful. Something *is* going on. Your life may be in danger."

The call finally ended, and Larry hurried toward his black

Tesla on the second floor of the hospital's garage. The hum of the garage's fluorescent lights buzzed in a dull background to the rush of his footsteps, creating an eeriness Larry had never noticed before. With a sharp shove, he plunged the phone into his pocket and walked to the driver's door and got into the car. The door closed with its usual smooth, controlled movement. His mind was still reeling from the disturbing meeting with David and Jasmine's scary warnings. Larry started the car, then glanced at his rearview mirror to reverse out of his spot and turned his head to check.

In the back seat, Jacob sat rigidly, eyes fixed on Larry, a silent intensity in his gaze.

Chapter 16

Larry stared at Jacob in complete and utter disbelief. In the blink of an eye, he tried to open the door. Nothing happened. A desperate flick of his eyes to the backseat, assessing Jacob's reaction, then a frantic glance to the cool, smooth door handle, his only hope of escape. The door remained locked. With a sharp press of the unlock button, he tried the door again, the faint *click* repeating in the stillness. Again, nothing happened. Panic tightened its icy grip around Larry's chest, making his breath catch in his throat and his head swim. His own car had trapped him.

With a deep breath, Larry slowly turned to face Jacob. The tightness in his chest finally eased as he accepted the reality he could not get out, leaving him able to breathe. The same surge of adrenaline, the same tightening in his chest, occurred when he faced a difficult surgical issue. An initial panic gave way to a sense of calm focus, allowing him to think clearly and find a solution.

Jacob held the Tesla fob aloft on his fingertips and gave it a little shake. "I've locked you in," he said, the words menacing in the confined space.

Larry searched Jacob's face for any hint of hostility, but only found calm. His eyes softened as he gazed at Larry. A long silence preceded Larry's barely audible words. "What is it you want?" he asked, his eyes narrowed in suspicion.

At first, Jacob was quiet. The stillness hung heavy in the car's confines. "I need your help."

Larry stared, his mouth slightly agape, unsure of how to respond. A confused expression clouded his face, eyes narrowing with suspicion. Unspoken questions rattled in his mind.

Larry watched as Jacob lifted his shirt. A plastic bag taped with a silver duct tape clung to the right side of his abdomen. The bag seemed full of green bilious fluid. The air, disturbed by the lifting of his shirt, carried a sharp, metallic smell, like rusted iron. Larry estimated a litre had filled the bag. "How long has that been draining like that?" he asked.

"Six weeks."

"Since the injury on the sailboat?" asked Larry.

Jacob nodded.

"Look," said Larry, "we have a history of having a disagreement when you slammed me against the wall and choked me. I would not be the best one to look after you. I also have a peace bond against you. You must not come within 100 metres of me. If I were to help you and things did not go well, they could accuse me of exacting revenge. The College would discipline me for unprofessional conduct."

Lost in thought, Jacob slowly chewed on his lip, pondering the implications of Larry's statement. Not a sound could be heard. The silence hung heavy and oppressive, thick as a wool blanket. Jacob's suggestion came as an indistinct murmur, "What if Dr. John Hegland takes care of me, and you give him a hand? I don't trust anyone else. People are trying to kill me. I trust you two to be discreet. Call him."

Larry realized that the power had shifted, and now he was the one calling the shots. A surge of control coursed through him. His racing pulse slowed, but his mind raced even faster, a chaotic storm of half-formed ideas. *Jacob spoke with a gentle tone and a calm demeanour, conveying sincerity. His injuries are severe, clearly requiring the immediate attention of a skilled surgeon. John is just as deeply entangled in this complicated situation as I am. With John's help, we can work through this.*

Larry retrieved his phone from his pocket and made a call. "John," he said, "I need you to come to my car on the second floor of the parking lot."

***

The magnified laparoscopic image, a vibrant, high-definition display of internal organs, filled the giant screen in the operating room. The darkened room had only a few dull lights casting long, dancing shadows across John and Larry's faces, the air heavy with anticipation. Recurrent beeping of the monitors and the low whirr of the anesthetic machine were the only sounds in the otherwise silent operating room, a sterile and still void.

After a few minutes, with the operation underway, John said, "I expected a lot of adhesions with bowel stuck everywhere, but this doesn't seem too bad."

Larry replied, "While the upper abdomen looks fine, the small intestine is stuck to the pelvis with thick, almost glue-like adhesions. If we need to go down there, a laparotomy may be necessary. The fistula to the small intestine is in the mid abdomen. We'll have to free up enough small bowel to resect the fistula and anastomose the two ends. Let's review the CAT scan again to see if we missed anything."

With a flick of a switch on the laparoscope, John watched as the CAT scan image flickered into existence on the monitor. Larry scrolled. The grainy images flickered past until the fistula site appeared, its contours sharp against the blurry background.

"Judging by the X-ray, I suspect the injury created just a single perforation in the small intestine," he said, his voice low and serious. Larry's finger jabbed at a spot on the screen, his eyes narrowed in concentration. "Miraculously, the spear avoided his bladder and other vital pelvic organs. The pus that Jacob witnessed draining from his groin wound three days after the injury may have been what ultimately prevented him from dying of sepsis. He said that the infected fluid, likely originating from the small bowel injury, had a putrid odour and viscous texture. I suspect it leaked into the pelvis before forming a fistula. Lucky for him, no evidence of the abscess remains."

After flipping the screen back to the laparoscopic image, John fell silent, the sterile scent of the operating room almost comforting. He felt calm and confident that this might solve the problem with Jacob. With renewed focus, he resumed the surgery, the delicate feel of the laparoscopic scissors against the small intestine as he separated it from the anterior abdominal wall. It was a tedious process, filled with repetitive tasks that seemed to stretch on endlessly. He was cautious to avoid puncturing the bowel.

"Did you believe him when he told us he didn't come on the boat to harm us but to warn us we were in danger?" asked John.

"It seems a little farfetched, doesn't it?" replied Larry, shaking his head slightly.

"He insists he possesses irrefutable evidence, the details of which are so compelling they'll dispel all uncertainty. He confidently declared that the alias he assumed, Brian Harper, would throw anyone off his trail. No one would know it was him except for us. The anesthesiologist said he swiped his health card, and the word Valid appeared on the card reader's screen, the green light blinking.

This was the only reason the anesthesiologist allowed us to proceed. The card must be legitimate."

"At least we'll get paid, too," laughed Larry.

John continued with his dissection, dividing the small bowel adhesions stuck to the abdominal wall. "I think this is the fistula," he said excitedly as Larry pushed his finger against the abdominal wall over the fistula opening. As he pushed, the laparoscopic image showed the finger indentation, a pale impression against the darker organs. Using the scissors, John made a clean cut across the fistula. A rush of bile spilled from the open small bowel and spread through the abdomen.

"Pass me the stapler," said John as he turned to the scrub nurse.

The sharp click of the tool punctuated the silence as John stapled the small bowel on one side of the fistula. With a high-pitched hum, the ultrasonic scalpel cleanly separated the mesentery, leaving only a few tiny droplets of blood. With a second application of the stapler, he divided the bowel on the other side of the fistula. He carefully placed the specimen into a clear plastic bag, then retrieved it through one of the larger port sites.

John created holes in the staple line of each end of the small bowel for the stapler jaws to slide into. With a quick motion, he fired the stapler. Larry could hear the satisfying click of the mechanism creating the anastomosis. John carefully closed the open edges of the bowel using a V-lock suture. Tiny, almost invisible barbs along the suture clinched it in place, preventing it from loosening. The anastomosis was watertight.

After washing out the abdomen with saline solution and suctioning the spilled bile, John removed the laparoscope. With practised hands, Larry and John closed the small incisions, the quiet snip of the sutures punctuated by the rustle of dressing materials. After the anesthesiologist removed the endotracheal tube, the beeping of heart monitors faded as they carefully transferred Jacob onto a gurney, rolling him toward the recovery room. John's voice, crisp and clear, filled the room as he dictated the operative note, then he completed the postoperative orders.

He met Larry in the doctor's lounge, the indistinct murmur of conversation a backdrop to the clinking of cups. "That went surprisingly well," said John, settling into the plush leather sofa, the rich aroma of his steaming coffee filling the air.

Larry nodded, a slight smile on his lips. "He should be ready for discharge in two days, so we'll have an opportunity to find out everything he has to say, and hopefully get some answers. I'm particularly interested in finding out what he has to say about the centrifuge project from 10 years ago."

"According to Jacob, the man who had tried to take our lives with a gun while we were aboard the boat was from Iran. Someone ordered him to eliminate us, but also to capture and hold you captive. We need to find out what they wanted from you."

"I think I know—" An overhead page cut off Larry.

"Code yellow; code yellow; code yellow. PACU, bed 10!" blared the intercom.

"Bed 10," shouted John. "That's Jacob!"

In a rush to get to the recovery room, Larry and John ran down the hallway, which was located just past the doctor's lounge. Nurses dashed about, their movements a whirlwind as they checked closets and the areas beneath the stretchers, seemingly in a state of controlled chaos. Larry stopped one of them. "Nina," he shouted as she ran by, "what happened to Jacob?"

As Nina stopped, a look of bewilderment spread across her features as she turned to face him. "Who's Jacob?"

Recognizing his error, Larry corrected himself, and said, "I apologize. I actually meant to say Brian Harper."

Nina's expression changed, her features relaxing into a softer, more compassionate look. "He explained he needed to use the bathroom, indicating a pressing urgency." With a pointed finger, she gestured toward the open bathroom door, which was in the far corner of the room. "I went back to the nursing station because I had unfinished charting to complete. Since he hadn't emerged after a few minutes had passed, I went and knocked on the door to check on him. I asked if he was alright. When he didn't answer, I pressed the emergency button to open the door, and the bathroom was empty."

With a gentle touch, John tapped Larry on the shoulder, interrupting his conversation with Nina. "I want to show you something."

With Larry following closely behind, John led the way to the stairs designated as the fire exit. To gain access, John used his security badge. There, on the landing, was a blue hospital gown, its fabric rumpled and lying haphazardly on the floor. The IV line, secured to the intravenous pole, swayed slightly from a draft coming from the staircase. Beneath the intravenous line, a small puddle of fluid had collected, a small and insignificant spill of saline solution.

Jacob was gone.

Chapter 17

Jacob felt stronger and healthier than ever, the accident fading into a distant and less impactful memory. The surgery, while significant, only accounted for about 10 per cent of the agonizing pain he'd endured since the accident. The lingering ache in his groin was a constant, dull reminder of the trauma. He felt a lightness in his step as he walked, no longer burdened by the drainage bag attached to his abdomen. Although the rash persisted, the searing pain was gone, thanks to the surgeons' work diverting the caustic bile and digestive enzymes from his skin back into his intestines. The area felt strangely numb. Impatient and anxious, he couldn't bear to wait in the sterile hospital halls, hoping to remain unnoticed. Outside, the comforting darkness allowed him to melt into the shadows, safer from prying eyes and the sounds of the city.

Jacob's timeline was a complex web of interconnected events. He allotted seven full days for his body to heal from the invasive surgery, hoping for minimal pain and discomfort. Then he would silently and swiftly make his move. Although he'd lost 30 pounds since his injury, a week had passed with no further weight loss. He swallowed 10 packages of high-protein supplements daily. His intestine absorbed their protein and calories, leaving him with a persistent, slightly nauseous feeling. With the fistula finally closed, he could focus on rebuilding his muscle mass, although he realistically knew it would still take six more weeks to regain his previous strength. The lingering weakness was a constant reminder. Though wounded, his strength far exceeded that of most men. He could out-muscle 90 per cent with ease.

A triumphant smile spread across Jacob's face as he realized his carefully planned exit from the hospital had been a success. From concealing his street clothes in the dusty, rarely used hospital fire escape staircase to transforming his identity into that of a visiting Russian Jewish rabbi, Aaron Hart, he had meticulously planned his escape. Cloaked in the city's anonymity, he moved through the bustling streets, hiding in plain sight, wearing his black suit and dress shoes. It was his towering height and wild, tangled beard that made him stand out from everyone else. He covered the top of his head with a black *kippa*, its material worn and faded, almost a dark grey in places.

The Uber pulled up in front of the Four Seasons Hotel in downtown Toronto on the circular driveway. The only other vehicle was a yellow cab that left when Jacob's vehicle stopped at the entrance. He entered the front lobby.

"Good evening, Rabbi Hart," said the concierge.

"Good evening, Bruce," said Jacob.

"Is there anything you need from me tonight? I haven't seen you for a few days."

"I had some business to attend to for the past few days. If you could, please make certain I am not disturbed for the next few days."

Jacob pressed the button for the elevator, the lights flickering slightly as the doors opened. He stepped inside once he was certain he was alone. A soft hiss announced the closing of the doors before he rose to the 14th floor. At the suite's door, he swiped his card key, the electronic click signalling that 1407 was unlocked. Inside, he quickly scanned the space, searching for anyone who may have been waiting.

Flicking on the lights, he confirmed he was alone. Jacob pulled back the king-sized sheets, then carefully placed the pillows beneath them to resemble a sleeping human body, the soft cotton a familiar comfort in the deceptive charade. Exhausted, he lay down on the cool, hard carpet on the far side of the room, closed his eyes, and plummeted into a deep, dreamless sleep.

***

Hidden in the shadows of the hospital parking lot, Jacob could hear the distant hum of traffic and feel the chill of the night air on his skin. It had been a full week since the operation, the sounds of the hospital still ringing in his ears as he thought of John and Larry's work. During the past week of indulging in calorie-dense foods and liquids, he had gained five pounds, feeling the extra weight in his clothes. Each day, he dedicated six hours in the hotel gym, the rhythmic clang of weights punctuating the *whoosh* of the treadmills as he focused on his intense weightlifting and aerobic routine. He would continue his regime for six more weeks of rigorous training to regain his previous bulky physique. He could feel the strength slowly return.

If his intended target maintained his observed weekly pattern, he should arrive to drive to his home within 30 minutes. He had hacked into David Graham's Google Timeline. Jacob saw the chief of staff's predictable sequence of locations confirming his established routine. He would replicate them to cover his own involvement. The door to the parking lot opened. David walked to his Porsche Boxter and opened the car door.

Jacob moved silently behind him, his breath held, careful not to make a sound. With his right hand, he pressed the chloroform-soaked gauze over David's mouth and nose, the pungent smell of the chemical stinging his nostrils as his powerful left arm pinned the doctor's chest, restricting his movement. After a brief struggle, David slumped unconscious in his arms, his body limp and his breathing shallow. Jacob heaved David into the passenger seat with a thud and slammed the car door shut. He hopped into the driver's seat, the scent of vintage upholstery filling his nostrils. He pointed the cold, metallic video-freezing fob at the garage's video camera and clicked the button decisively. The grainy hospital parking lot video would now capture the Porsche Boxter's departure, its taillights fading into the distance, yet offered no visual evidence of the abduction. The dark tint on the windows, almost opaque, would prevent the video from identifying Jacob as the driver.

Jacob stopped in the parking lot behind the convenience store. The chipped paint on the building and the litter strewn across the parking lot hinted at its age and neglect. Only a flickering security light illuminated the parking lot behind the building. The rental van he'd left there a few hours ago sat alone in the vast emptiness. He retrieved a brown canvas bag with some things he would need later and loaded it into the tiny trunk of the Porsche. With the zip ties, he bound David to the cold leather seat. Jacob stuffed a white handkerchief into his mouth and secured it with duct tape, the sticky adhesive clinging to David's cheeks, in case he woke up.

Five minutes later, he pulled up onto David's driveway in the Porsche. The tires crunched on the stone and he pressed the garage door opener on the driver's side sun visor. He parked in the garage and got out. Leaving David's cell phone on the workbench, he plugged it in to keep it charged, showing on the Google Timeline he had followed his predictable daily pattern. Reversing the Porsche, Jacob drove down the driveway. He pushed the garage door opener, listening to the whirring motor as the door descended.

Backing onto the main street, he adjusted the rearview mirror and drove off, leaving a cloud of dust in his wake. Glancing at the passenger seat, he saw David softly snoring, his head lolling against the worn faux wooden panel of the door with the sound of a low rumble from the finely tuned engine. He slept soundly until the jarring halt of the Porsche roused him. They had arrived at a dilapidated barn in King Township, north of Toronto, the smell of damp earth and decay almost overwhelming. Jacob carried David to a chair in the middle of the barn and secured him to it, and tied a bandana around his mouth.

Now fully awake, David's eyes darted around the faint light of the room and pulled at his restraints. Jacob removed his gag. Fear and confusion lined David's face. Panic appeared in his eyes as he looked around the barn, as if not understanding where he was. He shook his arms, trying to loosen the zip ties, but the movement only made the grip tighter.

"What the fuck are you doing?" David shouted. "Do you know who the fuck I am?"

Jacob stared at him, his jaw clenched tight, a silent scream trapped in his throat. His voice was sharp as he demanded, "Who paid you?"

David stared back, his eyes wide with a mixture of fear and fascination. "What in the world are you talking about?"

"I want names," Jacob said, his voice tight with barely suppressed anger.

David's face broke into a smirk. "Fuck you."

Jacob, a towering figure at six foot six, walked forward until he stood directly before David; his shadow fell long and dark across the floor. He reached for David's left hand, tightly gripping his little finger before forcefully bending it until it popped out of its socket. He twisted with increasing force, his knuckles white, until a sharp crack, like a twig snapping, announced the painful fracture. A bloodcurdling scream ripped through the air—David's terror palpable in the raw, desperate sound. The shrill noise that clawed at Jacob's ears continued until he loosened his hold on the deformed finger. Tears, hot and relentless, streamed down David's face. He was sobbing now, his shoulders shaking with each choked breath.

Jacob stared at David, a neutral expression on his face. He dragged a worn wooden chair across the floorboards and settled heavily into it. Jacob waited patiently for David to quiet down before asking again, "Tell me, who was the person who paid you?"

With a frustrated shake of his head, Jacob saw the hot tears prick David's eyes and roll down his weathered cheeks. His shoulders had slumped. The cocky attitude he started with had disappeared. He appeared defeated. Jacob let David writhe in pain for a few more minutes, the sounds of his sobs still ringing in the room before moving to another finger. David's agitation grew as he thrashed against his bonds, his face contorted in a mask of terror, sweat beading on his forehead.

"I... I... don't know the name," he stammered. "A man approached me a few months ago. He explained he wanted me to suspend Larry Klapman, one of our new surgeons. He said they needed something from Larry and would use the suspension as leverage. If Larry did what they wanted, they would ask me to drop the suspension."

"How much did he pay you?" asked Jacob.

David's mouth opened as if to say something, but no words came out at first. He swallowed as if to clear something stuck in his throat. "I had no choice," he croaked. "He knew something about me. Something... something I am not... not proud of. He threatened to tell the press. It would have ruined me."

Jacob continued to stare at David, his burning gaze making David squirm under the intensity. David continued to thrash in the chair, not able to move too far with the zip ties restraining his arms and legs. Swollen to twice its size, the mangled finger hung at a sickening right angle to the rest of his hand, its flesh already discoloured. His body went still, and David's head dropped to his chest. He whispered, "$250,000," the number hanging like a dark cloud.

Jacob rose, his joints cracking slightly. He now stood facing David. "What happened to my daughter? What happened to Melodie?" he asked, his eyes searching David's face.

"What... what do you mean?"

Jacob reached down and clasped David's warm right hand in his. In a flash, he violently twisted his index finger, hearing a sickening crack as both joints dislocated with a sickening pop, and felt a sharp crack in his hand as the bone disintegrated. Again, a scream ripped from David's throat, a sound like tearing fabric. This time, the piercing, high-pitched wail tore through the air for a full minute. His body shook with each sob, a torrent of tears streaming down his face as he wept uncontrollably. His face was a mask of desperation as he looked up at Jacob, his eyes glistening with unshed tears, pleading for help.

"Please... please... let me go.

In a slow, deliberate movement, Jacob's calloused hand reached for David's left thumb, the skin soft and sweaty.

"No! No!" David's high-pitched sliced through the silence. "I'll tell you everything I know."

Jacob let go of his thumb. He remained planted in front of David, his fists clenched, prepared to inflict further harm if David didn't comply. A silent threat, but a threat nevertheless.

"A nurse, the one assigned to looking after Melodie, approached me. She told me about Melodie's nasty wound infection, describing the angry red, swollen flesh. With Larry Klapman, she'd gone over the patient's case, their discussion highlighting the gravity of deciding whether to administer antibiotics. Larry told her that antibiotics were not suitable for treating a wound infection. She said his voice was serious and low, telling her improper antibiotic use can develop stronger bacterial strains, causing worse infections. With a worried look, she asked me to intervene in the escalating argument. I went to the pharmacy and prepared an intravenous bag for her to hang. She hung the bag at night when she was sleeping. They discharged Melodie from the hospital the following day."

"What was in the intravenous bag?" asked Jacob.

His hands, now a gruesome mess of swollen flesh and bruises, trembled slightly as David glanced down at them before stating, "Eight thousand grams of ibuprofen, commonly known as Advil. Sufficiently toxic to cause widespread gastrointestinal ulceration with resulting hemorrhage and perforation, potentially life-threatening."

David gasped for air, his chest heaving, words catching in his throat. "They... The Iranians suggested I file a complaint with the College of Physicians and Surgeons, hoping that a formal investigation would convince you of Larry Klapman's culpability in

Melodie's death. They wanted you to take care of Larry, relieving them of the bloody business of killing him after he'd given them the information."

Jacob let out a long, weary sigh. *Just as I had suspected. This wasn't a coincidence—my daughter's tragic death, Larry Klapman's presence, and their intertwined past. It all points to something more sinister.*

His hand shot out, fingers closing roughly around David's head. He twisted it to the right, feeling the resistance until the sudden snap, a sharp, brittle sound. Although alive, David was unconscious. His skin was pale. His breathing was faint. Paralyzed from the neck down, he was completely immobile, his body unresponsive.

Jacob reached into his canvas bag and wrapped a tourniquet around David's right arm. Using the engorged vein at the inside of the elbow, he injected pure ethanol, enough to give him toxic levels greater than 0.40 per cent. Jacob carefully inserted a nasogastric tube into David's stomach before pouring 20 ounces of Jack Daniel's down the tube. He stopped pouring the nearly empty bottle, the last drops sloshing inside, before placing it on the plush floor of David's Porsche. Jacob carefully cut the zip ties and lifted David into the passenger seat, then drove off.

Reaching the crest of the hill, Jacob hopped out of the driver's seat, the engine still purring. He carefully positioned David in his place, the doctor's body slumped over the steering wheel, making sure his head was resting gently against the cool leather. He pressed his hands firmly over David's nose and mouth to make sure he was no longer breathing before closing the door. With the emergency brake off, he pushed the car to roll down the hill. The beautiful Porsche, a machine of polish and chrome, gathered speed before Jacob's eyes, then launched itself off the cliff with a terrifying roar, disappearing into the mist rising from the Humber River.

Jacob unzipped the brown canvas bag, revealing the sleek, black electric bike. He unfolded it, the metallic parts gleaming faintly in the dim light. He headed back to Toronto, an hour's bike ride through the pre-dawn darkness.

Chapter 18

"Sure, I didn't like him, and our last interaction was confrontational, but to die so tragically... I wouldn't wish that on anyone," said Larry.

"The coroner isn't saying much about David's death," John muttered, his eyes scanning the room nervously. The harsh fluorescent lights of the doctor's lounge reflected off the pale, chipped mugs as they sipped the gritty, industrial coffee at the end of a gruelling operating day.

"According to news reports," continued John, "David drove his red Porsche Boxter into the fast-flowing Humber River near King City. The frightening details included the mangled flesh of his hands and a broken neck. What the heck was he doing up there?"

"I had a feeling something was wrong with David," said Larry. "His behaviour was off. His last conversation with me was a chaotic jumble of accusations and nonsensical ramblings. It sent shivers down my spine. The psychotic break was evident in his erratic behaviour—he was shouting, his body trembled uncontrollably. Something was up with him."

"Being chief of staff is a thankless position, requiring immense responsibility and problem-solving skills while receiving little credit. Every day brings a fresh wave of unsolvable issues that might leave him feeling overwhelmed and defeated. Maybe the relentless pressure, the constant deadlines, and the overwhelming workload had finally caught up to him?"

Larry let out a loud, booming laugh that echoed through the room. "John, come on. In your role as chief of surgery, you have avoided experiencing a psychotic breakdown. You seem to navigate through problems with an ease that suggests its second nature to you. You are like a seasoned sailor navigating through stormy seas. Even the most arrogant and egocentric surgeons among us hold you in high regard."

"What do you suspect was wrong with David, then?"

"Apart from his arrogance, controlling nature, and narcissism?" Larry smirked. "Often in our high-pressure medical environment, where the stakes are life or death, doctors turn to drugs or alcohol for solace. Maybe he was just one of those?"

John paused, his eyebrows raising briefly and eyes widening as he considered the matter. "That's not my impression. The possibility of substance abuse among surgeons is something I am always looking out for. I maintain a high level of awareness. One hallmark is a change in behaviour, including things like restlessness, unusual aggression, or lethargy. The dopamine rush from years of alcohol abuse masks the underlying issues of highly functional alcoholic surgeons. When their bodies stop responding to the effects of the dopamine release, their carefully constructed world comes crashing down. This is the real devastating result of substance abuse."

John paused to take a sip of his lukewarm coffee. "I suspect your initial assessment of arrogant and narcissistic personality traits is more accurate than any other. I never saw David touch a drop of alcohol, even at the hospital's boisterous social events. His need for control was too overwhelming to be blunted by the effects of booze. His behaviour has always been the same, a predictable pattern, never deviating from its course."

With a quick glance at his watch, Larry gasped. He jumped up in a panic, his eyes wide. "Shit! I promised Chantelle I would pick up the kids from school today, relieving her busy schedule. I'm off! Catch you later." Larry rushed to his car, the sound of his own breath loud in his ears as he raced down the corridors and to the parking lot. He glanced at his watch; only 15 minutes remained, but if he hurried, he could still make it... and if there were no accidents to slow him down on the way.

Larry pulled up at the school. He was only one minute late. He sighed a huge breath of relief. A space was available in front of the school. It was next to a fire hydrant, marked with a 'no parking' sign. He parked there and raced into the school. The quiet was deafening. He walked into his oldest child, Sheldon's home classroom. Martha, the teacher, sat at her desk on the laptop. She looked up when she heard Larry enter.

"Hi, Larry," she said. "If you are looking for your wife and kids, they just left."

Larry stopped in his tracks. "What... what are you talking about?" he asked. "Chantelle had a late appointment and asked me to pick them up."

Martha looked at the room and swept her hand around the empty space. She let out a soft, melodic laugh that filled the air. "Well, they aren't here, are they? You must have got your wires crossed."

Larry's face crumpled into a mask of confusion. With a frustrated shake of his head, he pushed through the heavy school doors and stepped out into the bright sunshine. Reaching his Tesla, he noticed a crumpled, yellow parking ticket stuck to the windshield; the paper felt stiff and cheap under his fingertips. With a frustrated growl, he yanked it off, the rough edges scratching his skin, before roughly stuffing it into his pocket. *What was Chantelle thinking? I should make her pay for this!*

He drove home, the tires whispering on the asphalt as he meticulously obeyed the speed limit. Another ticket was certainly not something he wanted. The crumpled parking ticket in his pocket fuelled his frustration. He thought about calling Chantelle, but the anger still simmered beneath his skin. He needed the drive home to cool down before he spoke to her. As he pulled into the empty garage. Chantelle's car was not there. With a sigh, Larry called her from his Tesla. He tapped his fingers against the dashboard. The call went to voicemail, the familiar beep noticeable to the silence of unanswered expectation.

"Chantelle," he said, his voice a low rumble, "call me when you get this. I recall you asking me to be the one to fetch the kids today. My efforts have earned me nothing but a parking ticket."

He quickly scanned the empty driveway, then his eyes moved to the street, where only a few cars were parked. The security guard's usual parking spot was empty; his car was nowhere to be seen. *He must have followed Chantelle to the school and then to wherever she took them afterwards.*

The house was silent, a departure from to the usual children's laughter and the playful shouts at that time of day. The quiet was so profound it felt unnatural, a heavy blanket stifling any sound. Larry sank into his chair in his office, the silence of the empty house pressing down on him as he waited for them to get home. He logged into his bank account on the computer. A stack of five bills— hydro, gas, utilities, and property taxes—lay on his desk, their crisp edges a gentle reminder of impending deadlines. With the first bill paid and a sigh of relief escaping his lips, the doorbell's chime cut through the silence.

Larry walked to the heavy oak front door and turned the brass knob to open it. A man stood there, his face obscured by the shadows from the roof overhang. Dressed in a crisp, charcoal grey three-piece suit, the man in his mid-forties stood a head taller than Larry. The man's dark, intense eyes, like pools of midnight, pierced into his. A sudden chill ran down Larry's spine, making the hairs on his neck stand on end. At first, the man said nothing, the silence razor sharp.

"Can I help you?" asked Larry.

"Yes," said the man. That one word alone held the unmistakable sound of an accent for Larry; it was a musical lilt that resonated with a hint of Farsi. He continued, "I think you can."

Larry stared at the man, his eyes narrowed in suspicion, a knot of unease tightening in his stomach. A strange feeling washed over him. Something was definitely amiss. He glanced to the street, noticing Chantelle's familiar red car parked in front of the house. Its shiny paint gleamed in the sunlight. *What was he doing with Chantelle's car?* A wave of confusion washed over him, and he turned his gaze back to the man, searching his face for answers.

"I need you to come with me," he said.

"What... what is this about? Where are Chantelle and the

kids?" His eyes darted to the car to see if they were there, but he couldn't tell because of the tinted glass.

"They are safe. I will take you to them."

Larry recognized in a flash what was happening. "I'm calling the police," he shouted. Larry shut the door, but the man's foot prevented it from closing. The man kicked the door with his other foot, knocking Larry to the floor. Once inside, the man kicked Larry in the face. A searing pain shot through his face, then darkness.

Chapter 19

It was pitch black when Larry woke up, not a single ray of light piercing the darkness of his room. A throbbing pain pulsed in his nose and face, making his head pound. Larry gingerly touched his swollen, throbbing nose, the pain a dull ache that made him worry it might be broken. At first, a fog hung in his mind, obscuring the events of the afternoon. Then the image of a tall man took shape, his dark eyes and the sound of his accented words coming back to Larry. A jolt shot through him, his heart pounding in his ears. *My kids... Chantelle!*

"Hey!" he yelled. "Anyone there!?"

His question remained unanswered, save for the oppressive quiet. He felt around with his hands. He found himself in a cramped room, the rough-hewn walls cold against his back. Small, dented cans and plastic buckets overflowed from the shelves onto the dusty floor. With his groping hands, he could feel a well-worn broom and a slightly damp mop occupied one corner, the head resting against the wall. Despite attempting to measure in the complete darkness, the room appeared to be approximately six feet by six feet and resembled a utility closet. Larry could smell damp concrete and resiny cleaning supplies. A heavy wood door, bound with iron, stood on one wall. Larry stood, steadying himself. Then, with a decisive twist, he turned the door handle, hearing a faint creak as it gave only slightly before he felt resistance. It was locked, firm and unyielding.

Larry pounded on the door, the wood groaning under the force of his blows, and yelled at the top of his lungs. "Hey! Hey!" he called, his voice hollow in the small space. With increasing frustration, Larry continued to bang on the door, each thud shaking the frame. With his ear against the wooden door, he strained to hear anything above the rhythmic *thump-thump-thump* of his own heart. The weight of defeat settled upon him like a physical burden as he sat down heavily on the cold, hard floor. He was confused and shaken. The horrifying thought of his children and Chantelle being abducted filled his mind.

With a sigh, Larry's head fell into his hands. He focused on slowing his racing heart, the frantic beat a drum against his ribs, and calming his panicked thoughts. He'd survived worse. The boot camp of the Israeli army training lessons drifted into his thoughts. What he needed was a rational mind, a clear and logical approach to the situation. Whoever had abducted him needed something from him, so they surely would keep him alive. If he were to believe Jasmine, it might be something he'd worked on when he had spent that year in the Israeli Army, the centrifuge project. His priority would be to get Chantelle and the kids to safety. He had to put their safety above all else, making sure they were out of danger before making any other moves.

The Psycho

Larry heard the steps—a *thump-thump-thump* of shoes on the unforgivingly hard floor. A faint, yellowish light appeared at the bottom of the heavy oak door, forming long shadows across the floor. *Someone was coming.* Larry pushed himself up from the floor, his joints cracking. Searching in the dim light from the sliver coming under the door, he scanned the surroundings for any object that he could use as a weapon. With a decisive movement, he grabbed a broomstick, the wood smooth and cool beneath his fingers. A slow, deliberate *click* warned that someone had unlocked the door. It creaked open, revealing a barely illuminated room. With his arm raised and ready to plunge the end of the broom's handle into the person's face, Larry stood firm. No one appeared.

"Dr. Klapman," said the voice. "Please step out of the room where I can see you."

Unsure of what to do, Larry stood completely still, listening intently. He sighed, heavy with frustration, before the makeshift weapon clattered to the floor. Given the risks, the aggressive approach—a dangerous gamble—would have to wait. With trepidation, Larry stepped into the long hallway, the silence amplifying his every footstep. The tall man from before, still sharply dressed in a three-piece suit, stood in front of him, his Persian accent resonant.

"Come with me," he said, his voice low, and he spun away,

disappearing up the creaking wooden stairs at the end of the long hallway.

Larry followed. Reaching the top of the stairs, he found himself in a darkened hallway that opened into a vast room with a concrete floor. Someone neatly stacked several sleek, silver laptops on a small wooden desk and chair in a corner. A bulky desktop computer, connected to the laptop by a tangle of wires, sat on the floor. "Please," the man said, gesturing to the worn leather chair.

Larry was puzzled, but obeyed the instructions and sat down in front of the laptop on the desk.

"We need you to unlock the codes that you placed on the worm from 10 years ago when you were with Unit 8200," said the man.

With a look of utter disbelief, Larry glanced at the man, his jaw slightly agape. "If you think I can recall eight months of relentless work and magically solve your problems in mere hours, you're delusional. Additionally, that technology and coding are outdated. Since I left, I have not been involved in that line of work. There is no way I am going to be of any use to you."

"Maybe this will help with your memory," he said, the glow of the laptop screen illuminating his face as he powered it up. A time stamped video appeared on the monitor. The footage captured Chantelle in a small room, sitting on a bed with their two boys snuggled close to her, one on each side. The boys sat quietly, their eyes closed, as Chantelle's fingers gently stroked their hair. Her soft touch always calmed them. A hushed whisper passed between her and their older son. The sounds appeared muffled and indistinct in Larry's ears. After a minute, the man turned the video off.

"Where are they?" shouted Larry as he tried to get up.

The man pushed him back in the seat. "They are safe. We will let them go when you have delivered what we want."

"That's bullshit! I know what you did to Benjamin. You tortured then killed him. You are going to do the same to us. I am doing nothing until you release them. They have nothing to do with this."

The man remained silent for a moment before he spoke. "This is exactly what I expected from you. The Unit 8200 provides foundational skills in resisting information extraction, but our expertise lies in efficiently getting the information from you, despite your training."

The only door in the room creaked open, and two large men walked in, their boots thudding heavily on the floor. They could have been twins; identical in features, height, and build, down to their mannerisms. Both wore tight white T-shirts, their steroid-induced muscles bulging, straining the seams. The tight spandex stretched over their muscular buttocks clearly outlined the dysmorphic body habitus. The overdeveloped thigh muscles made their gait awkward. Their strides were too far apart, and they seemed to waddle rather than walk. Their legs slapped against each other with each step.

"I have instructed these gentlemen to give you a taste of what to expect if you do not cooperate with us," said the man. "I'll be back in about half an hour to check on your progress and see how you're getting along."

The man turned, his eyes lingering on the hulking figures as they passed, their muscles rippling beneath their skin. The men looked at each other. Grins spreading across their faces as they smiled and waddled by the tall man. They stood beside the desk and motioned for Larry to stand. When he didn't comply, two powerful hands clamped down on his shoulders, hoisting him into the air. Larry felt sharp, searing pain as the fingers dug into his skin, a scream ripping involuntarily from his throat. With a grunt, the muscle men continued to lift him, then in a smooth motion, flung him on the concrete floor, the impact winding him. Each shallow breath was a struggle, the world fading as Larry felt his consciousness slipping away. Just before he passed out, he gasped as his diaphragm kicked into action, pulling in a deep, ragged breath. Taking a deep effort to breathe in, he felt the pain like fire in his chest as he felt the sickening crunch of broken ribs, his inhalation catching in his throat.

All Larry could do was to lie there and struggle with his winded breathing attempts. He saw the two men standing over him. He felt himself cowering, trying to make himself as small as possible, dreading what was next in store with him from these monsters. One took a step towards him to reach down as if to grab him. Larry closed his eyes. He heard a loud thump and the floor beside him vibrated. Another thump and a similar vibration followed. Larry opened his eyes. Both of the steroid-induced muscle men lay on the floor. Their heads lay at right angles to their neck. The neck, twisted 180 degrees, added to the bizarre mass of muscles lying on the floor. Neither man moved.

Jacob loomed over them. "Follow me," Jacob said, his voice low and urgent. He turned around and headed to the door. Larry lay on the floor, his mind reeling from a confusing jumble of thoughts and images. With a groan, he struggled to his feet, the blood rushing to his head, and he stumbled back down into the chair beside the desk, his breath coming in ragged gasps. Taking a deep breath caused a searing, agonizing pain in his chest. Larry focused on standing, pushing himself up with a grunt. He followed Jacob down the hallway, limping by the open door of an office. He stopped dead in his tracks, a chill crawling up his spine.

The tall man, unmistakable in his three-piece suit, sat inside the office, the glow of the laptop screen illuminating his face as he sat behind the cluttered desk. His eyes, a vacant stare fixed on something just above the doorway, unsettled Larry. Panic seized Larry as he realized what he was looking at, his lungs burning as if he were drowning in air. The man's neck, grotesquely bent to the right, made his head loll into an unnatural position.

A gasp, involuntary and sharp, tore from Larry's throat as Jacob's light touch on his shoulder and the quiet, "Let's go" jolted him.

Larry followed. Jacob headed down the long hallway to another door that led into a garage, the heavy door groaning as Jacob pushed it open, revealing a black Lincoln SUV. Not a single vehicle was in any of the other spaces. The darkly tinted SUV windows, like a mirrored surface, prevented Larry from seeing inside. Jacob flung open the passenger door, the hinges groaning a rusty protest, and beckoned Larry inside. He slowly lowered himself into the passenger seat, each movement causing a dull ache in his broken ribs. He glanced at the back seat.

His frightened wife, Chantelle, and his two children stared back at him, their faces a mixture of fear and confusion.

Chapter 20

"How can we be certain no one will find us here?" asked Chantelle.

Larry looked up from the electric winch he was greasing. He had spread out its innards of on the cockpit floor. Cleaning the components with the gasoline, the only solvent he could find, they were now free of grime. He was putting the winch back together.

"No one knows we're here except for John," Larry whispered, glancing nervously around the marina. Taking a deep breath was still painful, but the fractured ribs had become less bothersome over the past week. "Our IDF contact, Jasmine, has digitally placed us in Israel, using our cell phones and emails as bait—a cool digital trick. Each day, she taps out frantic text messages and emails, hoping to leave an online trail. Should anyone search for us in Israel, they could expect immediate apprehension and thorough interrogation by the Israel Defense Forces."

Chantelle sighed. "This is not something I signed up for. I thought your past was behind us when we started our life together in Toronto. You need to fix this. I don't feel safe!"

"We have a security guard sitting at the end of our dock 24/7." Larry waved at the man wearing army fatigues and carrying a rifle who passed by the boat. He waved back. "It is cheaper than hiring guards in Toronto, about a quarter of the price."

"Huh," she said, a worried frown twisting her lips. Her eyes clouded with apprehension. "They found our last security guard dead, a bullet wound in the back of his head. They crammed him into the trunk of his car, just a block from our house. It was useless having them protect us, wasn't it?" A palpable sense of regret filled the air, heavy and still, like a dark, oppressive cloud. "What makes you think this is any safer?" she asked.

"Shep, the Armada assigned to the marina, has his off-duty colleagues, clad in crisp uniforms, standing guard," Larry said confidently. "The government's stingy paychecks leave them all desperately needing extra cash to make ends meet. To kill even one would mean facing the might of the entire armada, an unstoppable force bearing down on them with devastating weaponry. I don't think the Iranians would be in favour of that."

"Despite their familiarity with violence in the Dominican Republic, the lure of money could sway them to look the other way if they are desperate enough. The Iranians seem to have huge amounts of money for this."

Larry looked around the marina, taking in the salty air and the sounds of seagulls. At least half the slips were empty. Seasonal moorings filled most of the occupied slips, and their owners were absent. Several large catamarans that bobbed on the water near the four-star hotel held families with boys who looked to be about his kids' age. Beaming, Sheldon and Abe had already made new friends. Laughter and the excited chatter of children filled the air as they raced back and forth along the docks, playing some imaginary game.

"The Iranians are trying to get information from me, which I don't think I can retrieve from my memory banks. It was so long ago," said Larry. "The details are now hazy, like a distant dream. Besides, consider the vast improvements in technology since then. It's a completely different digital landscape." Larry shook his head, sighing in frustration. "It's astonishing that they still haven't figured out that part."

"That," she said, pointing a finger at him, "is your problem. Just hand it over. Whatever they want from you. Give it to them and we can go home. They're not going to change their minds. We are stuck in this shithole of a country hiding from men that want to kill us. You have recklessly endangered your children's safety and well-being. Worst of all, the fear is a gnawing presence, a constant dread that permeates every moment of our existence. I don't think I can take much more of this emotional rollercoaster. My heart is constantly pounding and I feel sick to my stomach."

Chantelle's tears rolled down her cheek. She sobbed, emotionally defeated. She wrapped both her arms around her shoulders, rocking gently as if to comfort herself. Larry wiped the grease from his fingers on a cloth near the winch parts he was working on and sat down to hug her. He put his arm around her. Chantelle pushed him away.

"Don't you dare touch me," she whispered. She retreated into the main salon of the boat. The winch grease scent of the cockpit filled Larry's nostrils as he sat down. Unease settled in his gut. This sickening feeling was not new for him. He had lived through bad times with Chantelle before, and the thought of living through them again filled him with dread.

A few years after moving to Toronto, Chantelle had experienced a similar overwhelming feeling of abandonment. His second year of surgical residency was a whirlwind of intense learning. The responsibility weighed heavily on his shoulders from the insecurity of managing extremely sick patients. A gruelling 90-hour work week left him with precious little time to spend with Chantelle and their only child. With a tremble in her voice, she threatened to leave him unless he made significant changes.

Although he had met with the residency supervisor, they could do little about the one night in three on call responsibility. Chantelle said she hated spending the evenings alone. When Larry came home late on the nights he was not on call, he was so tired, he would often fall asleep at the dinner table. She said it was like living alone. Somehow, they navigated that tumultuous storm as he desperately tried to balance his family life. The painful experience of the histrionic screaming and the threats of leaving him that occurred with increased frequency for the next two years while he finished his surgical training left him with emotional scars.

Larry sat with his head in his hands, the scent of her perfume a reminder of their usual joy now replaced by the bitter tang of her tears. As a resident, they had tried couples' counselling, but his demanding job made it nearly impossible for him to carve out time for Chantelle, something the counsellor suggested. Chantelle explained to the counsellor that her life felt like it was slipping through her fingers. The feeling of constant missed opportunities weighed heavily on her. She confessed to spending many nights Larry was on call in dimly lit bars and boisterous nightclubs, the noise a strange comfort compared to the silence at home. During one of their tearful sessions, Larry discovered this heartbreaking truth, the silence punctuated only by her sobs. The shock of this discovery left him reeling. An icy dread settled in his stomach as he wondered what other secrets she held close.

These painful memories would return with every accusation and blame that Chantelle hurled at him. His kids interrupted his thoughts as they raced up to him.

"Daddy, daddy," shouted Abe and Sheldon in unison. "Can

we go swimming?"

"Count me in!" he replied.

With a quick trip to the boys' cabins, Larry grabbed their brightly coloured bathing suits and fluffy towels. He asked Chantelle if she wanted to join them, but she just grunted, the sound muffled by the magazine she was reading on the bed.

The infinity pool, seemingly endless against the backdrop of the vibrant blue ocean, beckoned the boys, who plunged in with joyous splashes. Although they could swim, Larry's eyes never left them as they splashed and played, the chlorine scent sharp in the air. Two other boys joined them in the cool water for a lively game of Marco Polo. The barkeep brought Larry's Heineken. He took a long sip and stretched out on the comfortable chaise lounge, feeling the sun's warmth on his face.

The marina boasted three restaurants serving fresh seafood, two inviting swimming pools, a state-of-the-art exercise room, a billiard room, and a relaxing spa suffused with aromatherapy scents. The sailors enjoyed the comforts of warm showers, fresh laundry, and ample provisions. Though forced to hide, Larry couldn't help but admire the stunning vista before him—a picturesque ocean bathed in golden sunlight, palm trees swaying, and the air alive with the songs of birds. He only hoped that Chantelle could see this as an opportunity to experience things in life she would not normally get to appreciate.

After an hour of splashing and swimming, the boys, tired and sun-kissed, traded the pool for the thrill of racing scooters borrowed from their friends. With shouts of laughter, they sprinted back and forth along the concrete docks, the rough concrete vibrating beneath their wheels and feet as they pushed for speed.

When Larry returned to the boat, he found it empty. Chantelle was gone. The expansive hotel's open-air lobby was visible from the boat's cockpit. He could make out the intricate details of the architecture and the vibrant colours of the furnishings. He glanced across the dimly lit bar and saw Chantelle, her face softly illuminated by the candlelight, sipping a glass of red wine. She was talking on the phone, her words impossible to hear from his vantage point.

With all the parts cleaned and greased, he used this opportunity to reassemble the winch, feeling the smooth motion of each piece as he worked. After an hour of careful labour, the winch was finally back together, its gears meshing smoothly. The test results were perfect. It functioned exactly as intended. Glancing back at the bar, he could hear the clinking of glasses, a dull background to Chantelle still talking on her phone. Her wine glass sat empty on the table, the condensation still clinging to its side.

Larry hopped on the dock and made his way toward her,

dodging his kids, who whizzed past him on scooters, shouting and laughing. Chantelle saw him approaching. She said something on the phone that he did not catch, then watched as she hung up. Larry sat in the empty seat beside her at the bar.

"Are you feeling any better?" he asked.

She turned and faced him, remaining silent for a moment.

"Larry, we have to talk."

Chapter 21

"Everything has happened so quickly. I can barely process it all. My head is spinning," she said between the sobs. They had made their way to the privacy of the sailboat, where the soothing rocking of the boat did little to calm her. Though the sun was setting, yet dark, and the kids were still playing on the dock with their friends, their laughter ricocheting across the water.

"We've been here a week now," said Larry. "Surely you feel safe here. It's a Caribbean paradise."

"I cannot get rid of the fear I felt. It plays over and over in my mind. I've never been so scared in my life," she continued, tears welling up in her eyes. "The man knocked on the door, his voice hushed as he explained the guard was ill and he was the temporary replacement. Urgently, he told me to gather the kids because your Tesla had failed again and wouldn't start. He needed me to come with him. He mentioned you had phoned him. I cancelled my hair appointment. We took my car. He said he would drive. When we got to the school, I returned with the children. He drove away, locking the doors. He explained they needed something from you and when you gave it to them, he would set us free. The way he looked at us, his eyes cold and hard, I knew that wouldn't be the case. I screamed. He slapped my face again and again until I stopped screaming. The kids, whimpering softly, shrunk down in the back seat, trying to disappear. His voice was low and gravelly as he threatened to hit them, too, unless they remained silent."

A wave of guilt washed over Larry as he looked at her, the silent accusation in her eyes a reminder of his failure to shield his family from harm. The bitter taste of regret filled his mouth. He reached for her hand, his fingers brushing hers before she abruptly pushed him away. Larry opened his mouth to speak, but nothing came out.

"He locked us in that cramped little room," she continued. "All I could smell was the mildew. After what seemed to be a few hours, the door swung inward, revealing Jacob. I recognized his distinctive build and facial features, which matched your description perfectly. My initial thought was that he was there to kill us. The unsettling silence and his grim expression only confirmed my fear. I let out a scream, a primal sound born of pure fear and adrenaline. The softness in his eyes, a quiet pool of compassion, convinced me he was telling the truth about wanting to help. He gently scooped up Abe and Sheldon. Their tiny bodies looked soft in his hands. And then took my hand. He asked us to close our eyes when we walked down the hallway. With a start, I opened my eyes, my heart pounding. On my way to the car, I saw at least three dead men on the floor. Their faces were pale, and their eyes were vacant. Their necks were twisted. He told us to wait in the SUV. His voice was low and urgent. He told us absolutely not to open the door for anyone. You showed up five minutes later."

"Honey," said Larry, "It's over now. We are away from them. It won't always be like this for us."

Chantelle looked at Larry, her gaze locking with his. Larry saw a flicker of something in her eyes. Tears still glistened on her cheeks, her eyes red and swollen. "Maybe for you it won't be like this, but as long as I am with you, an icy dread will cling to me like a shroud. I will forever remember the sheer terror and overwhelming sense of helplessness I felt. I will always wonder when the next assault will happen."

Chantelle seemed to choke, then took a deep breath. "This will not be over anytime soon. For the rest of your life, you could be a marked man. I will not live my life like that. I will not let our children live their lives like that."

Larry felt a pain in his chest as he thought he knew what was coming next. "What are you suggesting?" he whispered.

"I'm leaving to fly back to Toronto. I'm taking the kids with me. We leave tomorrow afternoon. Richard is flying in tonight and will take care of us."

A puzzled expression crossed Larry's face. "Who's Richard?" he whispered.

Chantelle took a deep, shaky breath, her eyes darting away

from Larry's intense gaze. "I've been seeing Richard... even before we took that fateful sailboat trip a few months ago on this boat. I wanted to cancel the trip, but the excitement of the adventure, the thrill of the unknown, was too strong to ignore. Anyway..." her voice trailed off, a hint of uncertainty in her tone. "It wasn't the hair appointment I had organized that day when I asked you to pick up the kids. I was meeting with Richard."

Larry's eyes widened in disbelief, his mouth falling agape as he stared at Chantelle. Then he could feel his face go red, a blush that spread quickly as his heart hammered in his chest, a frantic rhythm like a speeding freight train. A wave of dizziness washed over him, followed by a rising tide of nausea. Gasping, he stood up, his lungs burning for air. A terrible, sharp pain shot through his chest, intensified by the fractured ribs. He attempted to stand up, but the world swam before his eyes, a dizzying blur. He knew he needed to sit.

"I met him in the gym about three months ago," she continued. "We were both in the same peloton class. We talked for hours after that first class. I told him how I needed more in life than raising kids and how it felt being underappreciated. We would have a drink every day at the Orange Theory bar at the gym. That's why I was always late for dinner. I told him how you had endangered our lives with the threats of Jacob. He told me he would never let anything like that happen to me. That was the start of the affair. He took me to his apartment and made me feel like I was on top of the world."

With his mouth still hanging open, Larry, unable to move, sat on the hard wooden cockpit bench. The emptiness inside him was a cold, heavy weight, pressing down on his spirit. *The signs were all there, but somehow I missed every single one. Obsessed with my problems, I didn't even register what was happening. The mistakes I've made, the pain I've caused, it's all my fault.*

"I am going to stay in the hotel tonight," she said. "Richard will get here at around 11 p.m. Our flight tomorrow is at noon—direct to Toronto. You can meet us in the hotel lobby with the kids' bags at 9:30 a.m."

Larry stared at her, not sure what to say. Chantelle went into the forward room and emerged five minutes later with her small carry-on bag with wheels. Larry remained sitting in the cockpit, his head spinning, seemingly unable to grasp what was happening. He stared as she left the boat and stood on the dock.

She turned and said, "And Larry... I'm sorry..." Chantelle walked to the hotel lobby with her bag and got into the elevator. Larry watched as the door closed, still trying to understand what had just happened.

***

Larry tossed and turned, the weight of Chantelle's revelation pressing down on him, preventing him from sleeping. *I should have seen it a mile away. The clues were so blatant, so how did I not see what was coming? Sure, our marriage hasn't been without its challenges—fierce arguments and hurtful words—but I believed we'd overcome them. Maybe I should return with them, let the Iranians capture me, and end this agonizing torment. But that would only put them in more danger, exposing them to more threats and escalating the situation. I must shield them from any harm that may come their way.* A maelstrom of anxieties and half-formed plans, Larry's thoughts swirled chaotically in his mind, a dizzying mix of images and emotions.

It was still dark, the room only barely lit by the moon, when Larry rolled out of bed. He made a cup of Nespresso, the dark roasted scent a comforting contrast to the metallic smell of the cockpit. He sat down and contemplated what to do. His children's needs always came first, regardless of the cost. Larry reminded himself, with a determined nod, that this was his top priority, pushing all other thoughts aside. Safely hiding Chantelle and the kids reduced the probability of anyone harming them to get to him. Although he could evade the Iranians through digital trickery, their relentless pursuit was inevitable. *The absence of Chantelle and the children's vulnerability will make hiding much simpler for him and safer for them.* A quiet ease settled over Larry's mind as he acknowledged that Chantelle's plan, however painful for him, might be the only way to keep his children safe. The weight of this realization was crushing. His fractured ribs suddenly sent a shooting pain across his chest. He felt like he couldn't get any air into his lungs. He focused on shallow breaths, the sharp sting of the pain slowly fading to a dull ache.

When 8 a.m. rolled around, he roused the kids and fed them Nesquik cereal, their favourite. "Your mom is taking you back to Toronto today," said Larry.

Sheldon, with a mouthful of the chocolate cereal, shouted, spraying bits across the table, "We want to stay here with you! We just made some new friends. They have scooters."

"Sheldon, don't talk with your mouth full," rebuked Larry. "You've had fun here, but it's time to go home. You've missed too much school already. I'll get back home as soon as possible."

"How come you get to stay and we have to go?" said Sheldon. "Not fair!"

Larry thought about that for a moment. "You've right. Many things that happen in life are not fair. Sometimes we just have to live with unfairness. I'd rather be going home with you guys, but I can't."

Larry glanced at his watch. "Look at the time," he continued.

"We need to get ready to go."

He swiftly stuffed the boys' clothes and toiletries into the small roller bags, the zippers straining slightly, and then carefully placed them on the dock. The boys, energized and ready, hopped onto the sun-weathered dock, the morning warmth radiating up through their worn sneakers, and agreed to pull the surprisingly weighty bags to the main lobby. Chantelle was already there, patiently waiting, smiling faintly.

Beside her stood a tall, thin man, his dark, curly hair catching the light, a faint scent of sandalwood emanating from him. *This must be Richard.* He had a short, fashionably trimmed beard. His eyes, dark and bottomless, stared directly into Larry's, sending a shiver down his spine. His brow furrowed with concern upon seeing Larry. A silent question hung in the air, as if he was uncertain what to expect from him. Despite being nervous, Larry offered his hand, his fingers slightly damp with sweat. The sudden gesture startled the taller man, his eyes quickly glancing at the offered hand before a somewhat hesitant shake at first. It turned into a firm handshake, his grip strong and unwavering, as if asserting his dominance. A heavy silence stretched between them, thick with unspoken tension.

The taxi waited. Larry carefully placed the boys' bags into its trunk. Peeking in to where the kids were sitting, Larry leaned down, inhaling the sweet smell of their hair, and softly kissed them on their foreheads. "I love you," he said.

Chantelle hopped into the back seat, settling between the two boys, while Richard sat in the front. Larry watched the taxi speed away, its red taillights disappearing into the distance. He walked to the sailboat and sat in the cockpit, the smell of salt and canvas strong in the air, the sun warm on his face. A wave of grief washed over him, leaving him breathless and unable to control his emotions. The weight of crushing sadness filled his soul. With a choked sob, he covered his face with his hands, his body wracked with silent weeping.

Chapter 22

Jacob sat rigidly before the glowing screen of his laptop, fingers hovering over the keyboard in the dim light of his room at the Four Seasons. He had meticulously traced the digital trail of text messages and emails, each click revealing a new step closer to a government office in Tehran, Iran. He wanted to delve deeper into his existing knowledge, seeking clues to guide his next move. The familiar information felt strangely new. The Iranians had actually sent the emails and texts, many urgent in tone, that he'd supposedly directed to Larry to throw them off. Jacob felt a chill run down his spine as he realized they'd accessed and sent his private information. He had successfully blocked further texts and messages, but the damage was done. The Iranians' attempts at hacking emails and digital sleuthing were clumsy and easily detected.

Further investigation had led him to an email. David Garner, chief of staff, had addressed it to Sidney Acker, undoubtably a fake name, and sent it to a Gmail account that was obviously fake. It read:

Hi Sidney.

Thank you for the email instructions. I have done as you have asked. We are actively pursuing the death of Melodie Ashinoff and I have already found fault in the management. I will ask the College to assist us in punishing Larry Klapman. I will move for a suspension of his license to practice. This should give you plenty of leverage to get what you need from him. Convincing the father that Dr. Klapman is responsible for the death of his daughter will be the natural conclusion. I agree he will probably do what is necessary in retribution.

Please send the agreed upon money to this account in the Cayman Islands:

HSBC Bank, Acct: 235099; Swift: HSBC437; address 200 Elgin Ave, Georgetown, Cayman Islands

Please be aware this email will permanently auto-delete after 24 hours.

David Garner, MD FRSP(C)

Having exhausted all possibilities with David Garner, Jacob found himself invigorated by a new lead, a breath of fresh air after the previous fruitless search. Had the Iranians been more subtle in their attempt to cover their tracks regarding David Garner, a connection driven purely by David's financial greed, the outcome could have been different. Their plan was sinister: it involved getting the information they needed, no matter the cost, and then eliminating David, making sure he couldn't talk. The sounds of their actions would be forever silenced. This confirmed the revenge he had exacted on David was a victory, but it left him feeling unfulfilled. He had needed the irrefutable evidence—a smoking gun—and this written evidence placed David at the scene of the crime and proved he'd murdered Melodie. The thought, a dark and persistent seed, fuelled Jacob's ever-growing obsession.

With a click, he activated the miniature cameras in the sailboat. He could almost hear the quiet hum of their mechanics. Their camouflage was so sophisticated that only someone intimately familiar with their technology could hope to spot them. He watched the GPS signal, a small but steady line, showing that Larry was on the move. The map pinpointed him heading north, towards the turquoise waters and white sand beaches of the Turks and Caicos Islands.

Jacob reflected on Chantelle's phone call to Richard a few days earlier. She had unintentionally ignited a storm of digital activity in the hidden corners of the internet, a frenzy of clandestine communications and hushed whispers. Having listened to the video of her disturbing conversation with Larry, Jacob heard she was going home with her new lover, Richard. Jacob had then texted Gavin, the harbour master, relaying the message to Larry. The urgent instructions were for him to leave immediately. Chantelle's phone call had exposed his location, leaving him vulnerable. Jacob knew operatives were on the way.

His thoughts drifted back to the rescue of Larry and his family, remembering the chaotic scramble. The meticulously planned timetable had quickly unravelled. He raced them home after their escape from the warehouse, giving them just five minutes to grab what they could carry. Their bags packed, they hurried to catch their flight to Samana, Dominican Republic. The new forged passports officially recognized them as the Jamesons, while their first names remained unchanged.

"Keep these old passports hidden in your bags," he advised. "Their importance might resurface once the dust settles."

Five hours later, they were sitting on John Hegland's boat, *The Ileana,* in Puerto Bahia Marina, a few miles west of the small town of Samana.

"I'll be staying in the hotel," he told Larry, pointing to its open lobby next to the boat. "I'm leaving in the morning, so I won't see you again for a while."

"How will I reach you?"

"I'll find you when I need to." Jacob pressed a smartphone into his hand. It looked commonplace, but felt strangely heavy. "I have programmed it to accept calls only from my number. You can reach out to me by phone as well."

"Why are you doing this for us?" asked Larry once they were alone when Chantelle took the excited boys swimming. Larry was drinking a cold beer. Jacob had a glass of water with ice cubes in front of him. They sat in the cockpit. Jacob remained silent.

Larry continued. "Jasmine, my Israeli contact told me a bit about you. She suspected my involvement with the centrifuge worm was the reason you were pursuing me. When you found out I was your daughter's surgeon... Well, she suggested you went off the deep end."

Jacob turned his piercing eyes to Larry. After a moment, he responded. "My initial judgment involving your management of my daughter was unfair. I now know the truth about what happened to her. Rarely do I make mistakes like this."

"What happened to her, then? What truth are you talking about?"

"In Russia, I was their top nuclear physicist, a position that demanded long hours and intense focus in a secretive environment. My expertise included the intricate computer programming essential for the precise calculations of nuclear weapons production. Following the disastrous centrifuge incident, Iranian officials accused me of failing to identify the malicious code, a worm, that crippled their nuclear weapons program."

He paused and took a long sip of his water before he continued. "The Russian government, with its shadowy operatives and efficiency, also wanted me dead. I knew too many things about their nuclear program, too many secrets. I've been in hiding for more than 10 years now. Melodie, with her bright smile and unwavering support, was all I had left. The threads of this mystery are still tangled, but one thing's certain. The same shadowy figures pursuing you are after me, their presence a palpable threat. They used Melodie to flush me out. I'm going to find every person involved in the scheme to sabotage America's nuclear weapons and the murder of Melodie. I will not rest until I have punished them for their crimes and disrupted their plans. Our shared past and future inextricably link our destinies. I need to help you so I can help myself."

Jacob watched Larry's startled expression as he talked. Larry shook his head, as if in disbelief. "So, we must keep hidden until you have done what you need to do? That's no way for us to live."

"That is the only way you will get to live. You have no choice. If you stayed in Toronto, they would come after you with a vengeance. You have fought back and some of their operatives are dead."

Upon his return to the boat after midnight, while Larry and his family slept, Jacob discreetly placed six cameras strategically around the boat, focusing on different areas like the cockpit, stern, and bow. With a delicate touch, he connected a minuscule wire to the solar panels, ensuring a continuous power supply for his videos. The video images would go directly onto his laptop. The cameras, equipped with GPS locators, allowed them to track Larry's movements as he moved the boat, providing a real-time map of his location. With its blazing-fast processor and stunning display, his laptop was undeniably the most powerful and advanced on the market. Impeccably secure, the Four Seasons Hotel stood as a fortress of calm amidst the city's bustling chaos. Its security was unmatched. Satisfied that Larry was at least temporarily safe on the sailboat, he watched him move away from the danger, a relieved smile on his face.

Then Jacob turned his attention to Jasmine, the woman Larry had spoken of after his rescue from the tall man. The memory of his steely gaze still lingered. Jacob shivered momentarily at the thought. Jasmine's company website was easy to find. A simple Google search brought up the clean, modern homepage immediately. Yet hacking into her computer proved far more challenging than expected. Each layer of security felt like a new wall to breach. The firewalls protecting her business were exactly as Jacob predicted, but he possessed unique methods, unknown to others, to circumvent them. With a brief investigation, she would probably uncover the digital fingerprints of a hacker on her computer. However, if she tried to track down the digital trail, it would lead her to David Garner's now-empty Cayman Islands bank account, raising more questions for her than answers.

Among the documents Jacob stumbled upon were the ones she had forwarded to the IDF. Opening them revealed a raft of hushed whispers and cryptic messages from the dark web, a digital underworld teeming with secrets. Much of the message made no sense to Jacob, but one thing was glaringly clear amid the confusion. The hushed, urgent chatter seemed to centre on the disabling of the United States' nuclear weapons capability. Jacob found most internet information useless—a vast expanse of impressive-sounding but ultimately unactionable ideas, leaving him frustrated and unproductive.

Jacob copied what information might be relevant and pasted it into a file on his heavily encrypted laptop. Then he sent a note to Jasmine:

We need to talk. You know how to find me.

Jacob.

Chapter 23

Larry squinted at the chart plotter, his finger tracing the course line. Although his boat sliced through the water at a brisk eight knots, the ominous shadow of Silver Bank Reef, a shallow, 60-mile stretch of ocean north of the Dominican Republic, loomed ahead. To bypass the rocky area barely submerged beneath the surface, he needed to head further east. That would mean a close reach into the northeast trade winds, making for a rough ride in the enormous waves, which crashed against the boat with a deafening roar. He was also contending with a looming area of low pressure, the ominous weight of its approach a palpable presence. While it was too early in the season for hurricanes, the threat of smaller, unnamed storms was ever-present, their approach heralded by gusty winds and darkening skies. The predictions of shifting winds to the northeast suggested an arduous journey to Turks and Caicos, with the possibility of strong headwinds.

Larry weighed his options, a knot of anxiety tightening in his stomach. Great Inagua Island, the southernmost island of the Bahamas, lying further west, with pristine beaches and turquoise waters, would be easier to reach, allowing him to avoid the treacherous Silver Bank Reef. A solid anchorage in Matthew Town, nestled in a sheltered cove, would protect him from the fierce northeast winds, allowing him to safely ride out the storm. Another option would be to duck into the charming town of Luperón, in the Dominican Republic. But he had another worry. The Iranians might find him when he registered the boat. The paperwork, the questions, and the official scrutiny... It would signal his presence. Jacob had warned him that the Dominican Republic customs website was vulnerable, using outdated software with minimal firewalls, making it easy to hack. The Bahamas website was marginally better, but the sheer number of islands—more than 700—offered him the perfect hiding place.

The boat sliced through the waves as Larry steered it towards Great Inagua, 190 miles to the west. A full day's journey, 24 hours of travel, lay ahead to reach his destination. Larry glanced around. Massive waves, like colossal elephants rising from the sea, approached from the stern, their crests white with foam. It was a smooth and gentle ride. The rhythmic rocking of the boat and the warm, salty breeze lulled him into drowsiness. The morning's bright, warm sunshine beat down on him, a harsh reminder of his sleepless night since leaving Samana. Larry slumped onto the plush cockpit cushions, the salty air filling his lungs, and was asleep within a minute.

The boat lurched violently, throwing Larry awake as a massive wave passed beneath him, the sound of the impact shaking through the vessel. At first, he couldn't remember where he was. A disorienting fog clouded his mind. He glanced at his watch, noting the time with a grimace. He had slept for four hours, his dreams a blur of chaotic images and disjointed sounds, and he still craved for more sleep.

Larry checked the chart plotter, his eyes scanning the glowing screen for any sign of trouble. With Great Inagua still 160 miles away, the relentless sun beat down on him as he continued his journey. He opened the weather app after noting the strong wind and dark clouds on the horizon. The low-pressure area was advancing more quickly than he'd initially predicted, the wind picking up speed and carrying the scent of rain. In three hours, the winds would begin their climb to a brutal 30 knots, a tangible pressure building in the atmosphere. For him, the good news was that he was sailing downwind, the gusts filling his sails and pushing him smoothly along.

The ocean-going sailboat, with its sturdy mast and reinforced sails, could easily handle even the strongest winds. John had bought the boat, a sleek Hanse 508 with a 51-foot waterline, specifically for ocean voyages. John had explained to Larry he planned to spend the next few years sailing his boat in the Caribbean Sea during his time off, learning the ropes, and enjoying the sights and sounds of the islands before attempting a daring ocean crossing.

Larry recalled his conversation with John when they were travelling on the highway in the Lincoln SUV as Jacob sped them home after he had rescued them. Jacob had told him that John was expecting to hear from him.

"I'm in a spot of trouble," said Larry when John answered the cell phone.

"I know," replied John. "Jacob filled me in earlier today. Thank God he could get you out safely. Are Chantelle and the kids OK?"

"Not really. They are shell-shocked, as am I. I cannot believe this is happening."

"You need a safe place. I suggested to Jacob you get back to the boat in the Dominican Republic if you can. With the AIS turned off, it will be hard for them to find you. Maybe things will settle down quickly and you can come home in a week?"

"I doubt everything will blow over that fast. This attack on me is 10 years in the making. It might last for a while."

"I'll cover your practice during your absence. If it drags out, perhaps we can get our minimally invasive surgery fellow to help. We can discuss these details later. Contact me using encrypted WhatsApp with the Starlink internet on the boat. Avoid using your email, which they can track. And Larry... good luck. Stay safe."

A powerful gust of wind slammed into the sailboat, bringing him back to the present. The boat pitched sharply to port, the sound of the squall whistling through the rigging. Larry knew he had to reduce sail. John had simplified the boat's rigging, making it easy for one person to manage the sails and lines. With a grunt, Larry prepared to secure a third reef in the mainsail. The mainsail flogged slightly in the wind, its surface vibrating with the sudden release of the mainsheet. A sound like a gunshot ricocheted off the rigging when he released the main halyard. The bottom of the mainsail dropped, its canvas whooshing and flapping as it piled into the boom's sail bag. By carefully tensioning the third reefing line, he reduced the sail to less than 50 per cent of its original size. When the strong winds hit the boat, though tossing him about, it would be easier to manoeuvre the vessel as the sails responded to the gusts.

With the boat bouncing over the waves, Larry sat in the cockpit and waited. A whirlwind of memories and regrets, a rush of self-reproach, swirled in his head. He pushed the thought of Chantelle and the gut-wrenching shock of her choosing Richard—over him, for their safety—to the back of his mind. Thoughts crashed around in his head like waves, a relentless tide threatening to pull him under. *I need to keep myself busy; otherwise, these negative thoughts will drive me crazy.*

Descending the narrow stairs to the salon below, Larry sat at his computer and downloaded the latest weather data. Scouring the internet for a suitable anchorage near Matthew Town, he carefully transposed the weather map, searching for a sheltered spot with minimal wind and waves. The small, sheltered harbour looked safe, and its calm waters would protect the boat from the raging storm. Larry scrutinized the harbour, continuing to search for a protected spot before marking his intended anchor position on his map. The updated intel suggested his boat would be the lone vessel when the storm reached its fiercest strength. As a solo sailor, it was not ideal. If he ran into trouble, no one would be around to help.

Drained emotionally and physically, he collapsed into his bunk, the rough fabric scratching against his skin and reminding him he wasn't in the comfort of home with his family. He set the radar to sound an alarm should any other boat come within a two-mile radius. Exhausted, he knew he needed to rest before the storm hit so he could think clearly to survive. With a sigh, Larry closed his eyes, his mind racing with worries as he drifted off into a restless, fitful sleep.

A scream ripped through the silence, jolting him awake. It was his own. The memory of the dream evaporated instantly as he shot up from his bed, the vivid colours and sounds fading into the mundane reality of his room.

Darkness had swallowed the outside world, so he flipped the switch for the navigation lights, illuminating the instruments' soft glow. He secured his life jacket and then fastened the tether, feeling the reassuring click of the clasp. Cautiously, he poked his head out of the companionway, the salty air washing over him. The rain hammered against the dodger's roof. A relentless *rat-a-tap-tap* riveted through the small space. A bright flash of lightning, jagged and white-hot, hit the water about a hundred metres from his boat, followed by a spine-chilling clap of thunder that shook the very air. His heart leaped into his throat, a jolt of adrenaline coursing through him as he realized how close the strike was.

Each step was a challenge as Larry fought to maintain his balance against the relentless rocking of the boat, the waves tossing it wildly, before finally reaching the helm. The auto helm groaned, protesting with each correction as the boat bucked and weaved, the sounds of the waves crashing against the hull punctuated by the wind's howl. Feeling the boat heel sharply, Larry knew he had to reduce the sails further, the wind now a raging beast. With a grunt, he turned the boat into the wind, feeling it respond to the shift, then released the halyard, the mainsail gathering itself into the boom sail bag. With the boat pointing into the waves, it plowed into the oncoming surf, stopping it dead in its tracks and sending a torrent of seawater into the cockpit, soaking everything before crashing down on the other side with a violent jolt.

Larry's flashlight beam danced across the mainsail, revealing the worn fabric and the salt spray clinging to it. Some of the sail remained outside the sail bag, not yet completely secured. The understanding of his task caused a wave of icy anxiety to wash over him. Between crashing waves with the salty spray stinging his face, he needed to haul himself up the mast to manually lower the sail. With a decisive snap, he attached the tether to the sturdy jacklines that ran along the side of the boat. Then he took a deep breath, steeling his nerves against the biting wind, and left the cockpit's safety behind.

Crawling on his hands and knees but moving forward as quickly as possible, Larry lay flat on the deck each time a wave washed over him. Tightly grasping the handholds, he prevented himself from getting washed away. Once he was opposite the mast, after a wave had passed, he leaped up and climbed up three rungs. Larry pulled on the main halyard, which loosened the mainsail, allowing it to fall into the sail bag. The process only took about 10 seconds.

A gigantic wave, its crest a churning white froth, loomed over him, and Larry looked up in horror to see it about to crash. With only three seconds to react, the wind screaming in his ears, he wrapped his tether around the mast just as the enormous wave broke. The water, a cold, heavy force, rushed into his lungs, and he felt a desperate, violent need to cough. Adrenaline flooded his system, making his breath catch and his hands tremble slightly. The pressure caused a sharp crack in his partially healed ribs, sending a jolt of agony through him. Larry could feel the bone fragments grinding together. Overcome with dizziness, he felt himself teetering on the brink of unconsciousness. Then he felt the strong wind on his cheek as the wave receded. He gasped in a much-needed breath.

The wave receded further, leaving him suspended at right angles to the mast, his tether taut and cutting into his leg. The relentless creak of the mast was a constant reminder of his precarious position. A searing, sharp pain ripped through his chest. His burning lungs forced him to gasp for air with each strained inhale. Larry swiftly assessed the situation, the cold metal of the tether latch biting into his palm as he released it. He plummeted six feet, hitting the deck with a bone-jarring crash, screaming as he fell. The fall winded him.

Darkness filled his eyes as he blacked out. The last thing he felt was the sharp pain in his chest.

Chapter 24

Larry opened his eyes. It was pitch black; not a single star pierced the inky sky. A fiery pain shot through his chest as he attempted to sit up, forcing him to lie back down gently. Glancing around the chaotic cockpit strewn with debris, he realized he was on the floor. How he got there remained a mystery, lost in the fog of his memory. Water drenched him, dripping from his clothes and hair. *Maybe a wave washed me here.* Larry looked at his raw fingertips. *I have no recollection of crawling here.*

A deep breath hitched in his chest, the metallic tang of blood filling his senses as he winced, pulling himself onto the cold, hard cockpit bench. With a slow, deliberate movement, he rose, his joints creaking softly, and settled in front of the glowing screen of the chart plotter. The time was 4 a.m. His world was still and dark, and a chilling wind swept through the air. Larry swiftly performed a mental calculation and realized that he had been unconscious for six hours. Although the sailboat continued to face the wind and waves, the wind itself had diminished to a calmer 15 knots blowing from the east. With the power winch, he hoisted the mainsail, starting a course change toward Great Inagua, a destination 150 miles distant in the northwest. As the boat picked up speed to eight knots, its motion smoothed out, harmoniously moving in sync with the wind and waves.

With a gentle gait, Larry made his way to the main salon, where he then flipped the lights on. Upon opening the refrigerator, his eyes fell upon a can of Diet Coke. He seized it and drained its contents in four massive gulps. Removing his heavy, waterlogged clothes, he gazed at his chest's damp skin. A visible deformity, a misshapen protrusion, was clear on the left side. He drew a breath, and the malformation sunk inward, creating a tiny concavity in his skin. *Shit. I have a flail chest. No wonder it hurts so much.* With his body completely dry, he changed carefully into a set of dry clothes.

Larry went to the cabinet where he kept medicines. For the pain, he took a massive 800- milligrams dose of Advil. He rattled the bottle of Percocet, and after a quick count, confirmed that there were 10 or more tablets inside. Clarity of mind was essential for him. Only by maintaining his concentration could he successfully navigate his way to the anchorage. He would have to endure the sharp, relentless pain until then, a torturous wait.

Making his way back to the cockpit, he checked on the chart plotter. The radar sweep showed the absence of any boats within a 20-mile radius, displaying clear waters. He reflected on the situation, trying to determine the optimal next move in this complex sequence of events. The initial plan to hide in the Bahamas, while spending quality time with Chantelle and the children, appeared to be a very attractive and appealing option. Now that they were gone, Larry felt a profound sense of uncertainty and questioned whether he could realistically hide without feeling the constant urge to resolve his situation. A powerful, almost irresistible drive to uncover and neutralize whatever the Iranians were seeking propelled his actions. The time in Israel was 11 a.m. With a sense of urgency, he dialled the now familiar number.

"Jasmine, it's Larry," he said.

"I know exactly who this is," she replied, an unnerving certainty in her voice. "With each incoming call, the caller's tone, background noise, and even their breathing patterns instantly reveal a wealth of information. I can tell you are in some pain and you have emotional stress. You are sailing northwest at approximately eight knots, and your location is about 50 miles north of the Dominican Republic. Aboard the 51-foot sailboat, *The Ileana,* belonging to your partner, John Hegland, you are sailing by yourself. As far as I can see, there is not a single other person present on the vessel. The attire you are currently sporting comprises a red T-shirt, brown cargo shorts, and a pair of flip-flops. Oh, my. I just witnessed you glancing upward towards the expansive sky above you. Yes, I can see you through high-resolution satellite imagery, which uses infrared technology at night to enhance visibility."

"Jasmine, you're scaring me. Can the Iranians see me?"

"Nope. This kind of technology is unique to our organization, and we are the only ones with access to it. Since Jacob successfully hacked into my computer despite our preventative measures, it's likely he could locate you, too."

Larry thought for a moment and then said, "Jasmine, I need your help. They kidnapped me and wanted something, but I don't know what it was."

"I spoke with Jacob. He filled me in what happened with the rescue. He also explained why Chantelle and the kids were no longer with you. I'm so sorry. It must have been quite a shock for you."

Larry felt his heart skip a beat. "How would he know? I never told him."

Jasmine paused for a moment before she spoke again. "Jacob possesses many skills that are not yet known to us. With surprising ease, he bypassed our security protocols and gained access to our computer system. As a cybersecurity firm, we boast the most advanced firewalls and protection. However, he bypassed them with unnerving effortlessness, a feat that sent shivers down our spines. With a few keystrokes, he could easily find your current location and activities. There's a multitude of areas where his help would be invaluable, from his technical abilities to his calm demeanour. Can we trust him, what with his past dealings with Iran?"

"He swiftly took out six Iranians with his bare hands. I doubt they have any love for him. In fact, he says they're out to kill him as well. They hacked into his cell phone and e-mail to send me threatening e-mails I thought were from him. They killed his daughter, Melodie. He is certain of that. He is out to seek revenge for what they did to her. As retribution, he says he will single-handedly destroy whatever they are planning."

"He's flying into Tel Aviv tonight. We have a high-level meeting with the IDF command to decide whether we should get him to help us."

"Jasmine, I want to help too. I did my time in the IDF. Maybe they could call me back as a reserve, like you. I'd rather help than sit on a beach in the Bahamas."

Jasmine paused before answering. "Hmm. Let me see what I can do. I'll get back to you."

"Thanks, Jasmine."

"Get someone to treat your injuries. My software that analyzes changes in your voice says your pain is off the scale!"

"Ha ha!" Larry hesitated. He went on, but his voice was strained. "It only hurts when I laugh, that's all."

***

Three days later, Larry showed up at the Grand Bahama Yacht Club. Larry bypassed Great Iguana Island and sailed to Freeport, the northernmost island of the Bahamas. He got John's boat to a big, safe marina. The decision was driven by his plan to fly to Israel. He had booked a flight from Freeport to New York City. From there, he would connect to Tel Aviv on an El Al flight. He reasoned that his physical presence would make it difficult for Jasmine to say no to his offer of help. His very presence would pressure her.

"Not sure how long the boat will be here," Larry said to Fabian, the dockmaster.

"Don't you worry about anything. We'll take good care of her," replied Fabian.

"What if there is a named storm? The insurance says there needs to be a plan to pull her out of the water and tie her down."

"We'll do all that. Besides, we got hammered with a hurricane a few years ago. It may be a few more years before it happens again."

"Or it could be this year..." Larry reasoned. "Well, just take good care of her. She saved my life in that storm that blew through a few days ago."

Larry piled into the waiting taxi, careful not to hurt his ribs. He boarded his flight to New York City two hours later.

Chapter 25

Jasmine glanced at the handsome man sitting beside her at the Havana Club in Tel Aviv. "You don't find me attractive?" he asked.

"You are probably the hottest guy I've met in... the last five minutes," she replied.

"Then what's the problem?"

"I'm not sure what it is you want from me."

"Let's go back to my place, and I'll show you. You won't regret it."

A look of utter disgust contorted Jasmine's features as she stared at him. "Is that really the best you can do? No witty banter, no charming conversation to tantalize me? How can I tell how wealthy you are with no conversation?"

He smiled and said, "I am wealthy. I've sold more diamonds than anyone else in my firm. Do you like diamonds?"

"Look, I'm sure you are a successful person. I have no interest in someone like you, though. You are wasting your time with me."

He frowned and shrugged his shoulders. "If you weren't interested in meeting a guy like me, then what was the point of coming here, the best place to meet someone in Tel Aviv?"

"The office team wanted to come here. Girls' night out. They are dancing out there." Jasmine waved, the bass vibrating in her chest as she watched the wildly gyrating crowd on the dance floor. "Frankly, I'm bored here. The monotony of the same old sights and sounds is driving me mad. I know your type. Your business is of no concern to me. I'm leaving!"

With a sudden move, Jasmine pushed herself up, grabbed her worn purse, and slowly made her way to the door and out into the street. A line of patrons, buzzing with anticipation, waited outside, the sounds of their excited chatter mixing with the city's hum. She stopped and pulled out a package of Marlboro cigarettes and lit one. Just as she took a deep inhale, she felt a tap on her shoulder.

"I didn't know you smoked." It was Samantha, her partner at the firm. She was the one who had convinced her to come.

Jasmine's vision blurred, overwhelmed by the thick and stinging smoke, and she sank onto the curb, her body trembling. "I don't smoke, but I thought I would give it a try," she said. Jasmine stubbed the cigarette out with her shoe and left it on the pavement.

Samantha sat beside her in a short skirt and a form-fitting cotton shirt that left little to the imagination and put her arm around Jasmine, the scent of her perfume a subtle cloud. "Ahhh honey, things will get better," she said, her glossy bright red lipstick catching the light.

Jasmine looked up at, her eyes searching Samantha's face.

"How will it get better? I feel so used. It's like a hollow ache in my chest, a constant dull throb. He was only with me to gain access to our company and advance his career. Now that he's our partner, I'm forced to interact with him, even though the urge to strangle him is almost overwhelming."

"He moved out of your place and into Sasha's a month ago," said Samantha. "It's time for you to get yourself together and meet someone new. Come back inside. The place is throbbing with testosterone. Getting laid would do you a world of good. It would help you forget and you'd realize how much of a jerk he was."

A slow smile spread across Jasmine's face, crinkling the corners of her eyes. "You are such a good friend, Samantha," she said, her voice full of warmth and sincerity. "I can't do that. The meat market atmosphere just turns my stomach. Anyway, I am not ready. My company would be dreadful. I'm a source of quiet misery and unmet expectations."

Samantha stood up. "Suit yourself. Don't be worried if I turn up late tomorrow."

Jasmine got up, stretching her stiff muscles. After a quick hug, Samantha headed back into the pulsing, bass-thumping nightclub.

Jasmine headed home to the quiet of her apartment. The breakup with Joshua had been brutal, leaving her emotionally drained and heartbroken. They had been together for three years, a journey marked by countless memories and a growing bond. She felt a sense of peace and belonging. Yes, he was the one. Marriage and children had been frequent topics, their hopes and anxieties interwoven with dreams of a life together, filled with the laughter of children. Her unexpected afternoon retreat home because of agonizing menstrual cramps led to a horrifying discovery. Joshua, entangled with Sasha, a computer programmer from a competing company, lying in their bed, leaving her dreams in ruins.

Jasmine's apartment was a short walk from the lively bar, the sounds of laughter and music still drifting through the night air. She enjoyed her regular strolls. The daily walk to her office was a tranquil time, the cadence of her steps a calming start to the day. She didn't own a car. Jasmine found that public transportation and walking suited her needs perfectly and were more enjoyable. Joshua's beat-up 2002 Toyota Corolla, its paint faded and scratched, sat unused in the parking lot. Their last trip to see his parents on the west bank was more than a year ago.

Jasmine could see her apartment building. Made of weathered grey stone and four stories high, the building looked a little run down, with crumbling mortar and chipped stone. Yet her one-bedroom unit was charming. It featured an outdoor terrace, where the scent of blooming jasmine flowers often drifted around them while they ate dinner. With Joshua gone, the apartment felt hollow, the absence of his laughter and familiar scent heavy in the air. That was the main reason she'd tagged along with the girls at the nightclub tonight. It was preferable to another lonely night in the empty apartment.

The key scraped in the sticky old lock, and she pushed open the heavy oak door, stepping into the corridor where the only light came from a far-off window; she climbed the stairs to the fourth floor. Flipping on the light, she gasped at the sight that met her eyes.

Sitting on the top step was Larry.

****

"I couldn't wait to find out if you wanted me to help," said Larry. "I figured it would be harder for you to say no if I landed on your doorstep."

"How did you find me?" asked Jasmine. They sat at a wrought-iron table on the outdoor terrace, sipping their tea and enjoying the warm breeze. From the fourth storey, the city's sounds were a mix of car horns that blared angrily, the high-pitched wail of a far-off siren and the faint, cheerful sounds of laughter echoing from the street below.

"Jacob told me where you lived and how to get in. He suggested I wait until you returned from the Havana Club. I'm surprised you came home so early."

"What? How did he know where I was going? Wait a minute... This is spooky. Even for a cyber stalker like me."

"Have you met with Jacob?"

"That's the weird thing. I don't have the foggiest notion of his location. It's driving me crazy. He prefers to work alone. I suspect he knew my movements, monitoring my face through Israel's sophisticated facial-recognition programs, which likely tracked my every move. To protect privacy, Israeli law prohibits us from using this software unless it's deemed necessary to counter the threat of terrorist organizations endangering national security. Last month, we detected coded messages from a known Hamas operative, hinting at a potential attack through online forums. Facial recognition, the telltale outline of explosives clearly visible beneath his clothes, picked him out of a bustling crowd. The IDF's timely arrival prevented any further escalation. If I tried to find Jacob using that technology without the correct credentials, they programmed the system to trigger an immediate system shutdown, cutting me off."

"He seems to have a better idea of what is going on than anyone else. Let me try to get in touch with him."

Just as Larry reached for his cell phone, it buzzed. A text message appeared:

I'll meet you at Starbucks. On Ben Gurion Boulevard at 7 a.m. tomorrow.

"What is it?" asked Jasmine. Larry showed her the message. "I'm coming," she said. "There's no way I'm passing up the opportunity to meet the most talented cybersecurity breacher in the world." Jasmine's face crinkled as she proposed, "Why don't you stay here tonight? You can sleep on the sofa in the living room."

"I don't want to be any bother," he replied. "I can stay at the Holiday Inn nearby." Larry got up to leave.

"Stay here. Really. It is no bother." Jasmine went to the closet and pulled out some sheets, a pillow, and a blanket. "I could use the company."

Larry, clearly exhausted after the long flight and time change, his eyes heavy-lidded and his shoulders slumped, signalled surrender with a weary smile, raising his hands. He helped Jasmine arrange the crisp linen sheets on the plush sofa. They exchanged soft goodnights, the sound barely a whisper in the quiet room. Jasmine watched as he crawled under the sheets, his clothes rustling softly, and within 30 seconds, his breathing evened into a gentle snore.

With a sigh, Jasmine entered her room, the door clicking shut as she collapsed onto the inviting coolness of her bed. The tension melted away as she instantly fell into a deep sleep, the first good sleep in more than a month, breathing deeply and evenly.

Chapter 26

Jacob waited outside the Starbucks until they arrived, his eyes scanning the area for any sign of pursuit, the silence amplifying his tension. Once he saw through the window that Jasmine and Larry were placing their orders with the barista, he sauntered into the alley. He scaled the weathered brick wall, the rough texture scraping against his hands, slipped through the grimy bathroom window. Then he found the nearest table in the restaurant's corner near the bathroom, where he could easily access the opened window. In an emergency, he could retrace his entry route if the other two exits were blocked.

Jasmine and Larry saw Jacob and waved. He motioned them to join him. Taking a sip from the plastic bottle, he tilted his head back, the cool water a welcome relief to his thirst. Jasmine and Larry sat together, their backs to the counter, sipping their warm, frothy vente lattes.

"What are you hoping to achieve, and do you think your goals align with the Israel Defense?" asked Jasmine.

"The more I am learning, the more important it is for us to share information," replied Jacob.

"What did you find out?" she asked.

"Something big is about to happen," he replied, his voice low and serious. "The evidence I have gleaned online focuses on Iran's scheme to carry out an attack on Israel. The plan appears to cripple the US military's offensive capabilities, making a swift and powerful counterstrike impossible. Despite technological leaps and bounds since the crippling worm attack on their centrifuges, unanswered questions remain about the details of the computer worm code, questions they feel might be answered by the 10 of you involved. After a meticulous search, they located eight of the 10 individuals involved in the cyberattack on their nuclear weapon capability. Larry and an elusive woman named Maria are the only survivors. I suspect she is more cautious than the others. She has erased her tracks. Even I cannot find her."

"I remember Maria," said Larry. "She was a quiet but brilliant commuter whiz. She was the one I could trust her to help me when I ran into a problem I could not solve. I hope they never find her."

"What can we do to help?" asked Jasmine.

Jacob sat back in his chair and quickly scanned the room. A couple in their early-twenties, holding hands and staring into each other's eyes, were the only customers in the coffee shop.

Jacob conceded, "In some areas, your expertise in technology and cybersecurity exceeds my own," his gaze acknowledging her skill. "Perhaps Larry could improve his computer skills and discreetly investigate online activity using your company's computers, accessing their superior resources for a more thorough search. You can keep me updated with anything you find. I'll do the same."

A figure, tall and slender, caught Jacob's eye as the man entered the brightly lit Starbucks. His faded blue jeans and his polished leather boots seemed out of place to the suits and ties of the men striding past the windows of the coffee shop. His skintight white T-shirt, clinging to his broad shoulders and narrow waist, revealed thick bicep muscles. He glanced over at Jacob; his black eyes, like chips of obsidian, seemed to pierce right through him. Jacob felt a surge of adrenaline, ready for the challenge that lay ahead.

"In exactly 30 seconds," Jacob said, his voice sharp and precise, "you are to get up and leave. Do not stop for any reason. Keep moving until you reach your office building, regardless of the sounds and sights along the way. I'll give you further instructions later this afternoon, around 3 p.m."

After Jasmine and Larry turned around to look at the front of the restaurant, Jacob used the distraction to disappear. Thirty seconds later, the pair got up to exit, leaving their half-finished lattes on the table. The blue-jean clad man faced them, blocking their way.

Jacob was at the front door, the man's back a mere eight feet away, an easy target for the dart he flung into the man's neck. The man immediately put his hand on the small object and swept it away. It fell to the floor and got knocked into a corner.

Jacob watched as the man turned around and collapsed on the floor. Using the distraction, he slipped out of the Starbucks as the panicked baristas ran from behind the counter and huddled around the unconscious man. Crossing the road, Jacob spotted Larry and Jasmine hurry to the office less than a block away. Scanning the road for threats and seeing nothing suspicious, Jacob slipped into the alley behind the Starbucks and disappeared.

***

Jacob sank into the plush armchair in his suite at the new Four Seasons Hotel in downtown Tel Aviv, relishing the luxury and comfort surrounding him. He had expected the Iranian operative at the Starbucks from the chatter on the dark web after he'd left some clues as to his whereabouts and his proposed meeting with Larry. He wanted to see the online reaction after he killed the Iranian assassin. When highly trained operatives got outsmarted and killed during a simple mission, often the result was careless threats lobbed online. This could lead him to those responsible for killing Melodie. He checked his computer.

"Find Jacob Ashinoff and kill him! He killed Mohammed!" screamed Massoud Hossein, the brother of the Iranian operative in the video, his voice raw with grief and rage, his eyes blazing. Jacob had tracked the video to a studio apartment in the city of Qom past the outskirts of Tehran. The man had gone on a 10-minute rant in the video, which gave Jacob time to hack into his computer. He quickly scanned the emails and browsing history and uploaded them to a cloud site. Further investigation identified a series of usernames and passwords he might find useful in the future.

Jacob turned his attention back to the data on the cloud and had his AI program search for keywords and phrases and names of Iranian operatives. In a few minutes, he had gained a list of names, many he was familiar with. This time, though, something stood out. The brother's language included phases one might expect from an academic nuclear physicist. Over the past 10 years, US or Israeli operatives assassinated five top nuclear scientists, though those governments denied involvement. The brother's name was Dr. Massoud Hossein, the lead nuclear scientist at the Fordow Fuel Enrichment Plant.

Jacob glanced at his watch. It was time to call Larry. "You need to stay somewhere else tonight," he said. "They might know where you're located. I have rented a fully furnished place for you. I'll text you the address. You get moved to a new spot tomorrow and the next day. A driver will pick you up. The name and phone number I will text as well."

"What's going on, Jacob?" asked Larry.

"I'll fill you in when I see you tonight."

Jacob hung up. He had a monumental task ahead, a mountain of work to conquer. In the time to have the conversation with Larry, the AI transcribed a recent phone call from Massoud Hossein to his brother, Mohammed, the one he'd poisoned with a dart in Starbucks. The time stamp of the conversation was from yesterday.

"Hi, Mo. I cannot believe how stupid the Russian is," said Massoud. "He is meeting Larry Klapman at 7 a.m. in Starbucks in Tel Aviv tomorrow. You need to bring him in for questioning."

"How am I going to do that?" asked Mohammed.

"Water is the only beverage the Russian consumes. I've arranged for a replacement barista at Starbucks; we accidentally knocked the previous one off his bike. He tumbled down the steep embankment and broke his arm in the fall. Got pretty scraped up from the rough ground, too. The replacement barista will surreptitiously add Rohypnol to the Russian's water bottle. At 7:20 a.m., after waiting 22-minutes, you can lead him to the unmarked van discreetly parked around the corner. His strength will drain away, leaving him as helpless and frail as a kitten."

"And what should we do about Larry Klapman?"

"Ask him to lend a hand in moving the Russian to the van

for a quick trip to the hospital. You are just a concerned citizen. You drive them to the warehouse, where we will question them both. News of their capture will bring a smile to the supreme leader's face, a smile that promises rewards and advancement."

The conversation continued for a few more minutes, describing a few other details of the plan. *Another reason I always bring my own water bottle wherever I go. I'm glad I emptied the Starbucks' water into the bathroom sink.* Jacob had little trust in many things that might harm him, including food that he had not prepared for himself and bottled drinks.

Using AI, Jacob looked for weaknesses in the plan he worked on. It was much too complicated for a human brain to find the scheme with the greatest chance of success. The principles he worked with were simple. They included:

1. Prevent the attack Iran was planning.
2. Stop the cyberattack on the US nuclear capabilities.
3. Punish those involved with Melodie's death.

Chapter 27

Larry's pulse finally settled as he sank into the worn leather chair in Jasmine's small office, the scent of old paper and coffee faint in the air.

"What in the world just happened?" he asked, his voice trembling slightly. He scratched his beard, the rough bristles a familiar comfort against his fingertips as he tried to calm his racing heart and ragged breathing. The sharp, stabbing chest pain had finally subsided, leaving a dull ache behind. He didn't want to alarm Jasmine, so he used a low, soothing tone, but her wide eyes and trembling hands betrayed her composure, mirroring his own unease.

"I think Jacob just saved our asses," she replied.

"I think we should do whatever it takes to stay on his good side," he said. "He's full of surprises."

"The best way to do that is to get him some useful information. Do you think you are up to doing some research?"

"I might need a minute to calm down and clear my mind." Larry frowned and shook his head. "What do you think happened to the man that Jacob attacked? Is he dead?"

"I suspect he laced that dart with a deadly poison. Its scent was faint, but unmistakable. I do not think he is still alive. Let me see what kind of online discussions are happening." Jasmine powered up her computer, the familiar whirring sound filling the quiet room, before beginning her search. "I've checked the usual chatter groups, but there's nothing yet; it might still be too early."

Larry said, "I think I can start on a computer. It will be a welcome distraction from what we witnessed. Perhaps I could begin with the files you have accumulated. I'm sure it will take me most of the day to skim through them."

Jasmine sat him in front of a second computer in her office. She logged him in and opened the files. "I have grouped them under headings. You could start with the one labelled Larry," she said.

Larry scrolled through the files. One, written in Farsi but translated to English, was from a cell phone conversation from three months ago.

Voice 1: "I cannot believe you messed it up."

Voice 2: "Someone snuck up behind me. He must have followed me to the sailboat. It was the only boat anchored there. Something happened to him to make him scream. I leaped over him in the cockpit to get away. It looked like a spear had gone through his body. No way the guy survived. I got one shot off. I think I hit someone, because another scream came from inside. Taking off was my only option. What happens now?"

Voice 1: "They are angry. You must not come home until things settle. You have failed again."

Larry flipped to a video, the screen lighting up his face. The image showed him walking away from the house, his footsteps crunching on the gravel driveway. He opened the door of his Tesla and got inside. Leaning out the door, he gave a friendly wave to the security guard, who stood stoically by the gate.

The next image showed Chantelle driving their kids to school. The security guard's presence behind her was a constant reminder of being watched. Following the two cars, the video showed the kids' school with the bright yellow buses parked outside. The next image, time stamped 3:50 p.m., showed a hazy afternoon light. Chantelle's car pulled up, the engine sputtering slightly before cutting off. With Sheldon and Abe in tow, she walked back to the car, her face aglow in the afternoon sun. Larry exhaled at the painful memory. In the last video frame, Chantelle's car disappeared around the bend, its taillights fading into the distance.

Another file listed a bank transfer to David Garner, his chief of staff. Larry gasped, and his eyes widened at the unexpected amount. Right before Melodie died, someone had deposited $250,000 into David's account from a discreet offshore account in the Cayman Islands, a notorious tax haven. David's bank account was a numbered account, and someone had traced it back to him in

Toronto.

There is no way this is a mere coincidence. An official email, bearing the Iranian Ministry of Finance letterhead and embossed seal, instructed someone named Hamid to retrieve the misappropriated funds. "The account was empty," he stated in the reply to the email.

The next item that caught his attention was the file of computer codes he'd created 10 years ago. Although outdated, someone had redacted a section. Larry suspected it was this part the Iranians were after. Leaning back in his chair, Larry pondered the blacked out parts. He had no recollection; his mind was a blank slate. Ten years had passed since the eight-month struggle to produce that computer code; now, looking at the outdated syntax, he could practically hear the whirring of the old computer fans. His part of the centrifuge destruction was to get the worm to update the latest software when the Siemens computer activated it. He was certain he couldn't repeat such a reckless act now. The sterile glow of the screens felt like a lifetime ago, a cold, distant memory.

Larry turned to Jasmine. "I think I know what the Iranians are going to do," he said. "They are going to annihilate Israel with a nuclear strike."

Jasmine smiled, a genuine laugh bubbling up from deep within, crinkling the corners of her eyes. "Since its inception, there have been ongoing plans to destroy Israel. This cause has consumed Iran. It is the driving force of their existence, their life's purpose. The IDF relayed all the intercepted communications to their US military counterparts. The prevailing fear is that they intend to eliminate America's ability to launch a nuclear counterattack, leaving Americans defenseless. We need to find out what they have in mind and stop it from happening."

"Jacob is the secret weapon they have underestimated," said Larry. "He has a plan. I also believe he is helping me because he needs me involved in what he is doing."

"Maybe he's using you as bait?"

"It wouldn't surprise me." Larry thought about that for a moment. "There is not much else I can do. I cannot go back home and put my family in danger." Larry paused and frowned before he continued. A worried look crossed his face. "I worry about putting you in danger."

Jasmine smiled again. "I can use a little excitement in my life right now. Do not worry about me."

"Jacob called earlier. He says someone might have compromised your apartment, possibly someone watching you. He insists I change my residence often, moving around a variety of neighbourhoods and lifestyles. You need to stay with me until we're sure it's safe to return."

Larry showed the text message to Jasmine with the address of the new apartment. "Huh," she said. "That's not far from here. We could walk."

"Jacob's sending a driver. He feels it is safer. I need to find out why he is doing all this for me, though."

Larry's phone buzzed. He opened a text message from Jacob:

The driver is in the garage. When you are ready, he will take you. I'll meet you at the apartment later this evening.

He turned to Jasmine and said, "Are you ready?"

"You go ahead," Jasmine said, a hint of worry in her tone. "There are a few tasks on my to-do list that need my attention. I'll meet you the address for dinner around 7 p.m. We can order takeout. Maybe some tasty Thai? No one is going to follow me. Obviously, I'm familiar with all the techniques of doubling back, taking shortcuts, and slipping out of stores through the back exits—"

"Skills honed by years of practice," Larry interrupted with a wry grin. He walked down the narrow stairs to the garage in the basement. A sleek Mercedes-Benz, its grey paint shimmering faintly in the sparse lighting, sat silently in the space beside the staircase. Josh, the driver, leaned against his door, the cigarette smoke curling around his face as he inhaled deeply. With a grunt, he crushed his cigarette under his boot, then smoothly opened the back door for Larry, gesturing him to enter. He drove up the ramp in silence, the engine purring beneath him, exiting the parking garage and driving five minutes until he reached the imposing, four-storey apartment complex.

The Mercedes door shut with a soft thud as Larry stepped out, the scent of expensive leather lingering in the air, and entered the apartment building using Jacob's code. Reaching the second floor, he punched in a unique code for suite 207 and entered the tiny apartment. The quiet hum of the refrigerator and the faint smell of coffee were noticeable. The apartment was like Jasmine's, but smaller and without the bright sunshine and fresh air of the outdoor terrace. A cozy feeling permeated the space, from the compact kitchen to the inviting sofa in the living room and the comfortable-looking queen-sized bed in the bedroom. Larry's carry-on luggage sat in the corner of the living room.

Ten minutes later, Jacob walked into the room. He sat at the kitchen table and opened his bottle of water. Larry glanced at him and sat in front of him.

"If you are wondering what I am up to, I am moving ahead with my plan. I need your help in order for it to work."

Chapter 28

"That is not something I will do," said Larry, his voice firm and unwavering. He sat with Jacob at the old kitchen table, its surface scratched and marked by years of use. The darkness pressed in from all sides, heavy and absolute. Jacob's explanation of Larry's role in the plan concluded with a pointed stare and a terse nod.

"You and John Hegland are the only ones I trust," said Jacob.

"John would not do it either. Surgeons uphold life, not bring about certain death."

"It is the only way to stop this. What is one death when millions could die otherwise?"

Larry shook his head and sighed heavily. The door swung open with a loud bang, startling him, as Jasmine entered, carrying a heavy brown paper bag. The spicy aroma of Thai food, with its hints of lemongrass and chilies, filled the air, making his mouth water.

"I got takeout," she said, the greasy paper bag already slightly stained with soy sauce. Seeing Jacob made her stop instantly.

"Hi, Jacob," she smiled. "Care to join us for dinner?"

"No thank you," he responded.

Jasmine laid out the food on the table, arranging the dishes neatly, and placed the paper plates before Larry, leaving a space for herself beside him. The spicy aroma enveloped them as they dished out the food. With a growling stomach, Larry realized this was his first meal of the day.

"So, I heard you arguing when I arrived," said Jasmine between mouthfuls. "What about?"

Larry glanced at Jacob. With a slight nod, indicating it was alright to fill in Jasmine, Larry said, "Jacob has a plan to stop whatever it is Iran is up to."

"Excellent," she said, "let's hear it."

"Well, he won't say what it is," said Larry.

Jasmine looked confused. "So what's your idea, then, Jacob?"

Jacob looked at her and explained, "I created this intricate plan with the help of artificial intelligence. There is a strong likelihood of success, although its course may shift depending on unfolding events, keeping the final result unknown to me. That is why I cannot tell you what the plan is."

Jasmine looked at Larry and asked, "So, what were you arguing about?"

"Jacob wants me to surgically implant explosives in his body, so when he gets close enough to his target, the resulting explosion will eliminate the Iranian threat," Larry said, his face pale. "I said I wouldn't do it. It goes against every ethical boundary in surgery. To knowingly do surgery that leads to the death of that person is unacceptable."

"Even with the right paperwork, Iran is nearly impossible to enter. Attempting to smuggle explosives makes it all but impossible," Jacob stated grimly. "They have explosive detection sensors everywhere, with their constant beeping, especially where I will be going. This is the only way to evade capture, a clandestine and dangerous tactic. I must pack an adequate amount of explosives inside my body to result in significant damage."

"Is there a plan that works where Larry could surgically implant the explosives, only to remove them before reaching the target?" asked Jasmine. "Incorporate that suggestion into the AI model's parameters and observe the generated output."

"I experimented with that scenario," replied Jacob. "The chances of success dropped 10 percentage points, from a hopeful 80 per cent down to a less certain 70. The challenge is to swiftly remove the explosives without being apprehended, a race against time. Doing this in a foreign country and with uncertain operatives complicates matters even more."

"Considering the Jacob factor, the 70 per cent odds will significantly improve, raising the chances of success," said Larry.

"Predicting that is beyond the capabilities of AI. Your resilience in the face of devastating hardship is something no computer program could ever calculate. I say we proceed with Plan B: carefully removing the explosives before detonation, ensuring your utmost safety."

Jacob thought about this for a moment. "OK, but that means you need to come with me to Iran. Are you up to that?"

Larry smiled. "What else am I going to do? I will not get my life back until this is all behind me."

"Eight o'clock tomorrow morning, Assuta Hospital, HaBarzel Street," he said, the words sharp and precise in the sterile air. "Don't be late." Jacob got up from the table, turned around, and left the apartment.

Larry and Jasmine stared at each other. "What exactly did I just agree to?" asked Larry.

"It seems you are an accessory to a terrorist," laughed Jasmine. "Or you will be after tomorrow. Do you really want to go to Iran?"

"I'm going to have to go now. I feel things are moving too quickly. My life has changed so much in the past three weeks, I feel like things are spinning out of control."

Jasmine looked at Larry and said, "I sense all is not fine with your marriage. What happened between you and your wife?"

A deep, weary groan seemed to erupt from Larry before he began the tale of Chantelle and Richard, his voice thick with emotion. He confessed his desire to protect them, his words spat out with the bitter taste of inadequacy, the memory of seeing her with Richard at the hotel stinging him. He told her that keeping them far away was the only way he could ensure their safety. A cold, hard certainty, like the glint of steel, filled his tone. By the time he'd finished speaking, a lump had formed in his throat, and tears welled in his eyes, forcing him to pause.

Jasmine's touch was warm as she took his hand and began recounting the story of her and Joshua, the betrayal still fresh in her voice. Tears welled in her eyes as she told him she felt used, a mere stepping stone to his partnership in her company. When she finished speaking, tears streamed down her face, filled with emotion, her words barely audible. Larry listened, the weight of her sorrow pressing down on him like a physical burden, his heart aching for her.

He looked at her and said, "We are both damaged goods," his eyes reflecting a shared weariness. "They cast us aside like broken toys, leaving us to gather dust and forgotten, through no fault of our own."

"But we are resilient," Jasmine said, her smile weak but

determined, a hint of bravado in her eyes. "Having endured the intense drills, sleep deprivation, and constant pressure of IDF basic training, we can certainly handle this."

They were quiet now, emotionally drained, the recitations of their confessions lingering like a soft sigh. The silence hung heavy and thick, like a tangible weight, until Larry cleared his throat and said, "I'll take the couch. You take the bed."

"You'll do nothing of the sort. This is your place. I am the guest. You are taking the bed tonight."

Jasmine spoke with defiance and certainty. Larry held his hands up in defeat and said, "OK, you win."

Larry went into the washroom and brushed his teeth in the faint glow of the night light. Afterward, he crawled into bed, sinking into the plush mattress. In under two minutes, he was fast asleep.

Past midnight, the sound of the bedroom door slowly opening stirred him. He heard footsteps padding into his room. Before he could react, with the quiet rustling of the sheets, Jasmine crawled into bed, snuggling her warm body against his. She murmured, "I don't want to be alone. Can you just hold me?"

With a contented sigh, Larry rolled over, pulling Jasmine close, and wrapped his arms around her. He felt her breathing slow, deepening into soft snores, a gentle vibration against his chest.

Overwhelmed by fatigue, he too succumbed to sleep, the gentle scent of Jasmine filling his nostrils.

***

With equipment in tow, the IDF's surgical team had arrived much earlier and set up the operating room. The air hung heavy with antiseptic and nervous energy as the soldiers, all in surgical scrubs, worked within the operating room.

"The Semtex is in a sterile bag," explained Wendy, the scrub nurse, her voice low and measured, "as cylindrical tubes, sealed and secured. We have attached nylon strings to the ends and you can bury them under the skin. Using local anesthetic, the retrieval process will be painless and straightforward. You make a small incision, and a gentle tug on the string reveals its hidden purpose. Each bag contains 200 grams of the potent explosive. We have five bags in total, enough to perform the task."

"Why can't he just carry them in his pocket?" asked Larry while he was dividing an adhesion to make room for the bags.

"The Semtex has a distinctive methyl-nitrobenzene odour that is easily detected," said Wendy. "The compound escapes through the plastic and other containers. When we bury the Semtex in the body, any of the methyl-nitrobenzene that escapes undergoes a process called hydroxylation. The new molecule then gets reabsorbed, then filtered. The kidneys remove the hydroxylated compound from the bloodstream and safely excretes it in the urine."

"Huh," said Larry. "You've done this before."

Wendy smirked and said nothing.

With a few clicks, the bright lights of the operating room dimmed, replaced by a low hum and the soft glow of monitors. The laparoscopic image on the screen showed the spleen, surrounded by adhesions. Having found a suitable spot within the abdominal cavity to enter, Larry inserted two other ports for the instruments. "Adhesions have fused together Jacob's abdominal cavity from all his previous misadventures," said Larry. "I think I just got lucky to find some space with only a few adhesions up near the spleen."

Larry continued with his dissection of the adhesions near the spleen. He used a Ligasure, a cautery device that seals blood vessels with heat, the device humming quietly in his hand. Only a few more adhesions, tough and white, connected the spleen to the diaphragm. By dividing them, the space above the spleen would open, leaving room for the five Semtex bags. Larry applied the Ligasure to the adhesions. Before the seal had completed, the spleen tore from the adhesion. Within seconds, the lens of the laparoscope became covered in blood, obscuring his vision.

"Uh-oh," said Larry. "Bleeding from the spleen! I'm going to need suction!" Larry re-inserted the laparoscope. Immediately, blood covered the lens. He pulled it out.

"Wendy, use the suction! I need to control the bleeding!" he yelled, his voice tight with urgency, the metallic scent of the blood filling the air. Larry carefully inserted the suction canula into one port, while simultaneously inserting a sponge into the other; the suction hissed quietly. As he inserted the laparoscope, a crimson burst briefly filled his vision before obscuring it with a bloody spray. He pulled out the laparoscope. A layer of blood completely covered the lens. Then he quickly cleaned and reinserted it. A quiet hush filled the OR. Wendy expertly suctioned the blood, allowing him to place the sponge and apply firm pressure, which finally stopped the bleeding. With the bleeding temporarily stemmed, Larry felt his racing pulse slow to a more normal rhythm. The relief was palpable. But he knew the bleeding would start again the second he released the pressure of the sponge.

"Please get me some Surgicel," he instructed Wendy with a calm voice. Larry removed the sponge in the abdomen and replaced it with the Surgicel, a hemostatic sheet used to stop bleeding. He used his surgical instrument to apply pressure. After 10 minutes, he gingerly removed the Surgicel. The visible blood vessel pulsated, but was no longer bleeding. He quickly placed a surgical clip on the end, which sealed the vessel.

"Phew," he muttered, "that was a near miss. We dodged a serious bullet."

Larry pulled each of the five bags of Semtex into the abdomen with his surgical instruments and placed them into the space he had created above the spleen. He buried the blue Prolene sutures under the skin. With a syringe full of India ink, he drew a one-centimetre line to mark the skin where he could later place an incision to retrieve all five of the blue sutures to pull out the Semtex.

With a few deft movements, Larry removed the laparoscopic ports. The metallic instruments clicked in the quiet operating room. He closed the small incisions with an absorbable suture. He placed a small, sterile dressing over the freshly stitched incisions. Injecting through the intravenous line, the anesthesiologist roused Jacob using the reversal drug agents. Once he awoke, the anesthetist moved him to the recovery room.

With a few swift keystrokes, Larry entered the postoperative orders into the electronic medical record system. He walked to the crowded, bustling waiting room, and the murmur of conversations, to talk with Jasmine.

"Remind me to never operate on Jacob again," said Larry as he slumped into the empty chair next to Jasmine. "Those adhesions were brutal. I almost caused a fatal hemorrhage."

"You mean after you remove the explosives?" said Jasmine.

Larry gave Jasmine a confused look, then realized she was referring to his reckless promise to Jacob—a promise to remove the explosives before Jacob detonated them with the remote hidden in his phone. The terrifying thought flashed through his mind.

He smiled, crinkling the corners of his eyes. "He is an imposing figure, a mountain of muscle and sinew, which speaks of his strength and resilience. I warned the recovery room nurses about him. He would likely attempt an escape and they should strap him to the bed to prevent this."

"You told them to restrain him?"

"I don't want him disappearing without me. He has a history of taking care of himself after surgical procedures."

"I gotta see this," said Jasmine. "The mighty Jacob tied up with restraints, unable to move. Can you take me to see him in the recovery room?"

"Let's go! This time he isn't slipping away."

Larry quietly guided Jasmine into the recovery room, the steady beeping of monitors in the background. Walking around the corner, they entered bay 23. Larry stared at the empty bed. His eyes were wide with disbelief. The crisp sheets and the indented mattress were the only reminders of where he had last seen Jacob.

Four thick leather restraints remained, each snapped in two, with their ragged edges uselessly dangling from the metal bedposts.

Chapter 29

A dull ache in his abdomen was barely noticeable as Jacob walked down the hospital street toward the Four Seasons Hotel. To be certain that no complications from the surgery occurred, his plans included two days of convalescence. Then he would be off. His first step was to get to the hotel's gym. He could already feel the burn in his muscles.

The air was ripe with the smell of sweat and exertion in the gym, where 10 stations of treadmills, Peloton bikes, and other cardio equipment stood in a row against one wall. Dominating the centre of the facility were rows of weight machines, the clanging of plates providing a steady soundtrack. In another large room, the 50-metre pool shimmered under the bright lights, the chlorine smell sharp in the air. The gym was quiet at noon on a weekday. Sunlight streamed through the windows, illuminating dust motes dancing in the air as a lone woman cycled on a Peloton. The only others in the gym were the three attendants, cleaning the equipment and oiling the weight machines.

Jacob started his workout with the treadmill, setting the distance of 21 kilometres, which meant he was committing to running a half marathon. Jacob placed four litres of ice-cold blue Gatorade on the treadmill ledge, the bottles sweating slightly, and began his run. He'd been jogging for 10 minutes, and the salty sweat already stung his eyes as he finished the first litre of Gatorade. The cool liquid was a welcome contrast to the burning in his muscles. By one hour and 10 minutes, he'd finished the half marathon. The four litres of Gatorade were gone, leaving only the faint taste of electrolytes on his tongue. With a sigh, he stopped the treadmill, dripping with sweat, and headed for the refreshing turquoise of the swimming pool.

Jacob showered, the steam filling the small bathroom, then slid into the cool water of the pool, feeling the temperature difference immediately. Waterproof bandages, still slightly damp, covered the small, barely there laparoscopic incisions from earlier that day. With a determined nod, he set his watch for the 3.2 kilometre swim and carefully adjusted his goggles before entering the water. With each stroke of the front crawl, his massive size 16 feet kicked up waves, propelling him swiftly ahead. Forty-one minutes later, his watch beeped, a shrill sound cutting through the quiet of the morning, signalling the end of his swim. He slid out of the cool pool, water dripping from his hair and skin. With a frustrated sigh, after checking his time, he shook his head, strands of hair falling across his forehead. He was a minute behind his typical time in both the run and the swim; the fatigue was evident in his laboured breaths and slower strokes.

Next, he approached the weights. His primary goals centred on building upper body muscle mass and strengthening his core, focusing on exercises like bench presses and planks. He began his workout with a gruelling set of pull-ups, his muscles already burning as he completed five sets of 20 repetitions. He then mirrored his actions, using only one arm this time, the muscles bunching beneath his skin. The plates clanged as he added more weight to the bench press, inching his way up to 1,000 pounds. His muscles strained and sweat beaded on his forehead.

Four and a half hours later, he walked out of the gym, the satisfying burn in his muscles a testament to his workout. The air felt cooler against his skin. His calculations showed a calorie burn of around 4,000, a number that brought a satisfied smile to his face. He sat in his room in the Four Seasons Hotel, and spent the next hour methodically mixing and consuming a high-calorie, high-protein drink, the artificial sweetness leaving a slightly metallic taste in his mouth. He finally drifted off to sleep.

***

Jacob awoke with a start at 4 a.m., the sound of his alarm cutting through the stillness. It was time to begin his exercise routine. In the gym that morning, he pushed himself through his usual routine, maintaining his pace for the upcoming half marathon and 3.2 kilometre swim. He spent extra time on the weights, focusing on his squats and deadlifts to build powerful thighs and a strong core. He emerged from the gym six hours later, smelling faintly of sweat and chlorine, his body tired but invigorated. With each passing day, Jacob felt his strength returning, bolstering his confidence in a full recovery.

After consuming 5,000 liquid calories—a sweet, syrupy concoction—he sat heavily in front of his computer, a sugar rush coursing through him. Everything was falling precisely in place where it should be, a silent testament to careful preparation. Even the air felt still and expectant. He meticulously checked the canvas bag, feeling the reassuring weight of the supplies—food, water, and tools—for the journey ahead. He was ready. His muscles were tense and his heart pounded with anticipation.

***

Under the harsh midday sun, Jacob handed his papers to the customs official at the Iraqi-Iranian border, the worn documents rustling slightly in the dry desert air. Thus far, the trip had been uneventful, lacking any notable sights or sounds besides the recurring thump of the minivan tires on the road. He'd crammed his vehicle to the roof with computer parts. The hard drives brimmed with innovative technology and his van hummed faintly in the heat. The papers, signed by the supreme leader himself, were to deliver the load to the Fordow Fuel Enrichment Plant, a clandestine nuclear facility carved deep into a mountain near Qom, roughly 160 kilometres south of Tehran.

With a curt wave, the customs official signalled Jacob to pull over to the curb for a thorough vehicle inspection. Currently, international law prohibits the transport of any goods, services, or technology—including materials like centrifuges or enriched uranium—that could aid Iran's nuclear weapons program. Iraqi officials implemented rigorous checks on all goods crossing the border into Iran to ensure compliance. They knew the consequences of incurring the wrath of the United States would be severe, so they avoided any action that might provoke it.

The inspection required removing all the boxes, their cardboard scratching against the pavement as Jacob dragged them to the curb. With a sharp knife, the customs official sliced open a few of the boxes, revealing their contents and confirming that the images on the cardboard matched the goods inside. A golden retriever on a bright red leash excitedly sniffed each cardboard box, his tail thumping a happy rhythm against the ground. A weary hand motioned Jacob toward the minivan. The official's sigh was almost audible as he indicated the computer parts could return to their place in the minivan. Ten minutes later, Jacob set off, the engine's rumble a promise of the journey ahead.

He arrived at the desolate Fordow Fuel Enrichment Plant 24 hours after departing the vibrant city of Tel Aviv. It was eight in the evening and the few sounds were the drone of machinery and the distant cries of birds. A gentle breeze rustled the leaves outside. He knew the facility well from his work a decade prior, but the lifelike mask he'd created with 3D printed, perfectly mirroring his expressions, gave him confidence in his anonymity. His eyes, sharp and intense, and his mouth, a thin, grim line, were the only things that might betray him.

The mask, which perfectly matched the photo on his passport with the same slight downturn of the mouth, also responded to the electrical signals from his facial muscles, mimicking his natural expressions. When Jacob smiled, the grotesque mask on his face seemed to smile with him, the lips curving upwards. When he frowned, the mask mirrored the expression, the rubber features appeared to slump with the weight of his displeasure.

His identity papers confirmed his Iranian nationality. He was a government official transporting crucial computer components and accessories from advanced Israeli technology plants. It had been trivially easy for Jacob to hack into the government files. The process was like walking through an unlocked door. Forging the documents was a simple matter of copying and pasting. He rattled off Farsi with a native speaker's fluency, his words clear and articulate, devoid of any foreign intonation. With practised ease, he navigated the servers and encrypted files of the government networks.

The van's tires crunched on the gravel as Jacob parked it on a side street next to a sprawling residential complex of an identical row of brick buildings. With a satisfied sigh, he reclined his seat, carefully adjusting the headrest until it perfectly cradled his neck. He closed his eyes, and almost instantly, the silence of the minivan lulled him into a deep sleep. Exhausted from the long drive, he knew he needed a good night's rest to prepare for the demanding tasks ahead.

Chapter 30

Larry and Jasmine made their way back to her office. It was early afternoon. "What do we do now?" asked Larry.

"Clearly, his plans no longer include you," replied Jasmine. "He deliberately left you."

"Maybe he'll call me before he leaves for Iran?"

"Not a chance. He's gone without you."

"Did you know the IDF was going to get involved before they took over the operating room? Did you speak with them?"

"That caught me off guard. But if you consider it, if he presented his plan to eliminate the Iranian threat without authorization to the IDF high command, what potential drawbacks might they foresee? It seemed logical to me they'd gamble on this madman, figuring they had nothing to lose. If he fails, and meets his end through torture or death, there was nothing that could come back and identify the IDF as the instigators. The conclusion would be that rage consumed him over his daughter's death. They would believe he sought revenge, acting independently and fuelled by his loss."

Larry's eyes narrowed in thought. "The scrub nurse gave me the sense she had done this before, loaded someone full of explosives with the purpose of removing them later. Do you think they might have secretly added a GPS tracking device hidden within the explosives to follow his every step?"

"Hmm," replied Jasmine. "That is a good thought. I wonder whether I could find out using my IDF credentials."

Jasmine turned to her computer, the glow of the screen illuminating her face. With a determined click of the mouse, she logged into the IDF website, the keys clicking softly under her fingers as she searched for the file containing Jacob's tracking information. Larry leaned in close, the scent of Jasmine's perfume filling his nostrils as he watched her search. Jasmine's fingers flew across the keyboard as she effortlessly moved through the website's menus.

"I personally constructed many of the website's security firewalls," she explained, a hint of pride in her voice. "I can access the site without creating a digital trail, ensuring my privacy."

Jasmine continued her journey through the website, the satisfying *tap-tap-tap* on the keyboard accompanying her progress. Finally, after a gruelling 30 minutes of searching, Jasmine opened a file labelled The Psycho.

A chill ran down Larry's spine as she did so. Jacob's picture suddenly popped up on the screen.

"Wow," said Larry. "See if they have a live GPS locator!"

Jasmine continued to look through the website and clicked on a map icon. A map of Tel Aviv appeared, with a glowing blue dot. Jasmine enlarged the map until the name Four Seasons Hotel filled the bottom of the screen.

"It looks like we found where he's staying," said Larry. "Let's go and visit him." Larry got up as if to leave.

"Hang on," Jasmine said, her voice tight with urgency. "If we visit him now, our presence will reveal our ability to track him. He might interfere with the GPS signal, scrambling the coordinates, and leading us on a wild goose chase. Let's wait and see where he's headed, monitoring him from a distance, observing his movements and listening for any clues."

Larry thought about this for a moment. "You're right," he said. "Let's follow where he goes."

"I've loaded the GPS signal into an app on my phone," said Jasmine. "We can now track him from anywhere. It looks like it sends a signal every hour."

Larry glanced at his watch. "It's getting dark. Let's go for dinner. I'm starving."

Jasmine smiled. "Let's go back to my place and I'll make dinner there. I don't think we are getting followed. Jacob's comments about someone tracking us were not true. I think he was trying to distract us. We can stop at the small local food store at the corner and pick up a few things. I make a wicked butter chicken curry."

They headed out of the office building and onto the street. "Just to be safe, follow me into this store," she said as Larry watched her disappear into racks of women's dresses hung on the walls of a small shop.

Larry heard the bell above the door jingle as Jasmine entered the local clothing shop, her eyes scanning the neatly folded sweaters and brightly patterned dresses on the shelves. Larry noticed her subtle glances toward the door and window, her eyes darting about, searching for any sign of pursuit, a nervous habit that spoke volumes. With a subtle nod, she urged Larry to follow, exiting through the back and into the twilight. A rickety door opened into a narrow alley, the sounds of distant city traffic muffled by the surrounding buildings. The alley, shadowed and barely wide enough for a compact car, led them to a bustling street. Jasmine peered cautiously up and down the street, then gave Larry a discreet signal to proceed.

They walked into the small produce store, greeted by the scent of ripe peaches and berries. With quick, efficient movements, Jasmine tossed the supplies—a loaf of bread, a wheel of cheese, fresh chicken, some spices, and a few apples—into the woven-rattan grocery basket. Everything seemed amplified in the whisper-quiet store. The cashier near the front door scanned her items, the beep of the machine ringing loud. With a crinkle of paper, the cashier placed the items into a brown paper bag. She held up a package of Indian spices.

"What are you making?" asked the cashier.

"My favourite recipe for butter chicken curry," replied Jasmine.

"Make sure you add enough *garam masala*. I suggest you try the Rani brand rather than the one you chose. It's the first one on the shelf. I find it brings out the flavours better." The cashier pointed to the location.

A relieved smile touched Jasmine's lips as she exchanged the package for the one the cashier had recommended. She paid the bill. With a subtle nod, Jasmine silently signalled Larry to use the back exit. They went through their usual routine, a practised dance of glances and quick turns, and ended up in front of Jasmine's imposing four-storey building, confident that no one had followed them. They walked up the stairs and went to her apartment on the top floor. The door shut with a solid thud as Jasmine locked it, leaving them in quiet isolation.

Jasmine prepared dinner while Larry checked the app on her phone. Jacob was still at the Four Seasons.

Half an hour later, Jasmine emerged from the kitchen, balancing a tray laden with delicious-looking curry. The spicy aroma slowly replaced the more generic smells of the busy city outside as she placed it on the breezy terrace table. With a blissful sigh, Larry said, "The explosion of flavour in this butter chicken curry is unparalleled. It's the best I've ever tasted!"

"Ahhh, thank you for the culinary compliment. I love cooking, but I love it more when I see someone enjoying it." A shadow fell across Jasmine's face as she studied Larry, her gaze intense and her lips pressing into a thin line. "It's been 10 years since you were in last in Israel. How do you think things have changed?" asked Jasmine.

Larry remarked, "People seem happy here." A thoughtful wrinkle creased his brow as he stroked the rough texture of his beard, while he collected his thoughts. "People seem to carry a quiet understanding that life is a gift to be cherished and experienced to the fullest. Being here makes every day feel special. The air itself seems charged with a unique energy. I saw it in the OR with the IDF staff, I see it on the streets, and I feel it when I am with you."

With a gentle pour, Larry refilled Jasmine's glass and his own with a chilled white wine, the scent of citrus and pear mingling with the curry. "The fast pace of Toronto is a symphony of sirens, construction, and the constant chatter of people rushing by. There's never enough time to delve into the specifics, like precisely which *garam masala* blend creates the perfect butter chicken. In Toronto's bustling city centre, a customer might have deemed the advice from a lowly cashier inappropriate, choosing to ignore it amid the city's cacophony. Food is not just sustenance here. It's a deeply valued experience, with dishes prepared with the utmost care and enjoyed with mindful appreciation. A unique blend of personality traits, skills, and experiences gives each person their own special qualities. They eagerly participate in making a positive difference in everyone's lives. That's a rare find. It's something you won't easily discover in other places."

"You don't think your positive experiences here are because they are in direct contrast to your recent negative ones with your life in Toronto?"

Larry thought about the question for a moment before he answered. "It's possible. When the turquoise waters and a gentle trade wind filled my sails in the British Virgin Islands, it created a similar vibe to what I feel here. The sun beating down, a warm breeze caressed my skin, and the vibrant coral reef beckoned during the magnificent scuba dive. The question lingered in my mind. What could compel someone to abandon this beautiful setting? Then I got shot in the leg. My perfect image of paradise, once so vibrant and full of life, shattered into a million painful pieces, leaving behind a bitter taste. Chantelle and the kids have left me. My surgical practice is uncertain, and I fear for my safety back home. I think you are right. Perhaps I'm psychologically driven to seek a better life, one with more meaning and purpose."

"Well, it has its perks. The beautiful scenery and the kindness of the people are examples, but ultimately, the human heart always seeks a better place to call home."

"Where would you prefer to be right now?"

"In this moment, with you beside me, I feel utterly content and wouldn't trade it for anywhere else."

Her fingers intertwined with his, giving his hand a reassuring squeeze. With a gentle smile, she lifted his hand to her lips and softly kissed it. She stood up and moved the table out of the way before settling herself on Larry's lap. She tilted his head back slightly and pressed her lips to his in a tender kiss, her fingers gently caressing his hair. Larry sensed a growing feeling of arousal taking over him. The moment their tongues touched, he felt a surge of warmth course through his body.

With a sigh, Jasmine stood and slowly unbuttoned his shirt, their breathing the only sound in the quiet room. Their kisses deepened, becoming more passionate with each passing moment. With a quick motion, Larry unfastened the buttons of her shirt and removed it in one fluid movement. Then he swiftly unclasped her bra, and it fell silently to the floor. Jasmine gently undid the button on his pants, her touch sending shivers down his spine. They too fell to the floor. In the same manner, Larry removed hers. With little delay, their clothes were gone, and they stood naked. In one swift motion, Larry picked her up and took her to the tranquil bedroom. With a forceful kick, he closed the door behind him before gently laying Jasmine on the soft bed.

With an anticipatory sigh, Jasmine leaned over and switched off the light, plunging the room into darkness.

Chapter 31

Jacob awoke in the minivan. It was 4 a.m. Four hours stretched before him until the Fordow Fuel Enrichment Plant gates opened, a seemingly endless expanse of time heavy with the smell of dust and the promise of danger. The day would start with a challenging 75-minute run. He stripped down to his running shorts, the cool night air raising goosebumps on his skin, and started down the road in the dark. A biting wind whipped around him as he noted the 10-degree Celsius temperature. His breathing ragged, his muscles burning, he felt the satisfying rhythm of his heart, a good feeling. He could smell his own sweat after only 10 minutes of intense exercise.

Finishing his run with the pre-dawn chill in the air, he quickly rinsed off with a gallon of cold water before returning to the warmth of the minivan. For breakfast, he consumed a three-litre jug of protein drink and water, totalling 2,000 calories—a thick, somewhat sweet liquid that left him feeling full but slightly nauseous. He put on his lifelike mask after cooling down, making sure everything he needed for the facility was in his bag. With the sun already rising, he finished his final preparations and by 7 a.m. A sense of quiet determination settled upon him. He drove the van to the gates, feeling the vibrations of the engine as he waited for them to open.

At the gate, a stern-faced guard in uniform shifted his weight from one foot to the other, the sound of his boots making a dull thud on the pavement. He quickly scanned the crisp, official papers allowing Jacob's delivery, each bearing the supreme leader's bold signature, to transport the goods to the facility. He motioned Jacob to drive through the garage and come to a stop. As he pulled up, the garage door lifted with a whirring sound, then descended with a gentle thud after his van was safely inside. A frenzy of flashing lights and sensors engulfed the minivan, creating a whirlwind of activity.

"Remove those boxes!" the guard barked at Jacob, his voice echoing in the cavernous room.

Unlike the cursory border check, this inspection was painstakingly thorough, each item scrutinized under bright lights. With a grunt, the guards opened each box one by one, carefully removing the contents and placing them on a nearby table. They removed the hard drives from their cases and disassembled them methodically, their metallic surfaces gleaming under the fluorescent lights. Then they plugged the hard drives into a much larger analysis system, meticulously searching for worms, viruses, or any unusual code hidden deep within the digital depths. A decade had passed since Jacob, as the lead scientist, had painstakingly crafted the process, so he was completely comfortable with it.

The Psycho

Once the security team had satisfied themselves that the contents and the minivan were safe, they helped him load them back into the van. The door at the far end of the garage swung open. The guards motioned for him to pass through. Jacob navigated the familiar drive lined with aging oak trees, making his way toward the imposing main office building. He pulled his minivan up to the loading dock at the rear, the rumble of the engine fading as he switched it off. The sun beat down on Jacob's neck as he removed the trolley from the minivan's roof and carefully loaded the boxes onto it; the wheels squeaking against the asphalt. Upon entering the code, a prompt appeared asking him to place his finger on the print analyzer for identification.

This was the part that made him feel uneasy, a knot of uncertainty tightening in his stomach. Since his last visit, the security technology had improved dramatically. He could feel the heightened vigilance in the air. Despite successfully navigating the facility's security system and registering his prints, he'd never tested the fingerprint scan. The complex computerized IA algorithms he'd used, with their intricate, interwoven code, had a secondary plan. One that required killing the security staff who were responsible for opening the door. This could leave him vulnerable to unforeseen problems, significantly affecting the mission's success rate, which dropped to a mere 55 per cent in this alternative scenario.

Jacob's heart rate increased a blip when the rumbling

loading dock door rolled up, the metallic screech a welcome sound as he entered the cool, dark building. With each bump on the floor, Jacob felt the weight of the load on the trolley as he made his way to the elevator. The room was empty and silent, except for the visually perceptible fingers of someone tapping on computer keys in a lone worker's glassed-in corner office, illuminated by the glow of his screen. With his gaze fixed on the computer screen, he avoided Jacob's eyes, his head turned away. Scanning the room for a suitable location, Jacob selected the creaky computer table holding the antiquated equipment. The old fans whirred as he methodically replaced it with the shiny, new components. With a grunt, he bent to connect his equipment, the plastic of the plug slightly warm against his fingers.

"What in God's name are you doing?" shouted a voice.

Jacob silently completed his task, then slowly looked up. It was Massoud Hossein, the brother of the man he'd fatally darted in Starbucks. The bitter scent of coffee still clung to his memory. Jacob stood, his muscles tense, ready to face his opponent.

"Who gave you permission to enter my facility?" Massoud continued.

Silently, Jacob offered the papers, the supreme leader's signature a weighty presence in granting the request. Massoud ran a skeptical eye over the papers, their rough texture and oddly pale colour immediately raising his suspicions. "These are obviously fake," he said, his voice dripping with sarcasm. "I'm in charge, yet I'm completely clueless about this. The supreme leader will be here within the hour to make an important announcement. I sincerely doubt he would allow something like this on a day such as today."

"Let me show you something," Jacob said, his voice low, pointing to the shadowy area beneath the desk. Massoud crouched down, his eyes scanning the ground intently. With a quick motion, Jacob seized the man's head and twisted it, causing his neck to snap, killing him in an instant. Glancing around, he observed no one else was around. The door to the glassed-in office hung open, revealing the bright sunlight illuminating the desks and computers within. It was Massoud who had been working there before approaching Jacob.

The largest box, a hulking cardboard crate, easily fit Massoud when he was bent into three. Jacob pressed down firmly, the brown tape sealing the box's edges with a satisfying rip and stick. With a grunt, he heaved the box onto the metal trolley.

He went back to his work and fired up the computer. Its startup sound was a comforting routine. With a few keystrokes, he accessed the server and downloaded the files containing the codes. The network's activity flickered across his screen. Jacob swept up the crumpled bits of cardboard and other discarded scraps, tossing them into the overflowing garbage bin. He left the computer screen glowing, its faint hum a reminder of his unfinished work, as he retraced his steps to the elevator and out onto the loading dock. He strained, the metal ramp groaning under the weight as he wheeled the heavy box containing Massoud up into the back of the minivan.

A large, imposing amphitheatre stood at the end of the long drive, its razor wire fence glinting menacingly in the sun. Guards stood rigidly at the gate. With a flurry of hands, they signalled for Jacob to pull over, their faces etched with worry. Having stopped, Jacob passed them the invitation embossed with the supreme leader's bold signature. The event was to begin in a mere half hour. Satisfied, they motioned Jacob toward the parking lot, its asphalt shimmering in the heat, and he carefully backed into an empty space.

Jacob hefted the heavy canvas bag onto his shoulder and headed for the service entrance, the weight pressing down on him. With a faint whirring sound, the lock released after a successful fingerprint scan and code entry. He walked toward the heavy oak door marked Private in brass lettering. As the door opened, the rich, plush texture of the carpet was immediately apparent, its colour a deep and vibrant red. Richly detailed, dark wood furniture, polished to a high sheen and outfitted with plush velvet cushions, lined two walls, separated by ornately carved coffee tables. A dark corner housed a bar. Bottles of amber liquor gleamed under the glow of a wall sconce next to a high-end Italian espresso machine. Beside was a cabinet where crystal glasses shone brightly, reflecting the light into a rainbow pattern against the wall. In the other corner, a heavy oak door stood slightly ajar, the private bathroom entrance.

With a determined stride, Jacob approached the room and stepped inside. Gleaming black marble lined the restroom. A shower and toilet shone under the bright lights. Neatly folded clean white towels sat on one corner of the counter.

The supreme leader was dealing with a prostate problem. With a few keystrokes, Jacob had breached the security of his medical files to find the information he sought. He chose not to have a Foley catheter in his bladder, opting instead to urinate every 30 minutes. That's why this room and bathroom, freshly cleaned and subtly scented with lavender, awaited his arrival. Jacob was confident that someone had meticulously inspected the room to ensure it was empty, spotless, and prepared for him. A guard stood silently outside the main entrance to the room. Few were aware of the hidden service entrance that Jacob had used to gain access. The cleverly concealed door hid within the ornate wainscoting, almost invisible to the casual observer. Jacob was certain they would not post a guard outside the service door. The narrow, barely lit hallway felt like a place easily overlooked.

Jacob's height surpassed that of the supreme leader, though only by an inch or two. He had meticulously studied the man's mannerisms, noting the precise way he walked, the subtle twitch of his hands, and the almost imperceptible tilt of his head. He'd spent the last few months honing his skills, practising until his movements were second nature. Now, he felt confident he could mimic them perfectly. Jacob slipped off his mask and replaced it with the new one. He glanced in the mirror. The appearance sent a shiver down his spine. His resemblance to the supreme leader was uncanny. He could have been a clone, from his stern expression to his similar posture. Jacob stood behind the door, listening to the faint sounds of movement beyond, and waited.

He did not have to wait for long. Shouting and hurried footsteps preceded the supreme leader's arrival, which he could hear from the other side of the door. The bathroom door opened. The sound of the door being closed and then locked resonated through the room after the supreme leader was inside.

Jacob had waited for his chance to seek accountability for Melodie's senseless death. To face the man who had such little regard for human life that he would take her innocent life had culminated in this remarkable moment. Confronting the mastermind behind the planned devastating attack on Israel was a necessary action to thwart more senseless destruction. The attack, if successful, would lead to Israel's complete destruction. It would have been an event surpassing even the horrors that Germany had inflicted on the Jewish people during the nazi era. Such complete annihilation, unimaginable suffering, and sheer scale of loss would have overshadowed the Holocaust's representation of human cruelty. The supreme leader's terrible mistake was a naïve belief that his actions would go unpunished, a complete disregard for the responsibility attached to the role of a world leader.

With his expression unreadable, the supreme leader turned to relieve himself, his heavy footsteps falling faintly on the marble floor. His face crumpled in confusion when he saw Jacob. The identical stranger before him was a mirror image, down to the faint scar above his eyebrow. Jacob's powerful hands quickly snapped the neck of his enemy before the supreme leader could even utter a word.

Jacob stripped the long black robe from the supreme leader. He knew the shoes, far too small for his size 16 feet, would never fit. Jacob had brought several pairs, each meticulously crafted to match the supreme leader's footwear, and selected the closest match. With a sharp *pop*, he detached the drop-ceiling panel, revealing the space above, and gently lifted the supreme leader into the dusty, cramped confines of the ceiling.

He carried the body along a wide, sturdy concrete ledge, offering a grim and unwavering surface that could easily hold the body. He carefully positioned the dead man across two ceiling tiles where he had selected that would support the weight. The chance of discovery was almost zero before Jacob had completed his task. Jacob carefully placed the bag with the mask, clothes, and other items into another part of the ceiling and snapped the panel shut.

One last glance in the mirror confirmed he would pass as the supreme leader. He unlocked the door and walked into the room with the plush red carpet, ready for the next stage of his plan.

Chapter 32

Larry woke to the warmth of Jasmine's arms around him, the soft feel of her hair against his skin. Her breath hitched in a gentle snore, a quiet sound in the stillness. The digital display of the clock on the night table glowed faintly, showing 10:03, the numbers sharp and clear against the dark background. Having stayed up until after 4 a.m., they'd slept in, the sounds of the morning world muted by the thick curtains and closed windows. A smile touched Larry's lips with the memories of their fiery embraces imprinted into his brain. A wave of pleasure washed over him, unlike anything he'd felt in the months since Chantelle confessed her affair with Richard. That memory of her betrayal was still raw. Aside from her flirtatious behaviour, they had abstained from sex for the past six months. He thought that a shrug and a slight roll of the eyes were a normal response after a decade together.

With a shake of her head, Jasmine had disagreed, her eyes flashing. "That was a huge red flag, obvious even after 10 years together," she said, a hint of frustration in her tone. She confessed, "I find it hard to stop myself from touching you."

Larry smiled at the memory. Jasmine had promised she would never do what Chantelle did to him. "I am the most faithful woman in Israel," she had explained to him earlier in the evening.

Without waking up Jasmine, he reached over for her phone and opened the tracking app for Jacob. The blue dot remained still at the Four Seasons Hotel, not having moved for the past three days. He felt Jasmine stir. Her eyes met his, an unspoken question.

"You know, something is not right," said Larry. "I do not think Jacob would remain fixed in one position, not moving for so long. I think we should check it out."

"You never know," said Jasmine. "He had laparoscopic surgery and would need a few days to recover. Even him. What do you suggest we do?"

"Let's go to the Four Seasons Hotel and check if he is there."

"We do not know what name he is using, or his room number. I doubt if we could find him unless we knocked on all 600 hotel room doors. I have a better idea."

Jasmine leapt out of bed and sat at the kitchen table wearing only her nightie. Larry looked over her shoulder as she logged into the IDF website from her laptop and into the folder marked The Psycho.

"Jacob froze the image at the Four Seasons Hotel. I refreshed the GPS search, and it is looking for the signal."

Both Larry and Jasmine had their eyes glued to the computer screen. The blue dot now zeroed in on a spot 20 miles northeast of the city of Qom. The map identified the Fordow Fuel Enrichment Plant.

"How did he get there so quickly?" asked Larry.

"Likely he drove," said Jasmine. "What should we do?"

"I already have a visitor's visa for Iran. I think I should fly there and track him down."

"That's crazy," she whispered, eyes wide with disbelief. "Should the Faraja, Iran's national police force, find you, expect a slow, agonizing torture before a swift, merciless death. What if their facial-recognition software identifies you, highlighting your image among the crowd, and you become a marked person? That fake passport of yours won't get you anywhere. It's completely useless."

"Jacob promised me he would let me remove the explosives I implanted in his body before he pushes on the detonator. I cannot let him blow himself up. I should never have let him talk me into it."

"Authorities strictly advise Israeli citizens against travelling to Iran. I cannot go with you. Please, Larry, don't do this!" Jasmine cried, her voice trembling with fear. Silent tears traced paths down her cheeks, leaving glistening trails in their wake. "For days, an unfamiliar, overwhelming joy has filled my thoughts. It is a feeling so pure and intense. I have never experienced this before. I have never felt so happy. Now, I could lose you. Please stay with me. I don't want to face the rest of my life alone. Jacob is a grown man. He does not want your interference. He wants you to stay out of it."

"I have to, Jasmine. I promise I'll be back. Jacob needs me to remove the explosives. Whether or not he likes it, it's my responsibility."

Jasmine sobbed. "I can't bear this."

Nodding slowly, Jasmine accepted Larry's viewpoint, a thoughtful expression on her face as she whispered, "Promise me you'll be careful."

Larry used Jasmine's laptop to search for flights. One was leaving for Tehran in four hours. He bought a return ticket. He reserved a small compact car from the airport in Tehran so he could drive to Qom and from there to the Fordow Fuel Enrichment Plant. Jasmine drove him to the airport.

Sobbing, Jasmine clutched Jacob tightly at the airport, whispering, "I love you, Larry." The sounds of departing planes and bustling crowds faded into the background as she spoke. "Ten years ago, I let you slip away. That will not happen again."

"I love you too," replied Larry. "I'll be back soon. You'll see."

***

Two hours later, the plane touched down at Imam Khomeini

International Airport. The tires screeched slightly on the runway. Using the passport Jacob gave him, everything worked perfectly. The customs agents barely glanced at it before waving him through. He quickly spotted the bright, gleaming logo of the Avis car rental booth and selected a sleek Peugeot 206. Two hours later, he drove through the bustling city of Qom, the sounds of the bazaar reverberating around him, then continued onward along the highway toward the Fordow Fuel Enrichment Plant.

He texted Jasmine to let him know he had landed and again when he got through customs. "I'm heading for the blue dot on the GPS map. I'll be there in about half an hour," he messaged as he got closer.

Larry pulled up to the security gates around the facility two hours later. The guard approached him and said something in Farsi. Larry shook his head, showing he could not understand. The guard motioned for him to turn around and drive away. Larry looked at his semi-automatic rifle and then put his car in reverse and turned around.

About a kilometre from the gates, as he was driving towards Qom, a cavalcade of armed vehicles drove past him, heading for the facility. At least 10 large black Nissan SUVs with dark tinted windows went by. Three Ford-150 pickup trucks with six armed guards, one in front, one in the back and one in the middle, escorted the SUVs. Larry pulled to the side of the road and called Jasmine.

"A motorcade, complete with flashing lights, just sped past me, heading towards the enrichment plant," Larry said. "I attempted to access the area pinpointed by the GPS signal as Jacob's location, but security personnel who refused my entry blocked me. Something big is coming down."

"I've been on the internet, noticing the rising tide of online discussions originating from Iran," said Jasmine. "The supreme leader is announcing something important this morning. The internet chatter suggests he will soon make the announcement, with the enrichment facility's impressive architecture as a backdrop. Larry, you need to get out of Iran. They are evacuating all western embassies in Tehran. Something big is happening. It could ignite a larger conflict, the first spark in a devastating war. Larry, this is the real thing. Get back to the airport, catch the first flight out— anywhere. Do it now!"

"I want to wait to see if I can help Jacob. Maybe they trapped him inside?"

"Frankly, you're not equipped to help him. It's beyond your capabilities. Your profession is saving lives through surgery, not sneaking around as a spy. Please, Larry, listen to me. It's urgent. Get out of there now! Your life is in danger."

Larry was quiet, contemplating his options, the rush of air

passing through the vehicle's slightly open window while he raced down the empty road. A sense of impending doom hung heavy in the air. Jasmine was certain something terrible was about to happen and he had to trust her.

"OK," he said. "Let me think about it as I drive towards the airport. Call me if you hear anything else." Larry hung up the phone.

The car sputtered to a stop at a gas station in Qom. Larry filled the tank, then walked to the kiosk to pay. The cool plastic of his credit card felt in juxtaposition to the punishing summer heat. At the side of the kiosk, above the cash register, Larry could see the flickering TV screen displaying breaking news headlines. A massive image of the supreme leader filled the screen, looming over a cheering crowd packed into the amphitheater. The crowd roared.

As the supreme leader prepared to speak, the small kiosk vibrated with the sound of clapping hands and cheers. Larry stared, mesmerized, as the video on the screen scanned across the dense crowd, the individual faces a sea of blurry movement. He squinted, trying to make out Jacob's face through the fuzzy image, but it was too indistinct to identify anyone. Larry slid his platinum credit card across the counter to the attendant. With a quiet click, the attendant handed Larry the card reader, and he punched in his security code.

The TV screen exploded with the image of the supreme leader, his body jerking as an unseen force lifted him off the platform, a gasp rippling through the crowd. Smoke filled the room. It seemed to clear within a few seconds. A spray of blood, thick and dark, splattered the stage as the supreme leader collapsed, his body hitting the floor with a heavy thud. Blood spread across the lightweight wooden stage, surrounding the supreme leader. The impact contorted his body at an unnatural angle, his eyes wide open but staring in opposite directions as the camera crept closer, the unsettling image growing sharper.

The surging crowd, a wave of flailing limbs and desperate cries, scrambled over each other to escape the amphitheater as the camera swept across them. Their faces were a mask of confusion and terror as they ran in different directions, desperate for safety amid the rising screams. A team of armed soldiers, their weapons gleaming under the stage lights, stormed the stage.

The camera focused on the lifeless body of the supreme leader on the stage. In the background, panicked and screaming crowds escaped through the open doors. The camera zoomed into the supreme leader's face. One medic, easily identified by the red cross on his arm, felt for the carotid artery, his head shaking slightly as he did so.

The camera flickered for a moment as the image returned to the supreme leader's face, which once again filled the screen. Larry saw a pair of hands with the red cross armband reach down and tug on something at the neck. It appeared he was pulling the skin off the neck. Now both hands struggled to grip at the neck. The camera zoomed in to reveal what appeared to be a rubber mask that the medic had discarded on the ground beside the body.

Zooming in, the image of Jacob's face filled the screen. His lifeless eyes were wide open.

Chapter 33

"You need to get out of Iran!" screamed Jasmine into the phone.

"I'm driving as fast as I can," said Larry. "I'm about an hour away from the airport."

"The location where they found the supreme leader's body was on the stage. The shocking story on the internet claims that a fall broke his neck. His body had exploded, spreading his guts across the stage. A person who appeared to be the supreme leader, but was in fact an imposter, dramatically exploded on stage. Do you think Jacob exploded himself?"

"I saw his face on the video from the news station at the gas station. He was the person lying in a pool of blood on stage."

"Oh my God. He did it then! That's awful. You must be upset. Are you OK?"

"I'm in a state of shock. If I hadn't seen it with my own eyes, I wouldn't have believed it."

"Just get back here as quickly as possible. I booked a flight for you to Cairo on EgyptAir in three hours from now. Text me when you are in the departure lounge."

"OK. See you soon!"

Upon returning the Peugeot, Larry proceeded to the Avis underground parking facility, where he settled his outstanding bill. He went to the EgyptAir counter, where an agent provided him with the boarding pass for his flight. Since he only had a carry-on with him, he could bypass the checked baggage area and head straight for the security checkpoint. Following the electronic scan of his boarding pass, he methodically emptied his pockets of their contents, carefully placing each item into a designated bin, along with his cell phone.

Larry passed through the scanner, and following the X-raying of his things, he retrieved them from the conveyor belt. A sudden and loud ruckus behind him made him glance back. Just as Larry turned, a soldier clad in army fatigues suddenly charged and tackled him to the ground. The impact of his fall sent a jolt of pain shooting through his sternum as he landed directly on his still-healing rib fractures. He heard a distinct crunch indicating a worsening of his injuries. He could not take a single breath, his lungs constricting, and his chest tightening with each desperate attempt. The force of the impact left him winded, his body reeling from the shock. His pulse was racing, and a confused feeling washed over him.

Larry felt handcuffs getting slapped on his wrists behind his back. When the soldier wrenched Larry to his feet, he felt his shoulder dislocate. Tremendous pain shot through his shoulder to his back. He screamed involuntarily as the soldier pushed him forward into a small room and sat him down. The pain in his shoulder was excruciating. He knew he had only a few minutes to push it back into place before the muscles tightened, making the reduction of the dislocated shoulder impossible.

"Please," he said to the soldier. "You dislocated my shoulder. I can push it back in place if you take off the handcuffs for just a minute." Larry tried to point to his deformed left shoulder with a nod of his head. The soldier ignored him and kept looking and said nothing.

After a few more attempts to talk to the soldier, Larry gave up. His shoulder throbbed. He tried not to move. A few minutes later, a man dressed in army fatigues and sat down in front of Larry.

"Welcome to Tehran, Dr. Klapman. We've been looking for you," he said.

Larry could feel the pained expression on his face and said through clenched teeth, "My left shoulder got dislocated when the soldier tackled me. Can you ask him to release the handcuffs, and I can try to push it back in place?"

Continuing his intense stare at Larry, the man then addressed the soldier in Farsi, uttering something that Larry couldn't understand. The soldier, his movements precise and efficient, extracted his keys and used them to unlock and remove the restrictive handcuffs. Using his right hand, Larry delicately raised and lowered his left shoulder until the arm was moving up and down by five centimetres. The intense pain caused a cold sweat to appear on his forehead. It dripped into his eyes. He abducted his arm, pulling it away from the rest of his body. Larry turned his hand over slowly, palm upwards, until it was facing the ceiling. Upon achieving 120 degrees of abduction, he experienced a palpable *pop* sound as his dislocated shoulder spontaneously reduced itself. The intense pain in his shoulder gradually subsided.

"Do you feel better?" asked the man sitting in front of Larry.

"Much better," Larry whispered. "Just a dull ache remains from the intense pain. The downside is the fractured ribs are more noticeable now that the excruciating shoulder pain is gone."

The man's gaze fell upon Larry. "Our supreme leader is dead. Do you know anything about that?"

Larry took a deep breath. "I'm a surgeon. I do not know what happened to him."

"Someone snapped his neck and then, by using a mask, went on stage pretending to be the supreme leader and blew himself up. We'll come back to this. Do you have any idea what the supreme leader was going to say today?"

With a slow and deliberate movement, Larry shook his head

from side to side. He truly and honestly did not know.

"Today, Iran had planned to issue a statement declaring the complete destruction of Israel, a statement that would undoubtedly have had severe international repercussions. The planners scheduled the nuclear attack to coincide precisely with the moment the supreme leader made his announcement. There was an issue that caused a malfunction or failure in the system, process, or task. The actions of a saboteur who had deliberately tampered with the explosives, is likely the same individual who rendered the bombs inert and incapable of detonation. Someone deactivated the computer virus we developed, a virus strikingly similar to the centrifuge worm you were involved with 10 years ago. What is the extent of your knowledge or familiarity with this?"

A look of sheer astonishment spread across Larry's face, his expression a mixture of disbelief and wonder at the surprising turn of events. *The military commander seemed to share information that he felt I already knew, prompting the question of why he was doing so. The commander's conviction seemed absolute. He has no doubt whatsoever that I am the individual who committed this act.*

"Look," said Larry, his tone implying a significant observation that required immediate attention. "Although I contributed to the centrifuge project, my involvement was quite minimal and insignificant in the larger scheme of things. The code I created for the worm triggered a download of the newest software upon the worm's successful connection to the Siemens S7 system. That was all there was to it. And that was 10 years ago. I'm a surgeon now. I know nothing about worms and viruses and certainly nothing about nuclear weapons."

"You are much too modest," said the commander. "Look at this."

The man slapped down a photograph depicting Larry, Jasmine, and Jacob engaged in conversation at a Starbucks, a moment captured just before Jacob fatally injected the Iranian operative with a dart. "Jacob Ashinoff's actions directly resulted in the deaths of several of our top undercover operatives, individuals who had proven their exceptional abilities in the field. Look, in this picture I see you are currently enjoying a cup of coffee in his company. How can you explain that?"

"I operated on his daughter, who unfortunately died after complications from surgery. He threatened to kill me, too."

"It doesn't look like he's trying to kill you in the picture, does it?"

Larry glanced at the photograph, unsure of what he should say in response to the image before him. This man possessed a significant amount of knowledge about him, and he was deliberately revealing this information in small, carefully measured increments.

Larry looked up to see that the man now had a self-satisfied expression on his face. Larry, in a curious and somewhat demanding tone, inquired, "What do you want from me?"

"We are arresting you for spying. I am transferring you to Evin Prison, where we have a team of interrogation experts waiting to talk with you. My advice would be to cooperate with them. Unlike Canada, we do not have 'due process' here. We caught you with a fake passport. You are here illegally. You are a known enemy of Iran with your past dealings with Israel, and you have information which we can use to protect ourselves from retaliation from the US."

Larry felt his heart sink into his feet. "Any chance I could get a lawyer?"

The army commander, overcome with sudden mirth, let out a hearty laugh before rising to his feet. "You're going to have to handle this situation all by yourself. There is no one else to rely on for help or guidance. There is a chance consular services may be available to you. No Canadian consulate exists in Iran, but sometimes other consulates help the Canadians. It all depends on how cooperative you are."

He glanced at the soldier and spoke in Farsi. With a sharp turn, he headed for the door, the sound of his footsteps echoing as he pulled it shut with a forceful slam. With a curt nod, the soldier gestured for Larry to extend his hands. He placed the cold steel handcuffs on Larry's wrists and, with a *click,* secured them. A forceful push propelled Larry forward and out the door. Their bayonets glinting in the sun, three other soldiers surrounded Larry and marched him into a waiting, dark-tinted SUV. The engine idled impatiently. Leaving the airport, the SUV bumped along the pot-holed road towards Tehran, the sounds of the city growing louder with each passing moment.

Chapter 34

Larry's gaze swept across the bleak, six-foot by six-foot cell. They had painted the rough-textured walls a brilliant, almost blinding white. It contrasted the smooth, cold floor beneath his feet. A metal bed lay along one wall, devoid of sheets. Its cold, sharp rungs dug painfully into his back as he lay upon it. Larry surmised he was in solitary confinement. The occasional drip of water from the leaky faucet in the corner was the only sound that broke the silence. A chipped, white metal toilet, showing rust around the edges, sat beneath the sink. A thick, cloying odour of urine and feces, heavy with the stench of decay, permeated the room.

He felt a profound sense of isolation. The silence was absolute, confirming his belief that no one knew he was there. He pondered his uncertain future, a knot of anxiety tightening in his stomach. Larry had calculated that a week had passed since they had locked him in the cell. It was seven days ago when the guards led him into the sterile, cold interrogation room. The only noise he could detect was the buzz of the ventilation system.

His mind replayed the interrogation like an endless movie reel.

The recording device that had been placed in front of him during the interrogation quietly captured his every word, which was later transcribed by AI and printed for his signature on crisp, white paper. He still had not signed the papers and stubbornly refused to comply until they answered his questions.

Larry felt a wave of nausea when he stumbled out of the building, the interviewer's words still reverberating in his ears. The gash on his forehead was healing, and no longer throbbed with pain. The mere thought of the interview sent a wave of nausea through him, his chest tightening with anxiety, beads of sweat forming on his brow. An overwhelming urge to pace would take over, his feet moving in restless circles, the sound of his shoes against the floor falling softly in the quiet room. He would pace sometimes for hours until his anxiety settled, only to return a short time later. As he reminisced, details from the interview replayed in his mind.

"So tell us from the beginning how you were involved with the centrifuge project," asked the man who introduced himself as Hamid.

Larry started with the story of his basic training for the army in Israel and told them about his involvement with the coding of the centrifuge project.

"Why would you want to come to Israel and do that?" asked Hamid.

"My grandfather pressured me to get a glimpse of my Jewish

heritage by joining the army for basic training," replied Larry. "When I applied for medical school, they wanted me to get some real-life experience. After that year, I received my acceptance letter to medical school, and five gruelling years of general surgery training followed." With a smile, Larry recounted how he'd met Chantelle during his time on the kibbutz—the bustling community life and, ultimately, their wedding day.

"I thought I'd left the vibrant tapestry of Israeli life behind, but then I ran into Jacob, bringing back a flood of memories." With a shaky breath, Larry explained how Jacob had cornered him at the hospital, the frightening details still fresh in his mind. He described the sailing trip, detailing the moment the gunshot rang out, followed by Jacob's pained cry. He described the subsequent surgery, recalling the small bowel fistula and resection of the damaged intestine. Larry nervously spoke of his abduction, detailing the harrowing experience before launching into his escape to the Dominican Republic. He mentioned how John had set up the sailboat like a condominium with all the amenities of a house.

"It was there when my wife admitted to an affair," said Larry in a shaky voice. "Chantelle told me she didn't want to live like this on the run. Richard, her new boyfriend, flew to Samana to collect them. I have not seen or heard from them since. I wanted to protect them from whatever fallout occurred."

Hamid sat back, fascinated with the story. "Ahhh, Richard," he replied. "We were roommates in basic training for the Iranian National Guard. Glad to hear is doing well."

Larry's heart skipped a beat. "What are you saying? Richard is part of your organization?"

Hamid smiled and said nothing.

"Tell me," Larry roared, spittle flying from his lips. "What is Richard up to?" Larry felt his face flush crimson, a wave of fiery anger surging through his body. "You need to tell me. What the fuck is going on with him? What does he want from Chantelle?"

Hamid continued to stare at Larry, all the while smiling. Finally, he knocked on the door and said something in Farsi. A guard came in and handcuffed Larry's hands behind his back.

"You cannot leave it like this!" Larry's face was red with anger as he shouted, the veins in his neck bulging. "You need to tell me what is going on with Richard!"

When Larry remained motionless, the guard roughly shoved him forward. Larry stumbled, his legs giving way beneath him, and landed heavily on the hard floor. He crashed to the ground, his head hitting the concrete with a sharp crack, the pain searing through him. A gash on his forehead spurted blood. He felt a throbbing pain and saw his blood mix with dust on the ground. With a grunt, the guard hoisted him up by his cuffed hands, the pain shooting up his arms and settling heavily on his shoulders. Warm blood dripped into his eyes, stinging and blurring his vision. He couldn't see a thing, his eyes straining against the overwhelming veil of crimson.

"You son of a bitch! Tell me!" yelled Larry as the guard dragged him away. The sounds of his desperate protests, a mix of anger and fear, filled the air.

***

Throughout the week, an unnerving silence reigned; not a single person, not even a guard, came to Larry's cell. One morning, they slipped the papers under his door so quietly he didn't hear a thing. They silently slid the trays laden with food under the door. The hallways were eerily silent, devoid of any sound. To Larry, their actions felt like a calculated move. The silence was deafening, the absence of others keenly felt. Locked in the white room, with no sound and colour, was a form of psychological torture—an emptiness that suffocated him. The artificial brightness, a relentless, glaring white, clashed with his body's natural rhythms, leading to severe sleep deprivation. They left him with his disturbing thoughts about what Richard would do with his children and whether they were in any danger. Larry paced the cold, damp cell, his frustration mounting as he felt utterly helpless to protect them.

Larry had kept track of the days by putting a scratch on the walls with his fingernail. So far, the marks showed seven days of isolation. *Maybe Hamid made up the story about Richard and him together in the Iranian National Guards just to torture me psychologically. The damage I am doing to myself is far worse than they could do to me. I need to get a grip. Hamid must be lying about Richard. The Israeli army warned me about psychological torture during basic training. I need to think about other things. I need to find things every day to be grateful for. Otherwise, my despair will consume me.*

Larry noticed that someone had discreetly pushed some photographs under the door. Hesitantly, he picked them up with trembling hands. The picture of his two sons eating cereal at the breakfast table struck Larry with a painful longing. They sat in his kitchen, oblivious to the suffering he endured in his isolated cell. He could feel his chest tighten with each breath as he gazed at their smiling faces. Chantelle, still in her fluffy pink bathrobe, with her hair a mess from sleep, looked as if she had just woken up. With a smile, she presented Richard with a cup of coffee, the dark liquid still frothing slightly from the espresso machine. Their smiles were genuine as they gazed at each other, oblivious to the camera capturing the moment.

Hamid and Richard grinned at the camera in the next photo, their arms thrown around each other in a display of obvious affection. Dressed in army fatigues, their polished boots a mirror finish, reflecting the sun's rays with a blinding flash. *They are screwing with me. I won't let this get to me.* Larry tore away the picture of his two boys and crammed it so it rested between a crack on the wall. He could see them while lying on the bed. With the rest of the picture and the one of Hamid and Richard, he tore into pieces and threw them into the toilet, flushing them away.

To survive, he knew he had to concentrate on each day as it came, without dwelling on the uncertainties of the future. The endless monotony of solitary confinement spurred him to consider his options. The absence of sights, sounds, and smells was a growing concern. Discovering things that would evoke feelings of thankfulness and appreciation was crucial for him; he needed that feeling of contentment. The memory of Jasmine's whispered confession of love and the feel of her hand in his flooded Larry's mind, bringing back the joy of their last night together. An unexpected rush of happiness flowed through him, bringing a comforting warmth. He sighed contentedly, imagining a sweet scent of lavender coming from his pillow, which lulled him into a peaceful slumber, certain everything would eventually be alright.

Chapter 35

Jasmine had accepted a week ago they must have apprehended Larry before he caught the flight to Cairo. With a sinking feeling, she'd contacted EgyptAir and learned that he hadn't been on the plane. The agent's flat tone added to her anxiety. He'd promised to text her if there was any news, but her phone remained stubbornly silent. To her dismay, she learned that Canadian consular help was unavailable in Iran. Turkey's consulate, the closest one geographically, had absolutely no power concerning events within Iran. He would be by himself. A profound loneliness settling in her heart.

Jasmine frantically searched the internet, desperately seeking any information about Larry. Someone had taken a picture of a person lying facedown in handcuffs at the Tehran Airport security area. The timeline showed a 12:05 timestamp on the picture, but whether it was Larry remained unclear. She knew he would have passed through the area during that time slot.

She knew the authorities would almost certainly find out his passport was a forgery. The telltale signs were too obvious. Many security areas used facial recognition. The cold, impersonal gaze of the cameras following his every move. The likelihood was that they stumbled upon him. His pale face would stand out in the software, identifying him in just a few seconds. Especially since the Iranians had been hunting him relentlessly. They would have had a team of agents at the airport, poised to intercept anyone fleeing after the botched attack on Israel. Jasmine would imagine that the atmosphere would have crackled with adrenaline. Hushed conversations and hurried footsteps would have filled the bustling terminal.

News channels endlessly replayed grainy security footage. The aborted attack dominated the headlines. Several details were indistinct, leaving much to the imagination. It was undeniably clear that Iran's nuclear capabilities had far exceeded the western nations' previous estimations. The implications were deeply unsettling. As the supreme leader made the announcement, a synchronized detonation of a nuclear bomb over Israel was to have happened. The Department of Defence in the US reported an aborted cyberattack on their defence system. It was unclear how they thwarted it, but many questions remained.

Jasmine watched the news video of Jacob's explosive performance on stage. Larry was right. Undeniably, it was him. The removal of the mask showing his face left no room for doubt. Like many of the rest of Jacob's victims, the supreme leader also had a fractured neck as the cause of death. All along, Jacob had planned to blow himself up.

Jasmine found this inexplicable, and it frustrated her. The supreme leader, responsible for the death of Jacob's daughter, had felt the full force of his revenge. The raw satisfaction was probably mixed with the bitter taste of loss while the murder of Melodie lingered in the air. He'd successfully averted the launch of the nuclear bomb on Israel by some miracle and the cyberattack to prevent retaliation from the US.

With every box checked, Jasmine couldn't understand why he would take his own life. It defied logic. Jasmine watched the video once more, studying every detail. There was no mistake. It was Jacob. Jasmine shook her head, strands of hair falling across her face as she tried to make sense of the situation.

Jasmine logged into the IDF website, the white screen momentarily blinding her before she located and opened the file labelled The Psycho. The picture of Jacob laying on the stage in a pool of blood came up. The short video icon, when clicked, revealed a shocking video of him exploding in a flash of light and sound. Jasmine clicked a link, and the Hebrew letters of an Israeli website filled her screen. As she read about the aborted nuclear attack, a chill ran down her spine. The website article examined the complexities of the Iranian-made virus, a sophisticated piece of malware intended to stifle American counterattacks. Its description included technical specifications and potential consequences. A brilliant coder had designed a complex algorithm to isolate the virus, effectively stopping it in its tracks and preventing any further damage. The Americans had identified a breach in their system's security—a gaping hole that allowed the virus to enter—and they quickly sealed it with a reinforced firewall.

A knot formed in her stomach as Jasmine examined some links to the dark web, the cryptic URLs promising both danger and intrigue. The report grimly described the death of a leading Iranian nuclear scientist responsible for the enrichment facility, noting the potential implications for the country's nuclear program. Someone had broken his neck and stuffed the body into a cardboard crate in the back of a minivan. Another report described a massive explosion at the office tower, the shockwave shattering windows for blocks and sending a plume of smoke billowing into the sky, as the six-storey building crumbled into a heap of twisted metal and debris. An aerial picture of the Fordow Fuel Enrichment Plant showcased the shocking before and after images, highlighting the scale of the changes. Only a depressing pile of rubble remained where the beautiful six-storey building and amphitheatre had been. Twisted metal and shattered stone now replaced the former grandeur.

The complex layout of the Iranian prison system website frustrated Jasmine as she searched for the information she needed. It was likely that Larry was being held in Evin Prison, known for holding political dissidents. Notorious for its inhumane treatment of prisoners and its confinement of journalists who spoke out against the regime, the prison was a place of unspeakable horrors, where the stench of fear and despair hung heavy in the air. Hanging, a gruesome and public spectacle, was the preferred method of carrying out the death penalty. They hoisted the condemned high, their bodies swaying in the breeze as onlookers gathered. Jasmine had no doubt this would be Larry's fate.

With a sigh, Jasmine considered the options, each one presenting a unique set of challenges and rewards. The heavily fortified building, with its thick walls and armed guards, was impenetrable. With half a century of unbroken containment, the prison stood as a grim monument to its success. There had never been an escape. The walls, thick with concrete and brick, muffled the sounds from outside. They moved the prisoners constantly to confuse anyone trying to track their location. Jasmine knew breaking him out was impossible.

The thought of Larry's impending execution, the cold finality of the gallows, was unbearable. A sense of urgency washed over her; she had to do something, anything, to change the situation. Finally, after an hour of listening to monotonous hold music, she spoke to Marjorie Hansen in the Canadian consulate in Ottawa.

"Dr. Larry Klapman is being held in the Evin Prison in Tehran," she said to Marjorie. "We need to get him out. They suspect him of orchestrating the latest assault on the regime and the death of the supreme leader."

"Iran has no consular services," replied Marjorie. "Often we work with the Turkish consulate there who have better relations. I'll need to make inquiries, but I should warn you, the Iranians rarely respond to our requests. I suspect they will deny all knowledge of Larry."

The conversation continued for a few more minutes, with Jasmine outlining her concerns they could hang him after they had extracted all the information they could from him. She told him about the fake passport.

Marjorie said, "I believe your friend is in serious trouble. I do not think we will be able to help. I'm sorry."

A wave of frustration washed over Jasmine as she hung up the phone. She felt a crushing weight of sadness settle upon her, and tears welled in her eyes. Hot tears streamed down her cheeks, each one a salty burn against her skin. She placed her hands on her head, her shoulders shaking with silent sobs.

Chapter 36

The cold, hard metal of the bed pressed into Larry's back. By counting the marks on the wall, he could determine that he had been there for 13 days. In contrast to the earlier tension, the silence that ensued after the interrogation was heavy. The sterile white walls, the same thin mattress, the unyielding buzz of the ventilation system— nothing changed in his cell during the 13 days. The bright lights and white walls only amplified the monotonous routine of the same food. Larry was certain the strategy was to leave him alone, to let him descend into madness in the silent, crushing solitude of his confinement.

Each day, Larry made a point of reflecting on something positive, feeling gratitude fill him with warmth. Today, the simple act of breathing was a victory he savoured. That he was in Tehran's Evin Prison, known globally as the world's most notorious, struck him. He could almost feel the oppressive atmosphere of the place. For years, the regime had imprisoned journalists who wrote negatively about them in this place. The regime silenced their stories before finally executing them as traitors. The cold stone walls seemed to whisper their dissent. A profound certainty, like a pressure lifting from his chest, filled Larry. The regime's accusations against him, laden with damning evidence, would carry significantly more weight. The death sentence, a seemingly appropriate punishment for killing the supreme leader and preventing Israel's annihilation, was almost certain. For now, though, he was alive. A shallow breath hitched in his lungs, a testament to his stubborn survival.

If he dodged the death penalty, he knew his imprisonment here would be forever. The thought, heavy and bleak, filling him with a sense of crushing disappointment. A life sentence. Freedom was not an option. He was also certain no one knew where he was. He felt the stillness of the sterile white surroundings pressing in on him. In the hostile country of Iran, he would simply be another missing person, lost among the journalists and freedom fighters, soon to be forgotten.

He lay there on the bed. A subtle creak broke the solitude. It was at his door, making his heart pound. A frown creased Larry's face, his lips pressed into a thin line. The barely noticeable scratch shattered the soundlessness of the past 13 days. It was like a soft rustle of leaves, surprisingly loud in the stillness. He quickly hopped up, placing his ear against the door, trying to hear anything. The sound seemed to come from behind a thick curtain. He could hear a distinct scratching just outside his door. Definitely, something was there.

The door burst open with a loud crash, sending Larry sprawling across the room into the empty corner, a cloud of dust billowing around him. The bright lights glinted off the man's massive frame as he filled the doorway, a dark silhouette against the brilliance. Larry could only stare from his position in the corner on the floor, his mouth agape at the breathtaking scene before him.

It was Jacob, his presence both comforting and slightly intimidating, who stood before him.

For Larry, time seemed to stop. The world went silent. The air was still. A wave of bewilderment washed over him. He felt utterly confused. During his 13 days of confinement, alone in the cold, damp cell, he had mourned the loss of this strange but magnificent man. The silence had amplified his grief.

Seeing him standing before me feels like a cruel illusion, a tactic the Iranians are using to break my resolve. The harsh fluorescent lights of the room only emphasized the surreal quality of the moment.

He watched as Jacob's heavy boots thudded against the concrete floor, each step bringing him closer to the corner where he lay. Jacob gently picked him up to a standing position and said, "Follow me."

Jacob turned and paced out of open the door. Then, with a burst of speed, ran down the hallway. With a furtive glance over his shoulder, Larry trailed after him, the smell of human sweat and urine a constant reminder of their precarious situation. The cold, hard metal of the cell doors lined up in a redundant pattern as they ran past, the air heavy and humid, until they reached a small service closet. Jacob opened the door, the hinges creaking softly, and motioned Larry inside.

Their eyes wide with terror, two bound men sat on the floor, gags muffling any sound. Save for the dingy, once-white underwear clinging to their lower bodies, they were naked. Sweat stained and dampened the fabric. Their crisp, starched guard uniforms lay folded neatly beside them. Their polished shoes and socks were neatly arranged in a pile. The semi-automatic rifles rested atop the pile of clothes. The men had fought against the binding ropes with all their might, but the knots held firm. Their struggles only tightening the bonds.

Jacob reached down and handed Larry one pile of folded uniforms and said, "Put these on."

Larry removed his prison garb. He quickly donned the brown uniform. He noticed out of the corner of his eye, Jacob mirroring his movements with the other pile of clothes. A silent, almost conspiratorial exchange. Jacob reached into a canvas bag and pulled out what appeared to be a mask and handed it to him. The thin, flexible rubber, cool to the touch, contained sensors on the inside and small LED lights that glowed faintly. The bright closet lights illuminated every detail as Larry stared. An exact copy of the guard's face sat on the floor before him, a shocking duplicate in every detail. Larry's eyebrows shot up in surprise as Jacob, with a flourish, produced a second mask from the same bag and slipped it on. It was a perfect replica, capturing every detail of the other guard's features down to the faintest lines on the forehead and a small scar on the right cheek.

Grabbing the weapons, Jacob opened the door and gestured for Larry to do the same. Jacob turned to the closet, pulled out a set of keys, and locked the heavy closet door. He indicated to Larry with a nod to maintain a position slightly behind, emphasizing a two-handed grip on the rifle, pointing it downwards. Jacob walked toward a glassed-in box containing a bright red emergency button. He shattered it, the sound like a gunshot in the stillness, and immediately pulled the knob. The overhead speakers suddenly shrieked with the high-pitched wail of a siren, and blinding lights flashed, momentarily causing him to flinch. A loud, resounding click reverberated through the hallway as each door locked, the sound heavy and final.

Larry followed Jacob through the labyrinth of hallways. The doors clicked open one after another as he used the pass hanging from his uniform pocket and the small set of keys on their chain. They entered another larger hallway, the sound of hurried footsteps running on the concrete as guards scurried in both directions. As they approached a tall, imposing door, another guard, with a curt gesture, indicated his intention to lead the way. Jacob barked a sharp command in Farsi, the guttural sounds bouncing off the walls, and the man nodded as if thanking him, and bolted in the opposite direction.

Jacob opened the door to reveal a sprawling, grassy courtyard. At least 20 guards, shouting orders and brandishing weapons, scattered in different directions as Jacob and Larry dashed across the courtyard toward the heavily guarded entrance. A guttural yell ripped through the air from Jacob, directed at the two guards who stood rigidly at the gate. With a groan of rusty metal, the heavy gate swung inward, revealing the road beyond. The gate swung shut behind them with a loud clang as Larry and Jacob sprinted past, their breaths coming in ragged gasps. Reaching the road, they spun right, the rough asphalt jarring their feet as they ran past the imposing stone prison walls. Other guards, yelling and sprinting, ran past them towards the prison entrance, barely noticing them in the chaos.

Honking horns and screeching tires filled the air as they hurried across the busy street, dodging speeding cars. They chose a quieter street to the left, slowing their pace to a stroll, the sounds of the city fading as they walked. The car horns and distant shouts almost obliterated the faint, high-pitched wail of the prison siren. Jacob led Larry down a narrow alleyway, where the smell of damp garbage and old bricks filling his nostrils. At the end of the road sat a heavily tinted black SUV, menacing and sleek. Jacob opened the side door and nudged Larry inside.

Sitting in the driver's seat gripping the steering wheel was Jasmine.

Chapter 37

Jasmine pressed on the gas and used Google Maps to guide her through Tehran. Larry noted she stayed within the speed limit and could see her concentrate on driving.

"I have a few questions," Larry said, his face feeling pale and his hands shaking from the shock. He paused, his gaze shifting between Jacob's tense posture and Jasmine's bright, expectant eyes. "What the fuck just happened?"

Jacob had removed his mask and gestured to Larry to do the same. They still wore the guard uniform, but a pair of blue jeans and a white T-shirt lay in a folded pile beside him. "We need to get rid of this stuff," said Jacob. "Then I'll explain everything."

Larry impatiently removed the starched, uncomfortable guard's uniform and pulled on the softer, more familiar clothing. With a sigh of relief, he traded his heavy leather boots and thick socks for the cool comfort of his flip-flops. A disorienting fog clouded his mind, leaving him unsure if the sights and sounds around him were tangible or figments of his imagination. Days had bled into nights in solitary. The lack of stimulation warped his perception of reality. An icy dread washed over him. He feared this was all a dream, that he'd wake at the end of a rope, facing certain death. With a grimace, Larry pinched the soft skin over his hand, his fingers pressing into the pale flesh. The pain was sharp and sudden. The gritty reality of the situation was undeniable. This was not a dream.

The SUV pulled up to a dumpster on the outskirts of town, the smell of garbage thick in the air. With a grunt, Jacob hopped out. The scent of stale sweat clung to the uniforms as he crammed the masks, guard uniforms, rifles, and boots into a green garbage bag. He tossed it into the already half-full bin with a thud. With the sun beating down, Jasmine headed the SUV down the highway toward the Iraq–Iran border, almost a thousand kilometres to the west, the heat shimmering on the asphalt.

"You were to be sentenced to death for killing the supreme leader, the nuclear physicist, and preventing the attack on Israel," said Jasmine. "I couldn't let that happen."

"But I saw you... Jacob... get blown up," said Larry.

"You cannot believe everything you see on the news," said Jacob.

"What's going on, Jacob? How did you survive that?"

A deep, world-weary sigh escaped Jacob's lips. "I've spent my whole life always looking over my shoulder, one step ahead of those who want me dead. The constant threat of a menacing presence always hanging over me. I needed undeniable proof, something irrefutable, that I had died. The Four Seasons provided the perfect backdrop as I filmed myself wearing the supreme leader's mask. To blend in, I paid the concierge a hefty sum to don a red cross armband, identical to those worn by the first responders in the amphitheatre. It was him, the concierge. He was the one who pulled the mask away, revealing my face. That red cross symbol on his arm was the key to my success. Remote in hand, I lay on the wooden floor and carefully zoomed in on my face for the video. I configured the news cameras to incorporate the video of the paramedic removing my mask remotely, and I timed it perfectly. I programmed the news to splice the videos together at the precise moment of the live confusion. This is the reason you might have mistakenly assumed my demise."

"That's crazy! Was that you on the stage?"

"I was the one on stage, but without the explosives in my body. I had made a tiny incision and pulled on the thin, blue Prolene strings you had left. All five explosive cylinders easily slide out. Then I used small tapes to close the incision."

Larry looked at him incredulously. "What did you need me for, then?"

"I didn't need you," answered Jacob. "That is why I was so shocked to find you searching for me. I never expected it. I contacted Jasmine the moment I learned they had taken you prisoner. She confirmed your fear that I was on the verge of a suicidal explosion. I never expected such a selfless act from you. The AI models did not account for that specific scenario among the possibilities considered."

"I saw you—or was it the supreme leader—come crashing down on the stage after the explosion?"

"A small blast ignited on the stage when I pressed the remote detonator, causing a smoke bomb to explode. Simultaneously, I detonated the bomb I had hidden in the supreme leader's rectum, causing a powerful explosion." For once, Jacob was almost animated, telling the sequence of events like it was some action-adventure movie. "In the confusion of swirling smoke and shouting, no one could see what happened. The flimsy ceiling tile gave way under the weight of the supreme leader, his broken neck snapping as he tumbled to the floor with a thud. With a deafening roar, dust and debris rained down around him. The impact spread his intestines over the stage. Panicked shouts and the heavy thud of running feet surrounded me as I slipped out with the crowd, careful to remain unnoticed."

"Hey, wait a minute," said Larry after a thought crossed his mind. "Your body? What about your body? No one ever recovered it. No one will believe you are dead."

Jacob stared at Larry, his eyes narrowed in disbelief. The

sight was so bizarre it felt unreal, like a fever dream. "With the amphitheater clear of people, I detonated the rest of the explosives. All that remained was a pile of rubble, dust, and broken stones, a testament of complete destruction. A reasonable assumption would be that I am buried under all that, suffocating in the darkness and weight."

"Are you the one responsible for thwarting the attack on Israel?" asked Larry.

"Yes. That was me." Jacob went silent, his eyes losing their usual sparkle. A stubborn set to his jaw and the glint of defiance in his eyes betrayed his unwillingness to tell Larry anything more. "I think it's time for me to take a break and relax." With a sigh, Jacob pushed the seat back until it was almost flat, the quiet motoring of the car a lullaby as he closed his eyes. Within moments, deep sleep claimed him, his breath slowing, and his body relaxing completely.

Jasmine glanced at the back seat. "Why don't you sit up here with me? I'll fill you in with the rest of the story."

With a grunt, Larry heaved himself into the front passenger seat. He reached for Jasmine's hand, his touch gentle at first before his grip tightened into a reassuring squeeze. With a tender gesture, he raised it to his lips, the scent of her faint but familiar as he kissed her hand. "I am having difficulty in believing this actually happened. You shouldn't have come to Iran. You know what they would do to you if they caught a Jewish girl in this savage country."

Jasmine took her eyes from the road and glanced at Larry. "I love you. I couldn't sit back and let them hang you."

Larry could feel his eyes moisten. He wiped them with his wrist. "How did you find me? The facility must have thousands of prisoners. Where did you know to find me?"

"There are actually 1,553 prisoners there," replied Jasmine, a grim expression twisting her face as if she pictured the overcrowded cells and the despair within. "The database Jacob and I hacked into meticulously lists everyone's location, each coordinate precise and in accurate detail. Ten years earlier, Jacob had interviewed a captured dissident nuclear scientist, and the layout of the facility was somewhat familiar. We got the rest of the details from online sources."

"Wait," Larry said, his voice tight with urgency. "Jacob had been in the prison before?"

"Apparently, one of the nuclear scientists who worked alongside Jacob, a man named Dr. Arya Petrova, leaked sensitive information to the US, jeopardizing Iran's national security. The police arrested him, then subjected him to hours of brutal torture. But the guards could not understand the jargon. The meaning remained elusive, despite their efforts. They summoned Jacob, the lead nuclear scientist, to decipher the complex information. No one has heard from the scientist since his disappearance, and a growing sense of dread suggests they sentenced him to death. Likely they hanged him."

"What was with up the guards we impersonated? How did Jacob do that?"

"That part was surprisingly easy, almost effortless. By hacking into the guard's work schedule, we quickly identified who was assigned to your block. Using AI and 3D digital printing, Jacob meticulously crafted perfect replicas of their faces, each pore and wrinkle faithfully reproduced. The masks, equipped with tiny sensors, mimicked every twitch and movement of the wearer's facial muscles. We reviewed the prison-break protocol, noting that the ensuing chaos would provide the perfect cover for you to slip through disguised as a guard. The sheer pandemonium would be your ally. No one has ever escaped the imposing fortress."

Larry felt his heart skip a beat. "Aren't you worried they will catch us at the border? Surely they will look for us."

Jasmine smiled. "Jacob has it all figured out. I think we will be alright."

***

As the sun dipped below the horizon, the SUV arrived at the Iran-Iraq border. The air grew cooler. The buildings' long shadows stretched along the road, while the setting sun silhouetted the border patrol guard as he walked a slow circle around the SUV. With a curt nod, he signalled Jasmine to pull over to the curb. Then he gestured for them to get out of the car.

Larry watched anxiously as another guard appeared. His eyes narrowed when he saw a large dog straining at its leash beside him. The dog bounded into the SUV, its tail wagging, and sniffed at the leather in the front seat. With a grimace, the guard opened the rear passenger door. The dog sniffed cautiously at the musty smell emanating from the back seat, likely the picking up the scent of where Jacob had rested. He repeated the same meticulous process for the rear compartment, carefully examining each area. After about 30 seconds, the dog bounded out, tail wagging furiously.

With a wave of their hands, they directed the three of them into the imposing customs building. They handed their passports to the official sitting in the kiosk, his eyes lingering on Larry's face, then his photo, before quickly glancing at Jasmine's, and finally at Jacob's. With a decisive thud, he stamped each passport and handed them back, betraying no emotion.

With a last nod from the border guards, they were free to leave after exiting customs. A wave of relief washed over Larry. The SUV started immediately and Jasmine shifted into drive, ready for the road ahead. Less than 500 feet away stood the Iraqi customs building, a low structure with a few people waiting outside in the heat, the sounds of their conversations barely audible from the distance. The customs officer was in a booth on the driver's side. They handed their passports to the man who stamped them. In less than 60 seconds, with engines roaring and tires screeching, they sped towards the Iraqi-Jordanian border, a gruelling 10-hour drive ahead.

Thirty minutes past the border, the SUV was silent except for the hum of the engine. Only then did they remove their masks—the ones that matched the pictures on their fake Canadian passports.

Chapter 38

"The only safe place for you is to stay with me," Jasmine whispered, her breath warm against Larry's neck as they lay tangled in the sheets. "If you return to Canada, they will discover you just as before, and murder you. They're relentless. The complexities of the Israeli political and social landscape would make an attack on you far more challenging. The threat of terrorists and those who seek our destruction is ever-present, and we remain vigilant, eyes and ears peeled."

Larry's voice was strained as he confessed, "I'm deeply concerned about my children and the impact Richard could have on their lives. I feel I need to protect them. Maybe I should warn Chantelle."

A burst of raucous laughter erupted from Jasmine. "A furious, cuckolded husband, confronting his adulterous wife, spitting out the accusation that her new lover was actually an Iranian spy." Tears streamed down Jasmine's face as she laughed uncontrollably, a sound filled with unrestrained mirth. Jasmine laughed so hard, an inadvertent snort emanated from deep in her throat. Larry, witnessing the infectious laughter, got caught up in the moment and could not stop himself from joining in.

Jasmine seemed to have difficulty getting the image out of

her mind that brought out the contagious laughter. "I doubt you would get out one sentence before she slammed down the phone."

Her demeanour changed to one with more sympathy. "I'm sorry, honey, but picturing you attempting to have a serious conversation with her dishonest thoughts is quite difficult. Well... it doesn't work for me."

Larry smiled. Jasmine was right. He would sound like a jealous husband trying to discredit her new partner with accusations he knew she would not believe. "You might be right, but you don't have to find it so funny," he laughed. After a moment to collect his thoughts, he said, "I need to do something, though. My children might be in danger."

"Jacob has given you the best possible advice," Jasmine replied, her voice calm and reassuring. "Lie low in Israel. Keep a discrete profile until this whole situation calms down."

"Jacob figured it would take a year or two before the Iranian people had other matters to deal with, hopefully, distracting them from me. Even after that, I would need to be careful."

"We can think about a solution for Richard's situation, but I could really use your expertise at the cybersecurity firm, working on data breaches and threat detection, which can be quite intense. We're drowning in customers and fighting a losing battle against the constant stream of sophisticated software attacks. I desperately need more support. Being Jewish, living in Israel grants you citizenship and a sense of safety."

Larry thought about her words at length. *This offer feels like a lifeline after enduring months of unimaginable trauma, a beacon of hope in the darkness. The sound of Jasmine's humming and the warmth of our shared home were like a dream come true. Living with her was as close to paradise as I'd ever hoped for. I'd longed for some financial stability, but the reality of earning a living doing this work exceeds my expectations, filling me with a sense of accomplishment. Yes, I'll miss the precision and the adrenaline of surgery after all those years of dedicated training. But perhaps once things calmed down, maybe I could reclaim my old position or find comparable work in this new location.*

"I should call John Hegland, my chief, and let him know what I am up to. I must accept I cannot go back to my old job as a surgeon anytime soon. In fairness to him, I think I should resign from the hospital so they can hire a replacement surgeon to distribute the workload."

"So you accept my offer to live with me and work at the firm?"

With a tender smile, Larry leaned down and gently kissed her lips. "You saved my life," he whispered, tears in his eyes, "and I'll spend every remaining moment making you happy. Each day feels like a gift, a precious loan from time itself. And yes, nothing would make me happier than to be with you."

***

It was 4 p.m. Toronto time when Larry called John, who picked up on the first ring. "Who is this?" he said, his voice a whisper.

"John? Is that you? This is Larry," he said.

The line went quiet for a moment, then John spoke again in a hushed tone. "La... Larry? I was told you were dead. I got a visit from the Canadian Security Intelligence Service, an agent named Robert Baker."

"CSIS? What?"

"They said the Faraja arrested you and sentenced you to death for murdering the supreme leader. They had some questions about what I knew. Unbelievably... Where... where are you?"

"Not sure if I should tell you where I am, except to say I am very much alive, thanks to Jacob and Jasmine. Let me tell you what happened since I left your boat in the Bahamas." Larry spent the next hour telling him the story about what had happened over the last few months.

"It wouldn't be safe for me to come back to Canada now," Larry explained. "I believe Richard to be an Iranian operative.

Canada has many Iranian refugees. Some are actually Iranian assassins. Some are spies. Richard is a highly trained assassin. I think my children are in danger, but I am reluctant to confront him, fearing he would harm the kids or Chantelle to get me."

"Chantelle called me after the CSIS agent's visit. She had received a similar visit and was extremely upset with the report of your death. You should call her and let her know you are alive."

"I can't do that, John. If Richard was an Iranian operative, he would know I escaped and would wait for confirmation of my location. His eyes would constantly scan for any sign of me. They might send a squad to take me out, guns blazing."

"What can I do to help, then?"

"For now, keep pretending I am dead—my life depends on it. Hire a surgeon to fill my spot. When things are better and I can safely return, I will definitely reach out and let you know."

Larry could hear silence on the other end until John said, "Good luck." It appeared he was about to hang up when he asked, "What are you going to do about Richard?"

"I have a plan," replied Larry.

***

Larry, together with Jasmine, uncovered significantly more details about Richard, including some surprising facts. With their expertise and years of experience, they'd breached the military's digital defenses, accessing Richard's top-secret file. Mehran Feradi, his true identity, was a name known only to a few. Having achieved the rank of *Sarhang*, a senior officer position, before joining the Ministry of Intelligence and Security (MOIS), he was a highly decorated officer. His file detailed his skills, including the assassination of high-ranking dissidents outside of Iran, with specific mention of the silenced pistol used in each operation. He had also earned a business degree from Harvard, graduating with honours and a strong network of connections.

The file detailed Richard's solo trip to the United Arab Emirates, where he abducted Ruhollah Zam, a dissident journalist. Specific dates, locations, and methods filled the account. After bringing him back to Iran, they accused Zam of "corruption on earth," citing his alleged incitement of the 2017–2018 Iranian protests, which involved widespread unrest and clashes with security forces. In the cold December 2020, they hanged him, fulfilling the Iranian court's death sentence—a gross last act. The government, in a formal ceremony, bestowed upon Richard, the Order of Fath, the nation's highest honour, for his crucial role in capturing Zam. The photograph showed him holding the heavy medal, a proud smile illuminating his face, the award's weight almost palpable.

Currently, Richard's whereabouts were a mystery, although

his botched assassination attempts in the US left a trail of unanswered questions and frustrated agents. Among the items Larry copied and placed in the file were pictures of Richard with several recognizable American political figures, their faces familiar to many. He scrolled through Richard's Facebook page until he found a picture of him and Hamid smiling. The disturbing image on the dark web showed his two sons enjoying breakfast, while Chantelle and Richard lurked ominously in the background. The sight still sent chills down Larry's spine.

Larry sent the files anonymously to the CSIS agent Robert Baker, explaining where they could find the Iranian operative. He also sent the same file to Richard.

***

"Have a look at this!" Jasmine shouted across the office, her voice sharp. With a quick hop, Larry peered over Jasmine's shoulder, the glow of the computer screen illuminating her focused yet strained face as she hunched over her work. Thirty-six hours had passed since Larry sent the emails to CSIS and Robert. The significance of his actions settled heavily on him.

"Iranian Spy Found Dead a Mile From The Peace Bridge, Neck Broken. Scene Suggests Struggle," screamed the headline. "For the past year, Richard Myer, also known as Mehran Faradi, had made Toronto, Canada, his home. Sources close to CSIS, speaking on condition of anonymity, confirmed he was an Iranian spy, citing intercepted communications and financial records."

A picture appeared, showing Richard and Hamid, clad in army fatigues, their arms warmly draped over each other's shoulders. "Though the RCMP held a warrant for his arrest," the article continued, "he slipped across the US border before they could apprehend him. The mystery of his broken neck deepened the suspicion of foul play. Perhaps a struggle ensued? As the death occurred within a mile of the border, agents from the United States Border Patrol are conducting a thorough investigation."

Jasmine stare at Larry with a confused look.

"Jacob," he whispered.

Chapter 39

"It's the tariffs that are sinking us," said the Vice President of the United States. He wore his expensive tailored blue suit and had trimmed his brown beard to cover his weak chin just before the meeting started. Puffing out his chest to hide his potbelly, he continued. "We cannot back away from them now. It would be a sign of weakness. We would lose everything we have gained."

"What if we slowly reduce them to a level that makes it seem we are not backing down?" asked the chief of staff, pushing back her grey hair behind her ears, a move she often did when she was nervous.

"That would be the same thing as saying we were wrong," replied the VP. "We never do that."

The entire room went quiet as the president stood up to speak. "I'm not going to talk about the tariffs. You will see it was the most brilliant economic move of the century. Americans will thank me for generations to come as the mastermind who created the greatest nation on earth."

The room erupted into thunderous applause, a wave of sound washing over him. All 18 members, a mix of young and old, rose to their feet with a booming cheer for their leader. A wide, bright smile illuminated the president's face. The past three months had been a whirlwind of deadlines and pressure, each day blurring into the next in a blur of activity. The Supreme Court's decision, blocking the executive order of deportation of criminals, was a major setback. He had completely ignored them. It reflected a callous disregard for the legal process, one of many. He knew they were powerless. No amount of effort could prevent his actions. Anyone who dared to stand in his path felt the full force of his wrath, facing punishment and possible deportation.

"While waiting for the tariffs to correct the trade imbalance, we need to create a diversion, something to distract the masses from the initial negative economic impact of the tariffs. The Americans are getting restless. They want instant results. I say we give them that."

Again, thunderous applause, followed by a wave of sound and motion, filled the room as people leaped to their feet, cheering wildly for their leader. For a full minute, the room reverberated with clapping before the president finally quieted the crowd by raising his hand.

"I am asking you for support in the next bold move, which is absolutely necessary if we want to achieve economic success. You can expect criticism, but we get that anyway. As the most powerful nation on the face of the globe, we must flex our muscle and show the world our capabilities. I can guarantee, after that, the talk about tariffs will fizzle out."

"What did you have in mind?" asked the chief of staff.

The president went quiet as he collected his thoughts. "Our talks with Canada have gone nowhere. I will not wait until they launch an attack against us. I have ordered a military strike against Canada. Our troops have assembled on the border with Canada. They are going to blast past the border towns, wiping out anyone who stands in their way. We will level the entire southern part of the country before repopulating it with Americans. The 51st state will be ours in a matter of hours. Any country that criticizes us, well... they will be next on the list. No one is going to prevent us from glory."

A hush fell over the room. You could hear a pin drop. The president waited for the uproarious applause that never came. Colour rose in his cheeks, his face burning with a deep blush. A heavy, suffocating silence pressed down, deafening in its intensity. He looked around the room, his heart sinking as he saw the faces of pure terror staring back at him, a silent scream in their eyes.

Finally, the chief of staff spoke. "What about all the innocent civilians? The slaughter of the women and children?" The chief of staff became choked up. "I cannot be part of this. This has gone too far."

The president boomed, "You're fired. You are nothing more

than a weakling. I knew I should have chosen someone who had a set of balls. Get the fuck out of here! Now!" Spittle flew across the room, landing on the faces of those closest, who looked too frightened to wipe it away. He could feel his eyes darting around the room, daring anyone to challenge him.

Everyone in the room silently watched the chief of staff pick up her laptop and trudge out of the room. Once she had left, the President continued. "Besides," he said. "It is too late. I ordered the attack..." He glanced at his watch. "One minute ago. I think we can close the book on the tariff discussion." He smiled a satisfied grin.

***

Jacob looked at his computer screen, watching the reaction of the participants. He had hacked into the video system easily and had witnessed the meeting. Those in the room could have easily predicted this would happen and prevented it had any of them had stood up to the president to oppose his actions. Instead, they all went along with his schemes and encouraged him to do more. He was just fulling their wishes. In the past, striking back at a foreign country always increased the president's popularity. This time, it would be different.

Jacob had inserted a worm, eerily similar to Larry's decades-old creation, into the American military's control system. The digital code felt alien and menacing. Jacob knew the cyber security world had never seen anything like the speed and precision of this attack before—it was unlike any malware he'd ever analyzed. Using AI, he'd developed a worm that effortlessly bypassed firewalls and other cybersecurity software, a silent digital threat slithering through networks. The software, a silent virus, had infiltrated every part of the digital military machine, its code weaving through networks, silently creating algorithms designed to predict and prevent attacks.

Jacob felt a surge of power, the weight of an averted catastrophe settling over him as he reflected on disabling Iran's nuclear launch system, saving Israel from mass destruction. He could replicate the same actions in other countries, such as now when the US attempted to do something similar.

The beauty of this digital worm was that it would adapt to the rigid firewalls, sliding through the digital defences like a phantom, always finding a way around them. Once attacked by the software, it would automatically update, its form shifting and evolving into a completely new entity, a process accompanied by a cascade of data streams and flashing lights. With each unpredictable event, Jacob's ability to predict the future crumbled, unable to reveal a path to peace amid chaos. This is when the AI-powered software would kick in and organizes a path preventing the aggression choosing the algorithm most likely to succeed.

The build-up had been intense. Over the past few days, Jacob had watched the US military, with their imposing equipment and camouflage uniforms, assemble along the US–Canada border. This mirrored the strategy Putin had employed just before the invasion of Ukraine three years prior. A veneer of diplomacy masked the swift, decisive move. Hidden in the shadows, he pieced together the plan by carefully listening to the president's tense discussions with the 10 four-star generals, their clipped tones hinting at the gravity of the situation. The US military, a sea of uniforms and weaponry, prepared to unleash a wave of destruction upon major Canadian cities, their march an ominous approach to seizing control. They were to shoot any Canadian who interfered, considering them an enemy force, their rifles primed and ready. Though Jacob was unsure of the AI's strategy, he felt a quiet confidence that this invasion would fail. The conviction born of faith in the AI machine's capabilities.

With a few keystrokes, Jacob accessed the satellite images and video. The high-resolution videos were precise and the clarity of the images amazed him. Each detail was sharp and vibrant, as if he could reach out and touch them. He watched, horrified, as more than half a million troops, a sea of uniforms and weapons, advanced across the border into Canadian territory.

The line of soldiers came to an abrupt standstill, the thump of their marching boots ceasing, leaving an unnerving quiet. Jacob zoomed in on the screen, his eyes straining to make out the details of the sudden stop of the advancement. The audio signal he picked up from one soldier was clear, filled with no background noise or interference. Each helmet, a marvel of modern military technology, buzzed faintly as the army had installed the latest audiovisual equipment. Jacob saw the soldier's surroundings, the same sights and sounds as him.

"This is Major Jacobs. Canadian troops have infiltrated the unit next to us, unit 171," barked the speakers in the helmet. "You need to stop them. Use what ever force is necessary."

Jacob then flipped over to a soldier in unit 171. "This is Major Litwin," boomed the voice in the other soldier's helmet. "The command post informed me that Canadian troops infiltrated unit 170, next to us. They are wearing American army uniforms, so don't let them fool you. Our instructions are to use whatever force is necessary to stop them."

With bated breath, Jacob watched the unfolding scene, his heart pounding in his chest. With their guns trained on one another, he could imagine the tension in the air that the soldiers felt as a palpable sense of dread before the deafening roar of gunfire erupted as the opposing side advanced. Fifteen minutes later, the intense battle concluded, the sounds of clashing steel fading into silence. The American soldiers were dead or lay groaning in agony, their bodies scattered across the blood-soaked ground, having followed the military leader's command to attack each other. This AI, a complex network buzzing with calculations, was working to find the most effective tactic to stop the incursion.

The invasion of Canada was effectively over.

Chapter 40

Larry and Jasmine watched the same video images as Jacob, the flickering light painting their faces in an eerie glow. Jasmine's face, pale and wide-eyed, spoke volumes about the shocking scene they had just witnessed. A wave of nausea and revulsion washed over Larry as he pictured the fallen American soldiers—sons and daughters of patriotic families—sacrificed in a deadly game played by a disillusioned president. The sickening reality of the massacre settling heavily in his stomach, the air reeking with the stench of betrayal.

AI, tasked with preventing international conflict, carefully selected the algorithms most likely to succeed in its mission. Jacob knew the consequences of initiating the attack would be brutal for the country, a devastating blow to its economy and international standing. Preventing future attacks was a key part of the plan's appeal. The colossal failure left nations reeling, struggling to understand the source of the false commands that misled their troops. Their confusion resonated across borders. That was the beauty of AI. Its seamless integration and problem-solving capabilities were awe-inspiring.

Larry felt a deep responsibility to intervene and lessen the catastrophic impact on the US as he watched their army tear itself apart. But the moment had passed. The death toll, the highest ever recorded in such a short time, was staggering. It was a grim, deadly statistic. It was both a marvel and a tragedy that Jacob's AI could compel a nation's military to follow instructions to avert invasion.

"This is not what I expected," Larry said, his voice tight with disappointment. The sadness in his voice was thick with unspoken grief. A tremor shook his head as he spoke. "Jacob pleaded for our help when he explained the AI needed our cybersecurity expertise to navigate the military's impenetrable firewall. Now we have blood on our hands."

Jasmine stared at Larry, a strange mixture of emotions swirling in her eyes, her expression unreadable. "Your existence as a Canadian Jew has been one of privilege and safety, shielding you from the harsh realities faced by others. The ever-present threat of annihilation is a grim reality for Jews and others in the real world. It's an ever-present cloud, a shadow that never fully lifts. Sometimes, a violent rebellion against the powerful is necessary to avoid utter annihilation. Otherwise, we face certain doom. Their plan was obvious from their raised voices and excited gestures, which you heard from video of the president declaring the invasion of Canada. As commander-in-chief, the president gave the soldiers the cold, hard order to kill anyone who stood in their path during the invasion. Without intervention, the death toll would have climbed higher, leaving a trail of devastation and unimaginable suffering. Could you stomach the crushing guilt, the knowledge that your inaction led to this? Innocent men, women, and children, their lives brutally cut short, lay slaughtered. A president, lost in a self-made fantasy, revelled in the power he wielded."

Larry stared at his trembling hands, his knuckles white as he clenched them into fists. A violent shudder wracked his frame, each breath a ragged gasp. The transition was jarring from the sterile precision of the operating room, where he'd dedicated his life to saving lives, to the chaotic, bloody battlefield. He'd unwittingly taken part in the slaughter of soldiers, all for the supposed greater good. Larry knew, with a sinking feeling in his gut, that he'd crossed the line of no return. Jasmine was right. The message was simple, yet grave. Every nation understood that exhibiting aggression toward another would invite swift and severe repercussions, potentially destabilizing the aggressors.

"It is going to take me some time to adapt to this role in establishing world order," whispered Larry. "You'll need to be patient with me."

Jasmine reached over and took his hand. "And you'll need to be patient with me. I have a lot to sort out as well."

The melodic chirp of Larry's phone, a familiar ringtone, pulled him from his thoughts. He glanced at the screen. The familiar caller ID of Jacob already filled him with a sense of dread. Larry read the message:

I have just sent you a link. The worm, in its relentless pursuit of its aim, eliminated the chance of another attack. Its algorithms are humming like a well-oiled machine. Check it out.

Larry transferred the link to Jasmine's computer. A video image appeared. "Mr. President, you need to come with us." A soldier with a brush cut and wearing army fatigues gestured to the president to follow him. He was in his early twenties and spoke in a loud, crisp voice.

"What's this about?" the president stammered, his face ashen and his body wracked with tremors.

"The White House is about to be stormed by protesters. The national guard is refusing to shoot any intruders. Your life is in danger. We have exactly three minutes to get you out of here. Please follow."

On the video, Larry and Jasmine saw the president quickly push himself up from the plush leather sofa, his face grim, then follow closely behind the soldier. A mad dash down the cold marble hallway led them to a steep flight of stairs. Breathless, they finally arrived at the roof. A military helicopter, its propellers whirling with an ear-splitting roar, waited for him, ready for a quick takeoff. The soldier cut short the president's protests as he shoved him into the back seat.

Jasmine and Larry stared in stunned silence and disbelief as they watched. Adjusting the earphones, the soldier gave the president a reassuring pat before quietly closing the door and giving the pilot the takeoff signal.

The helicopter's undercarriage camera revealed a dense throng of protesters surging through the Washington, DC's streets, their banners a chaotic splash of colour near the White House. A surging wave of people, a sea of faces and upraised arms, breached the fences and security, flooding into the grounds and up the stairs, a human tide rising to the building. People were running in all directions. The scene mirrored the earlier storming of the Congress building by protesters years prior.

"Maybe we did some good after all," said Larry. "Where do you think they are taking him?"

"Hmm," Jasmine paused, puckering her lips as she thought. "If they threw him into the ocean, the churning waves would be a fitting end. A finality as cold and vast as his crimes. With all the criticisms of him not allowing due process for criminals, I doubt that is what will happen."

The video image went to a satellite image. They could see the helicopter approach a superyacht. The name on the back was *Kosatka*. The chopper landed on the helipad. A minute later, the president got out. Jasmine and Larry could see him ushered into the cabin by two men. A minute later, the helicopter left and headed back towards Washington.

"Kosatka," said Larry. "Why does that sound familiar?"

Jasmine did a Google search. In a second, she had the answer. "That's Vladimir Putin's yacht!" she said. "What the...? What just happened?"

Larry's lips curved into a slow, sly smile. "It looks like the president and Putin were friends all along. Jacob's actions have led to peace between Russia and Ukraine, giving Putin a lot of free time. Like Bashar al-Assad, the deposed Syrian president, the current president could plan a comeback, using similar tactics to regain his position. Jacob will see that never happens."

"How do you feel about the concept of being held accountable?" asked Jasmine. "How does he evade justice so effortlessly? His actions leave a lingering scent of impunity in their wake?"

"He still commands a massive following of Americans who remain unwavering in their belief of his infallibility. Picture the upheaval. The streets teeming with protestors, the constant news alerts, the deep divisions in society—all stemming from a congressional impeachment. By remaining in exile, he distances himself from supporters, a lonely existence marked by silence and isolation. With him gone, the US can rebuild. Its economy would recover and its infrastructure would strengthen. The IA algorithm seems to have nailed it this time."

***

Larry hunched over his computer, the glow of the screen illuminating his tired face. He furiously typed, wrestling with an algorithm designed to help Jacob predict and mitigate an imminent Hamas attack on Kfar Azza, a small village near the Gaza border. Jasmine had detected the alarming internet chatter and the AI software was churning out the algorithms to prevent it from happening.

Jasmine had offered him a small office just down the hallway of her own. They poured their expertise and countless hours into Jacob's peacekeeping project, a testament to their dedication. The sudden knock reverberated through the quiet office, jolting him from his thoughts. He looked up. Abraham and Sheldon, his sons, came running, their breaths ragged with exertion.

"Daddy, Daddy," they cried, their small bodies launching themselves onto his lap, sending his chair crashing to the floor. His sons, both bawling loudly, rolled around on top of him, a tangle of limbs. Overwhelmed by emotion, Larry felt hot tears stream down his face, blurring his vision.

He glanced up at Chantelle, who stood silhouetted in the doorway, a slight smile in her eyes as she watched the spectacle. "They missed you terribly," she said, a catch in her throat.

Lying on the floor, tears in their eyes, they whispered, "Mommy said you've been saving the world."

Glancing at his children, he realized they were safe at last. A genuine smile spread across Larry's face, the weight of their ordeal lifting from his heart.

The End